CREATURE FROM THE CREVASSE

MICHAEL COLE

SEVERED PRESS
HOBART TASMANIA

CREATURE FROM THE CREVASSE

WWW.SEVEREDPRESS.COM

This novel is a work of fiction. Names, characters, places and incidents are the product of the author's imagination, or are used fictitiously. Any resemblance to actual events, locales or persons, living or dead, is purely coincidental.

ISBN: 978-1-925711-58-5

CHAPTER 1

Bob Ferguson felt the familiar pull of the 8-pound test line against his left index finger. It was a strong, steady tug; a classic example of largemouth bass. It was his first cast of the early morning, and the crawler harness had only been in the water for a single minute before the bite. With a complete grip of the handle, he jerked the pole up at a forty-five-degree angle. Not too gently, or else he wouldn't place the hooks. Not too hard either, or else he'd yank the harness right out of the trophy's mouth. It was just right. The line suddenly tightened, and the pole bent into a curve. The fight was on. Bob stood up at the center of his twelve-foot rowboat, hanging on tight as the bass went for a deep dive. It was a feisty one, and it had no intention of coming quietly. He didn't reel in. That would simply create extra tension on the line and possibly snap it. The goal was to let the fish wear itself out. After about a minute of continuous tugging, the exhausted bass quit its attempt to dive deep. Bob felt the tension on the line ease up, and seized the opportunity to begin reeling in. By the weight at the end of the line, it was obvious that this was at least a fifteen-inch bass. The fish attempted to resist by swimming to the side, but was still being dragged by this force unknown to it. By instinct, it went in the only other direction to escape the clutches of this predator: up!

Bob laughed out loud when the largemouth broke the surface, flailing its body three feet over the water. A large splashed followed its reentry, and Bob quickly reeled in the several feet of slack in the line caused by the jump. The fish went for one last dive. Bob could tell the fish was determined, because his pole had bent at a near perfect ninety-degree angle. It wasn't going to bend any further. The fish wiggled toward the shelter of the weeded floor of the lake, but it wasn't gaining any distance. Once again, its energy levels were depleted by the effort. Bob pulled up on the line, and reeled in the slack he created. He looked over the side of the boat and saw the bass coming up to the surface. The fight was over. He raised it out of the water and swung it over the side of the boat. It flopped along the floor, nearly crashing into an open tackle box. With his thumb and index finger, he gripped the fish by its lower jaw and lifted it, a technique that would paralyze it until he let go. Holding the fish in this manner, he pried the three crawler harness hooks from its mouth. The worm was completely gone, either eaten by the bass or shaken loose during the fight. With the fish unhooked, Bob took a minute to admire his catch. It was a sixteen-inch largemouth, and he figured it weighed at least a couple of pounds. Not bad for the first cast of the morning. He pulled the live basket from the water where it was chained at the stern and placed the bass inside. It splashed briefly as he lowered the basket back into the water. When fully submerged, it began pumping water through its gills and prodding its nose against the sides of the basket, unaware that it was now being stored for its captor's dinner.

"Hell to the yes," Bob said out loud to himself. He couldn't imagine a better way to start the trip. Every so often he'd come to this lake, usually by himself. It was a perfect escape from normal life. Not that life was bad; he had a well-paying job, caring wife, two grown kids at age eighteen and twenty-one. But a man even needed an escape from that once in a while. With his dirty blue jeans, white T-shirt, muddy boots, and three-day beard, he looked like a simple hillbilly. In actuality, he was formerly an assistant college professor of math and computer science at Washtenaw Community College in Ann Arbor. Five years ago, he was promoted to Dean. It was more administrative than it was educational, but the pay was a significant increase, and the hours were focused during the day. Also, a career there meant being grandfathered into a pension plan with good medical benefits and a free two-year education for his kids. The twenty-one-year-old had no problem taking advantage of that, and graduated with an Associate's Degree in Applied Sciences. The younger child had just graduated high school, and expressed no interest in furthering her education.

Bob gazed out onto the water as he began setting his crawler harness. The sun was just starting to come up over the tree line that seemed to encompass the entire lake like a prison fence. Streaks of light stretched over the flat surface of water, making it appear almost like a mirror as it created a reflection of everything above and around it. Looking dead ahead at a cove, he could see his camper inland, just beyond a stretch of water lilies that covered the shore. He had arrived the previous evening, cooked a couple of burgers on the charcoal grill and went straight to sleep, knowing he wanted an early start this morning. The grill was where he left it, and he looked forward to heating his bass fillets on it.

He grabbed a fresh nightcrawler from a blue tub. The slimy purplish-pink bait squirmed within his fingers as if it knew what was in store for it. He pressed the first hook through its purple head, the second through its midsection, and the third through its pink tail. It was a hot summer, which caused the fish to go deep. Bob cast the line out further into the lake, watching it splash about fifty feet from his boat. He reeled in the unwanted slack and patiently waited for the next bite. His eyes scanned the lake. At least in this portion of the large body of water, he appeared to be the only one out.

Fine with me, he thought. His attention returned to the pole when he felt that jerk of the line. It was a quick one, possibly from a bluegill. Usually, bluegills didn't typically run this deep, but it certainly wasn't out of the realm of possibility. Another minute passed. He stood up onto his feet. Another jerk of the line triggered his senses. This one was definitely a harder pull, rather than a brief tug. He yanked back on the pole and quickly reeled in the bit of slack he created. The pole bent again, and the line went taut. *Definitely another bass, or the granddaddy of all bluegills.* The battle went through the normal motions. The fish attempted to go deep, only to be exhausted by the effort. When it eased up, Bob took advantage of the opportunity to start reeling it in. It fought back by pulling from side to side, and finally it went airborne, flipping wildly above the water before crashing down roughly thirty feet from the boat. It attempted to reverse, creating a brief standstill while it tugged in the opposite direction it was being pulled. The maneuver didn't work, and Bob joyfully watched at as fish prepared to make a second leap. The fish broke the surface and writhed at least three feet above the water. Bob began to happily laugh at the occasion. That mirthful laugh suddenly turned into a loud, startled "Sweet Jesus!" when a second enormous splash engulfed the area his fish had jumped. It wasn't some small spray; it was an enormous upward eruption of lake water, as if a grenade had detonated beneath the surface. Bob fell backward onto his seat from the shock, his eyes still fixed on the event. Something huge emerged from the surface, mostly concealed by the blast of water. Whatever it was, it had a dark, scaly exterior, and had a very bulky mass. It crashed down into the water, creating another huge splash. Bob nearly yelled out as his pole was suddenly ripped from his grasp, disappearing under the churning water. Large waves rocked his boat like a bobber for a long minute. Once the water settled down, Bob silently stared at the surface. It was a mixture of shock and awe. He had no rational idea of what he just experienced. He swallowed hard, and then succumbed to his natural instinct of looking over the edge of the boat. All he could see was his own reflection on the glassy surface. He didn't realize his own face was the last thing he'd see. The water beneath him exploded upward, and he felt himself lifted off his boat. The motion was so fast, his brain couldn't register the fact that he was midair, and gripped in a powerful set of vicious jaws. There was another crash of water, and as quick as it all started he was underwater. He instinctively gasped, accidentally filling his lungs with lake water before the jaws crushed down on his back, rib cages, and breastplate. Blood spewed from his mouth and nose as he was driven deeper. The jaws opened and extended and then shut again, suctioning Bob further into the mouth of the predator. A few bloody air bubbles squeezed out from a set of gills behind the jaws as Bob was swallowed whole.

At the surface, the bow of the rowboat had been dunked into the water after the creature had crashed down. Water flowed over the submerged edge, filling the space between the seats. The stern rose slightly higher as the water drove the metal contraption further beneath the surface. After about thirty seconds, the rear of the boat vanished beneath the water. The ripples cleared and the lake returned to normal. The glassy reflection of the tree line returned to the flat, calm surface. It appeared like a peaceful, perfect summer morning.

CHAPTER 2

Sunrise in middle Michigan usually came around six in the morning during the month of July. For the small town of Rodney, it happened at precisely *5:59 a.m.* It was around this time that the initial early morning traffic would commence, typical for a Wednesday morning.

Rodney was a small, hexagonal-shaped area of 28.3 square miles and a population of 19,879 residents. Named after Rodney Earl, believed to be one of the greatest bass fishermen ever, Rodney was most famous for the large lake that rested dead center its map. Shaped like a capital "T", Ridgeway Lake was one of the larger regular lakes in Michigan. With the vertical stem of the "T" slanted slightly toward the west, the lake was three miles long, and two-point-three miles wide at the upper cross. The lake contained fish such as largemouth bass, walleye, pike, crappie, bullhead, perch, bluegill, and other panfish.

The northern segments of Rodney were composed mainly of residential communities, while the western side of town contained a large market area where residents and visitors could do their shopping. The number one source of revenue for the town was Birchwood Lodge, located on the western side of the lake where the north and south sections of the lake intersected. Throughout the lakeside were several cabins owned by this lodge, and during the summer, these cabins and campsites were usually completely booked.

The largest complaint from both the residents and tourist population were the blasts coming from Corey Mine, located east of the lake. Each day, dynamite blasts sent tremors through the earth, disturbing the fishing community. Equipped with a large crane and heavy-duty equipment, workers hauled minerals out of the deep pit from early morning to late evening.

In the southern part of town were a small hospital, a public school district, a fire and EMS station, and the most recently added addition being a police headquarters. For most of its history, the town of Rodney relied on the County Sheriff's Department for law enforcement services. However, during recent years, response times had increased significantly in town. People needing police reports for traffic accidents reportedly had to wait over an hour for a law enforcement officer to appear. With a lack of police presence in the area, petty crimes increased drastically, which then led to a higher rate of misdemeanors. Stores in town dealt with a string of shoplifters, who had no fear of being arrested, and often the business owners would have to wait long periods of time for police to make a report.

The final straw for the town had taken place over a year ago, when a robbery occurred at the local bank. Several gunmen stormed the building and immediately fired two shotgun blasts into the ceiling. After ordering everyone to the floor, they made off with several thousands of dollars. Two of the suspects were eventually caught months later, not by the Sheriff's Department, but by Michigan State Police near the Ohio Border, where these individuals were attempting another armed robbery. Although there were no physical injuries, the robbery left a mental scar on the clients and employees, and the town in general which rarely saw violent crime.

Tired of the worsening situation, residents of Rodney pressured the mayor to take action to ensure safety in the community.

In direct response, the town officials initiated a process for the town to have its own small police force. Thus, the Rodney Police Department was formed.

****

"He's pulling in now," Officer Tim Marlow announced to the police staff. He was standing near the edge of the front window in the intake lobby, keeping a few feet back to not be clearly seen from outside. Behind the intake officer's desk were several uniformed officers waiting near a hallway. Most of these officers were first-shift personnel, waiting to get an impression of what kind of day they were going to have.

"How's he look?" one called back. The five-foot-seven, twenty-three-year-old scrawny officer didn't answer right away. Tim raised his hand toward his co-workers as a way of asking them to be patient. From the window, he watched the grey Jeep Rubicon park into its designated parking spot. The driver door opened up and its operator stepped out. Marlow immediately recognized the slouch in his figure and the grimace on his face.

"We're in for a rough one today, guys!" he announced. He hurried across the lobby toward the hallway. The other officers had already made way to the briefing room and took seats, appearing as if they had been waiting there for several minutes. It was a tradition well practiced over the course of many months. As Marlow hurried down the hall, he could hear the familiar squeak of the front entryway.

Chief Morgan Sydney retained the pained scowl on his face as he entered the building. He stepped into the lobby and carefully shut the door behind him, rather than carelessly let it swing shut. Such discipline was something drilled into him from the early days of the Michigan State Police Academy, and it never wore off.

The smell of minted freshener immediately filled his nose, with the slight smell of fresh paint. Even after six months, he was not used to a police station being so clean, much less the intake area where suspects were usually brought in for booking. Usually, there'd be tobacco stains, wads of spit, food crumbs, and even sometimes urine on the floors and seats. Almost every department had this issue. But this building was relatively new, and maintained the cleanliness of a new facility.

Before walking into the briefing room, he paused in the lobby. He stood as a six-foot-two, lean built, clean-shaven man of forty-five. His weight shifted to his right leg to ease pressure off his left. He rubbed his hand over his left quad. Under the fabric of the black tactical pants was a leg whose muscle tissue had been mangled from a shotgun blast at ten yards. As a lieutenant in the state police, he was leaving a courthouse after a testimony. Upon returning to the station, dispatch had reported gunshots at a gas station near his location. He had located the vehicle with the given description and managed to block it into a corner with ease after a brief chase. Standing out of his service vehicle with his Glock 17 drawn, it had appeared both suspects were surrendering. Unknown to him, however, there was a second vehicle in the robbery. A Dodge Charger unexpectedly sped up, a Remington R12 Autoloader extending from the passenger window. The deafening blast from the barrel coincided with a sudden agonizing pain in his left leg, which dropped him to the pavement.

Three weeks and two surgeries later, Morgan Sydney was released from the hospital. Although repaired to the best of the surgeon's abilities, the thigh muscle was left ravaged, and Sydney subsequently was in perpetual pain. Although given accolades for his service and sacrifice, the state forced him into a medical retirement. Over the next several months, he attempted to find work in other police departments, only to be turned down for fear that his injury would limit his abilities. His luck would change when he discovered the opportunity in the small town of Rodney. After a series of interviews and a detailed presentation, he was offered the position. It was clear to him that the mayor thought of his position as more of an administrative one, therefore not having any concern of his limited ability to do "police work." But it was a job, and it was a peaceful town; an environment he wished to live in for several years.

He made his way through the small empty lobby, waving hello to the intake officer. She waved back, pretending not to notice his limp. The officers always paid attention to his physical state each morning. If he didn't limp too badly, the pain was kept at bay and, therefore, he would be in a good mood. Work on these days was fairly laid back and pleasant. If there was noticeable discomfort, it meant he'd be irritable and unpleasant. There'd be no room for error on the officers' part. On these days, he'd be highly critical of their work performance, leaving zero room for error. It was a Dr. Jekyll and Mr. Hyde scenario.

Marlow knew this was the kind of day they were in for as Sydney entered the briefing room. Seated in arranged desks were ten officers and a sergeant. Seven of them were about to begin their shift from *7:00 a.m.* to *3:00 p.m.*, while the remaining three and the sergeant were wrapping up from the midnight shift. The midnight crew sat in the back of the room, waiting for the clock to strike *0700*. The sergeant stood at a podium at the front of the room, waiting patiently for the chief to enter.

"Good morning," Sydney said, clearing his throat. He looked to the sergeant. "Go ahead with it." The sergeant proceeded with the rundown.

"*0039*, Traffic stop at the intersection of Meyers and Baker Street, doing fifty-five over forty. At *0408*, we had an arrest of two disorderly drunks at Gamby's Bar. They're sleeping it off in the holding cell. Owner not pressing charges for damages. At *0545,* we had a traffic stop at Monroe Street, doing seventy in a fifty. Then at *0615*, a traffic stop on Selene Road. Sixty in a forty." The sergeant put away his notes, eager as his staff to leave for the day. "That concludes our debriefing." The clock struck *0700* and the midnight officers did not hesitate to punch out and exit.

Sydney took to the podium, doing his best to hide his limp. He felt himself growing ever-more bitter with the throbbing pain. Looking at the seven officers who watched him at the start of each shift, he knew they questioned his abilities. Like the mayor, they only saw him as an administrator rather than a cop.

"As always, let me be clear," he said. "I expect you all to be prepared for anything and everything, and above all else be safe." The crew resisted the urge to chuckle. After the formation of the department, the rising crime rate almost instantly decreased back to normal. There were hardly any felonies reported in the past six months. But they knew better than to heckle the chief, especially after considering his mood. "However," Sydney continued, "I won't tolerate horseplay in this department. Officer Scott…" All eyes went toward a mustached officer in the front of the room. "…don't be seeing your lady friend while on duty." The officer felt himself turn red. The other officers' instinct would normally be to chuckle, but they knew Sydney wasn't done.

"Officer Allen, don't let me catch you sleeping again in the patrol vehicle. Same goes for anyone else. I don't care how quiet the shift is, you must keep a high degree of awareness." He paused a moment, resisting the urge to grab his pained leg. During this time, the crew felt a sense of relief, believing the verbal punishment was over. "Officer

Marlow…would you like to explain to me the classes you're taking?" That relief quickly retracted. Marlow felt the blood drain from his face.

"Sir?"

"The classes you've been taking at *1230* to *1400* every Monday and Wednesday. Let us know how it's been going." Marlow stuttered for a moment. He felt all eyes of the room turn toward him.

"The semester's over, sir." When he hired in, he was still taking classes at a community college. One class took place Monday and Wednesday. His shift was Wednesday through Sunday, so the Monday class was not a problem. But Wednesday was a different story. "But the class was very boring." Sydney burned holes into him from where he stood. Marlow winced, bracing for a verbal bruising in front of the shift. The chief simply shook his head in displeasure. *Patheti*c, he grumbled to himself.

"Get to work," he ordered with gruff posture. Without saying a word, the officers stepped from their seats and went to the parking garage where the patrol vehicles were stored. Sydney proceeded down the hall and entered his office, shutting the door behind him. With nobody to bear witness, he fell into his chair, clutching his leg. On this day, any pressure applied to his leg worsened the pain. He was given a cane by his physician and instructed to use it, but personal pride always got in the way. To him, walking with a cane was a sign of defeat—that he was less of a man.

He dug into his pants pocket and pulled out an orange prescription bottle. On the label read *Meperidine. Take one every eight hours as needed for pain.* Sydney hated taking these meds almost as much as he hated the pain itself. He usually resisted taking them as best he could. Often, they made him extremely drowsy, which worsened his mood. In addition, they would cause dry mouth and general fatigue. Of course, there was the constipation. He dumped one into the palm of his hand and cracked open a water bottle. Before he could take the med, he heard a knock on his door. With a sigh, he rolled the pill back into the container. "Come in," he said. The door slowly opened, and Officer Marlow slowly poked his head through. He nervously entered the office, almost in fear of getting chewed out some more.

"Hi, Chief," he said. He looked at the bottle. Sydney didn't bother to hide it. It was no secret amongst his staff that he was on pain medication. The chief leaned toward his desk computer, giving the impression that he was busy. In truth, he was not. He had a meeting with the mayor in nearly two hours, but other than that, there was nothing to do other than simple administrative duties. Those wouldn't take too long to do. He figured he'd patrol after that.

"What can I do for you, Officer Marlow?" he said, deliberately sounding disinterested. Marlow shut the door behind him.

"The class was *Advanced Business Administration,"* he said. Having a moral conscience, he felt the need to explain himself even though the chief already seemed to be done with the subject. "I only had a few weeks to go when you hired me. I still had an exam to go, and a final that was a third of the grade. I just wanted to finish things up." Sydney didn't offer a response, making Marlow slightly regret coming in. "I'll take a deduction for the time I missed," he offered.

"Any reasonable boss would fire your ass," Sydney said. "Listen, kid, all you needed to do was ask me. I'm a reasonable guy. Use that brain you have up there." He pointed at Marlow's head.

"Yes, sir," the young officer said. "If I may ask...how'd you know?"

"Are you serious?" Sydney said. "You think I didn't notice you disappeared at the exact same time every Wednesday?" Marlow bit his lip. It was a logical conclusion. "Did you pass the class?"

"Uh...yes." He was surprised to hear the genuineness of the question. "I got an *A*." He took a seat at the front of Sydney's desk. "I'm working on going to graduate school. I'd like to become a commander, or a police chief. I'm trying to work my way up."

"The first step in working your way up is coming to work and staying the whole shift," Sydney said. He leaned back in his chair. "So, you looking to take my job after I retire?" His tone became less intimidating.

"I don't know," Marlow said. "I'm extremely grateful for this position. But I would like to get a position where there is more experience to be had. I'd also like to work in other types of units, like S.W.A.T. or Customs. I guess... I'd like to do the things you did and work my way up." He hoped he didn't overstep his bounds by implying he didn't want to work in RPD permanently. In some work places, that was considered taboo. Luckily, that didn't seem to be the case with Sydney, judging by his nonchalant expression.

"You're saying you want to be like me?" the chief said with a small chuckle. Marlow nodded and smiled. Sydney rolled his chair over to the side of the desk, and slapped his hand on his leg injury. "This is what I got for all of that." Marlow's enlightened expression dimmed to one of discouragement. "Trust me, kid, it's not worth it."

"I believe it is, sir," Marlow said before standing up. "I seriously do." He exited the office. Sydney leaned back, thinking of the conversation he just had. That young ambitious cop reminded him of someone he knew long ago. That person went through the State Police Academy, considered to be the most grueling of any basic training. With a naive desire to make a difference in the world, he worked his way up the ranks. Twenty years and one-hundred and thirteen felony arrests later, it all came to an explosive end with the pull of a trigger. Now he was in command of the only police department that would take him. He felt like he was running a security agency, serving more as a deterrent. To others, the job title sounded like a promotion, but deep down, Sydney felt like he was at the lowest point in his career.

Thinking harder on it, he wondered if he was actually worried he'd live to see Marlow succeed in his goals, and do what he couldn't.

That's a mark of a great leader. Berate your staff in front of the others as a means to demand respect, and actually worry young aspiring officers might actually succeed in bettering themselves, he thought to himself.

He looked at the prescription bottle. Only one pill remained inside it, and he had no refills. With nothing much to do for the day, he figured he would patrol near the hospital and check in with the doctor for an updated prescription. He was told he could stop by whenever he wanted. Perks of being the police chief, he guessed. He scooped out the remaining pill and rolled it to the back of his tongue, splashing it down with a gulp of water. Now all he could do was hope that this one wouldn't make him drowsy. Lord knew the meeting with the mayor was certainly going to have such an effect on him.

CHAPTER 3

It was after *11:00 a.m.* when Sydney parked the white and blue emblazoned Chevy Tahoe in the lot of Readfield Hospital. The meeting with Mayor Greene felt like a grand waste of time, most of which was spent going over the same topics as usual. He wanted to know crime stats in the town, as if he still believed it was an issue even though nothing significant had occurred since the foundation of the police force. Sydney knew Mayor Greene was a good honest man, but very naïve when it came to law enforcement. He insistently brought up the complaints from residents regarding the rumblings coming from Corey Mine, only to act surprised when Sydney informed him there was nothing that could be done about that.

Then Greene brought up the topic of additional police training, which would take place at the County Sheriff's Department. No doubt this was an idea of Sheriff Logan, who clearly resented the fact that Rodney developed its own police force. From their meetings earlier in the year, it was clear to Sydney that Logan personally despised him, as if somehow he made the sheriff "look bad" when he took the position. Of course, RPD was formed specifically due to neglect in service by the county. Ever since, Logan has looked for ways to one-up the chief. Supervising training exercises for his department was a way of doing just that.

The parking lot was relatively small, with several empty spaces. Readfield Hospital was not a large facility. It had been built exclusively for the small town of Rodney. Shaped like a large rectangle, the building stood three floors high and was not very wide. Near the southeast corner was a helipad, where an emergency transport helicopter rested while not in use.

Readfield Hospital employed roughly two dozen nurses, three ER doctors, an oncologist, a maternity doctor, and of course a hospitalist, in addition to general staff and a chopper pilot. Basically, it was a step higher than a family doctor's office, which just happened to have an ER, OR, and a morgue.

Sydney entered the front lobby on the west entrance, away from the ER entrance on the south. Three people were seated, waiting for their turn to be seen. At the front of the room was a check-in nurse, wearing navy blue scrubs and her blonde hair tied back. All eyes instantly went to the dark blue police uniform. She recognized him from previous visits.

"Good morning, Chief," she said. "How may I help you?" Sydney forced a polite smile. The pain in his leg, while dulled by the meds, was still taking a toll on him today. The slight drowsy effect of the medicine was also making his mood worse.

"How's it going? I'm here to update my prescription." He placed the empty bottle on the counter. "It expired, and in order to refill it, I had to get a new prescription signed."

"Okay," the nurse said. "Do you have an appointment?"

"No, uhhh..." He glanced back briefly at the people waiting in the lobby. He leaned in toward the nurse. "Dr. Williams told me just to stop by whenever I had time." He spoke just above a whisper. Likely the people waiting wouldn't be too pleased for someone to cut ahead of them, even if he was the police chief. The nurse had a look of awkwardness on her face.

"Oh...I'm sorry, uh..." she said. "Dr. Williams retired." Sydney felt his eyebrows raise up in surprise.

"No kidding?" he said. "I had no idea."

"He'd been feeling ill the past few months, and figured he put enough time in. There is a new hospitalist here, though. I'll page her for you," the nurse said with a polite smile. She picked up the phone and started to dial an extension.

"I appreciate it," Sydney said.

"No problem," she said. "You may take a seat if you like." The chief didn't want to, but the pain in his leg dictated that he sit down. He immediately regretted coming in while on duty, seen in his police uniform by the few people in the building. He had intended this to be a quick in-and-out appointment, but now he had to wait like a regular patient. Hopefully, the new doctor would be quick.

****

Dr. Meya Nasr stood over the medical exam table where her patient laid on his back. The patient was a man of forty, complaining of a pain in his lower back and sciatica in his leg. Dr. Nasr had ordered him to lay flat as she lifted his right leg toward the white ceiling to determine range of motion.

"Let me know when it begins to hurt," she told him, lifting his leg up about ten inches off the table. She raised it up several inches, pausing a few seconds for the patient to register any pain. It was at this moment the page came through the intercom.

"*Dr. Nasr, please report to check-in,*" the voice said. Of course she couldn't respond at the moment, nor did she have to. The nurse knew she was in the middle of an examination. *It'll just have to wait.* She barely finished the thought when her patient raised his hand.

"Okay, that's good," he said in a pained voice. She slowly lowered his leg down. This was the last of a few exercises she was putting him through. She sat on her round wheeled stool and picked up a tan folder containing his file.

"Okay, Greg," she said, "What I think you have is likely a bulging disc in one of your lumbar vertebrae. I'm gonna order an x-ray for you, and then we'll be doing a follow-up. Just go to the counter, and the nurse will point you in the right direction. Otherwise, we'll be in touch." The patient slowly sat up and got on his feet.

"Thanks, Doc," he said. She held the door open for him and he left for the lobby. She opened his folder again and jotted down a few notes. Back in medical school, she never imagined she'd prefer the life of a simple country doctor. She was always one who enjoyed being on-the-go, which suited her perfectly as being an ER physician in McLaren Orthopedic Hospital. Each shift was an adrenaline rush, with patients coming in suffering from injuries from car crashes, gun shots, animal attacks, bar brawls, overdoses, and many others. However, the job took its toll. The sight of mutilated corpses of victims, especially children, haunted her at night sometimes. Even worse were the patients whose injuries were so severe, it sometimes felt as if the most humane treatment would be to put them down. On one occasion, during a prison riot, a correctional officer had been thrown into coiled razor ribbon designed to keep the inmates in. Each movement by the officer sliced his flesh, and the only way to remove him was to cut away the section of razor ribbon and transport him to the hospital. When he arrived, the flesh on most of his face had been peeled away, and yet he was forced to remain still to keep it from maiming him further. After nineteen years, she found herself longing for a simpler life. Then, through the help of kind references, a job offer from Readfield Hospital in Rodney, MI came her way. It had some demanding administrative duties, as the position required her to oversee many of the departments in the small hospital, from Cardiology to Pulmonology and most services in between. But it was nothing she couldn't handle, and being able to leave work at *5:00* every afternoon was a plus.

She finished jotting down her notes when she remembered the page. She stood up and left the exam room, making her way to the waiting lobby.

Hopefully, it's not some jerk demanding to cut in line.

****

A few quiet minutes passed by as Sydney waited for the new hospitalist to meet with him. He turned his radio down to muffle the blaring radio traffic, although there wasn't much of that. Usually, someone would radio in a traffic stop or if they were switching from mobile patrol to foot patrol, or vice versa. Other than that there wasn't much going on. It was a typical day in the town of Rodney.

"Morgan?" he heard his name called. He thought it was the nurse, until he looked up. His eyes went wide when he saw Dr. Meya Nasr standing before him. He didn't figure the new hospitalist would be the woman he was married to for nine years. But she was recognizable as ever, a five-foot-six woman of Middle Eastern descent, with perfect smooth skin, and black hair that hung in curly waves to her shoulders. Dr. Nasr's reaction was the same when their eyes met. She had no idea that the police chief was her ex-husband. She wasn't even aware he had gotten a new job. After the divorce, there had been no communication between the two of them. There were no kids or property binding them together.

There was a moment of stunned silence between the two of them.

"Come with me please." It was all she could muster to say at this moment. Sydney stood up and followed her to the exam room, managing his limp the best he could. They were in the final stages of divorce when the shooting occurred, and it was the first real time she had seen the aftermath of his injury. She had offered assistance in his rehabilitation, but he refused, wanting to finish the proceedings. The papers were signed, and there was no more connection.

They entered the exam room, and she shut the door behind them.

"Well, uhh…you're looking good," Sydney said. It was generic, but it was the only thing he could come up with. He wasn't lying though. She was a physically fit woman of forty-one, and he could instantly tell she was in a happier place…although maybe not in this specific moment.

"I understand you're here regarding a prescription," she said. He was somewhat surprised. She spoke to him as a patient, not wasting any time getting to the issue. She gestured for him to take a seat on the exam table while looking at a folder containing his file. He took a seat, feeling the pain in his leg starting to worsen…as it often did in uncomfortable moments. There were a few moments of uncomfortable silence as she looked over his records.

You'd think she'd know most of it by heart, he thought. He figured he'd be polite and try and break the ice.

"So, when did you move over here?"

"I started three weeks ago," she said without even looking up at him. Finally, she set the folder down. "So the pain in your leg has been getting worse?"

"It's different each day," he said. "I'm able to deal. Dr. Williams told me to just drop by whenever I had the chance, and he'd update the prescription."

"It's my understanding that Dr. Williams, and the doctor you were seeing before him, instructed you to use a cane," she said.

"Yeah, but…"

"Why aren't you using it?"

"Well…" Sydney felt himself growing frustrated, but kept his polite demeanor. "…uhh, let's just say it doesn't look too encouraging in the public's eye to see a police officer walking around with a cane."

"Trust me, seeing an officer hobbling around on one leg isn't really an improvement," she said. "I can assure you it wouldn't hurt quite as much if you used the cane. It would relieve pressure from the muscle and…"

"Pardon me, but Meya…"

"Dr. Nasr," she corrected him. He paused for a brief moment. *Wow, tell me how you really feel about seeing me.*

"*Dr. Nasr*…I only came here to get a new signature on my prescription so I can get a refill. I'll even say please." One frequent complaint during their marriage was a lack of good manners on his part. Ironically, it seemed to be the opposite today.

"Alright," she said. "Drop your pants."

"I beg your pardon?" Sydney said. He felt uncomfortable and anxious, but also slightly amused.

"You want a new prescription for *Meperidine*, right? That means a new exam needs to be done. Off with the pants." Now Sydney allowed his demeanor to fail a bit.

"Not without dinner and a movie, *Doctor,*" he said.

"In that case," she said, "I believe all you need is a high dose of *ibuprofen*. That, plus continued use with the cane, should ease the pain in your leg." She grabbed a prescription booklet and started jotting down her signature. Sydney raised his hand in protest.

"Oh hell no," he said, barely keeping his voice down. "That stuff screws up my stomach and barely dulls the pain." Dr. Nasr looked up at him.

"Then let me do an exam," she said. It wasn't as though she hadn't ever seen him with no pants before, but she had never seen him with his injury. Sydney despised his mangled thigh, and was in no hurry to allow her to make condescending remarks about it. He felt his temper starting to get the better of him, and knew he better leave before he succumbed to it.

"I'll take the script," he said bitterly. Without missing a beat, she finished filling it out. She tore it from the pad and handed it to him. He took it from her, and forced a smile. "Thank you." He turned and let himself out the door. "Welcome to Rodney," he said. What he wanted to say was "go to hell," but resisted…not out of personal pride, but because of his position as chief. He shut the door behind him as he left.

Meya savored a few quiet moments by herself in the room. She didn't want to admit it, but seeing the man she once loved made the heartbreak feel fresh once again. She immediately felt guilty for remaining so bitter about the turmoil their marriage went through. She was aware that her bitterness had shown during that exam, almost unfiltered. The realization that her ex-husband was the chief of police in town was still hitting her hard. For the past two years, she distanced herself to emotionally recover. She didn't want any connection. There was no alimony, no child support, and all assets were divided. She worked herself to exhaustion, and finally moved to a quiet town to find peace. But seeing the man who once proposed to her by the Old Presque Isle lighthouse on Lake Huron brought it all back.

She snapped out of her thoughts, remembering she had patients waiting for her, in addition to other duties. It was time for her to resort to the only way she knew to forget; work.

****

Sydney took a seat in his patrol vehicle after obtaining his prescribed ibuprofen from the hospital pharmacy. His blood pressure was still increased, worsening the pain in his leg. He looked at the bottle, contemplating taking one of the pills, even though he knew they wouldn't help much. In a fit of frustration, he threw them down into the passenger seat and started the engine. Before driving off, his eyes went to the doors of the hospital. He thought of his surprise from seeing Meya in the hospital, and how it slightly reminded them of how they met.

An armed robbery had taken place, which resulted in a vehicle pursuit of the two suspects. County and state police units managed to force the vehicle off the highway, resulting in it crashing into a tree. A brief shootout occurred, leaving both suspects injured. Sydney provided an escort for the ambulance to the hospital. The two suspects were admitted, one with a gunshot wound in the lower torso, and the other suffering from lacerations from glass.

While in the ER, the suspect with the glass injuries struggled in his stretcher, desperate to get free. A series of curse words came out of his mouth, directed mostly at the cops and his attending ER physician. It was the first time Sydney had met Dr. Meya Nasr. To Sydney's surprise, she was not intimidated by the criminal's threats and insults. Rather, she threatened him back, informing him that they would operate without painkillers to remove the deeply embedded glass if he didn't cooperate. He remained quiet from then on.

Sydney returned the next day to acquire information on the individual. Her first words to Sydney were, "You should have shot him as well!" Apparently, the suspect resumed his rude behavior during the course of the night. It was something about her straightforwardness which stuck with Sydney. The two began to connect and see each other more often, under better circumstances. They were married a year later.

Over the course of time, the stresses of their jobs got the better of them. There were shortages in both the hospital and the state police, resulting in mandated overtime for both of them. Opposite shifts affected their relationship greatly. There came a point where there was hardly any communication between them. In addition, there was no sex life, which only added to the frustration.

Then came a time when Meya seemed to be quite distant and non-interactive. Sydney eventually starting suspecting an affair between her and another doctor she had talked about. His mind ran away with the idea, jumping to conclusions. This resulted in an ugly confrontation in the hospital lot, when he threatened the other doctor. The truth ended up being that Meya was sad and distant because she had tried to save the life of a child who had been in a car wreck. The child passed away in great pain, which left her depressed and feeling guilty that she couldn't save him. It was this confrontation that caused her to serve divorce papers. Sydney offered attempts to save the marriage, but Meya wanted it over.

As the divorce came to a close, Sydney found himself shot in the leg. It was the perfect end to a miserable chapter in his life.

He snapped back into reality. He shifted the vehicle into *drive* and eased out of the parking lot.

The day can only get better from here.

CHAPTER 4

Birchwood Lodge rested near a beach, simply named Birchwood Beach where the lake curved westward. The beach stuck out into the water like a huge arrow, with water to the north, east, and south, making it a prime area for swimmers. There were two docking areas for boats, one for privately owned and another for those rented out by the lodge. The lodge was a large building, all ground level where people checked in for their reservations. The building included a bar and restaurant, small general shopping area, a separate bait and tackle shop, a gaming room, and a fish cleaning station. The west side of the lake had dozens of cabins spread out, allowing for privacy for the tenants.

Noon was the start of the really busy hours near the property beaches. Visitors and residents went out to swim or simply relax on the beach, while others went out on the lake to fish. The early birds who fished in the morning often came in around this time as well.

Joel Pobursky stood behind his counter in the fish cleaning station, watching several boats slowly coming in from several parts of the lake. He could see the dock, where other visitors and residents were actively loading their fishing gear into rented boats. He referred to this time as shift change. Dressed in jeans and a grey uniform shirt with his first name embroidered near the collar, he knew the busy hours of his shift were about to start. Soon the clean tile flooring would be covered in lake water and fish guts. Being a fish filleter was no glory job, but it was steady and the pay was decent.

The first of many boats was docking. Joel already had his knives sharpened and ready. With many years of experience with cleaning fish for the residents, he perfected the techniques to clean the catch to produce boneless fillets quickly. Mr. Tindell, the owner of the lodge, often praised Joel as the fastest filleter around. He was treated like a celebrity. But for him, it was the same thing every day. Arrive at *8:00,* leave at *5:00*, go home, and repeat. He appreciated his job and loved his family beyond measure. However, occasionally, he would catch himself longing for just one more day of his previous adventurous life. There were eight years in the Air Force as a Pararescue, during which he got to experience the rush of several adrenaline-filled missions, and save the lives of his brothers-in-arms. After he fulfilled his service, he spent several years traveling the world to hunt big game. He traveled to Asia and had gone on safari in Africa, where he hunted animals such as cape buffalo. He also hunted at home in North America, particularly for bear, but those were smaller trips. His safaris abroad often led to unforgettable adventures, where he often faced death. One such incident occurred when he was stalking a buffalo in South Africa, when he realized a lion was about to leap onto him. It had been stalking him for several minutes, unbeknownst to him at the time. He turned and fired his .358 Winchester, striking the cat in the heart as it sprung at him from a large rock.

After he met his wife, he decided it was time to settle down. He worked a few jobs in construction, but the hours were unsteady. He then found a job down in Washtenaw County as a security lead for a college, while also serving with the fire department as a volunteer EMT. However, layoffs ended his time there. After searching for work, he eventually he managed to get hired at Birchwood Lodge as a professional filleter. The glory days of adventure were gone, along with his barrel-chested physique. Over the years, that muscular chest had sunk about eight inches down, and had become more rounded in shape. He still thought his mustache looked good, although it varied in shade from black to grey.

He heard Mr. Tindell from the next room, leading a couple new tenants through the lodge. There was a lot of laughter coming from the customers, but it sounded drunken and obnoxious. There were times when people like that would come to the lodge. They'd spend more time popping a bottle tab than they would fishing. Joel forced a smile when Mr. Tindell came through the hallway with the two new tenants. They were just as he pictured they be, stocky, dressed in wrinkled clothes and khaki shorts, and with obnoxious grins on their faces.

"...and this is our fish cleaning station," Tindell said to them. He was a short, skinny, but professional gentlemen with a thin goatee. Joel could read his body language. Tindell was unenthusiastic of these individuals as well, but they were paying customers. In the end, that's all that mattered. "This is Joel," he said with enthusiasm. "He's our filleter. If you don't prefer to clean your own fish, bring it here to Joel anytime from eight to five. He's the fastest around. You can give him any fish, and he'll have it back to you that same minute." The guys chuckled. They seemed to be staring past Joel to his personal display behind him. On several shelves were framed photos of him; some were during his time in the service, and many others were of him during his various hunting trips. Under those shelves was a rectangular table, holding a farewell gift from his friends at the Ann Arbor Fire Department; a decommissioned jaws-of-life. He kept it as part of his display, as there was no decent place to put it at home.

"Ha! I'm sure," one of them said in a New York accent. It was sarcastic, and Joel wasn't sure if they were referring to the fish cleaning or one of his photos. The guy turned to his buddy. "Hey, Jeff, look at that." He pointed to the top shelf, above the photos, where Joel had propped his custom-made Bandelero sword in its sheath.

"Okay, Richie, I have a bet for you," Jeff said. "I catch more fish than you, you have to buy me one of those."

"My ass!" Richie said. "You can ask Brook or Diesel." Jeff's eyes went back to Joel.

"Where can I get me one of those?"

"You can't. It's custom made," Joel said. He hoped for that to be the last of the conversation. Naturally, Tindell stepped in to ruin those odds.

"Joel's hunted all over the world. He used that big knife when he was in Asia. A crocodile came up out of the water and snatched him! He used the sword and stuck its blade down the reptile's throat!" He spoke as if he was telling stories around a campfire. It was a true story, one that Joel regretted telling Tindell. He asked Joel to prop the sword up at the Lodge and tell stories of his adventures. What Joel found amusing was that Tindell often told the stories instead.

"Yeah, sure," Jeff said, while Richie laughed. At this time, another customer entered through a glass doorway on the other side. A thirty-year-old man walked up, sporting a twenty-eight-inch walleye. The fish, olive and gold in color, dangled from a stringer with a clip strung through its gills.

"Howdy! Can I help you, sir?" Joel enthusiastically said to the customer, happy to take his attention off the beer drinkers. "Nice work," he added.

"Thanks," the customer said. "I was trolling and picked this bad boy up. However, I'm not too good at gutting these guys."

"Hand 'er on over here," Joel said. The man laid the large fish down onto the smooth grey countertop. Joel removed the stringer and picked up a Rapala knife with a six-inch blade. He ran the blade over the walleye's scales, brushing off the slime. He whipped the blade clean with a rag and then grabbed the fish by the head. In a swift and smooth motion, he sliced the fish under the fins, then behind the gill covers. He slit the belly and on top along the backbone. He slipped the blade under his cut behind the gill cover and ran the knife along the backbone, cutting behind the ribcage all the way down to the tail. He flipped the fish over and repeated the same action along the other side. Both fillets and the tail came off the body, leaving the fish head connected to a skeleton and string of guts. He set it aside and peeled the rib bones from the fillets, then ran his knife between the meat and skin to peel it off. The customer's jaw nearly dropped, amazed at the speed in which Joel filleted his catch. He had noticed the clock on the wall; the second-hand couldn't have moved for more than thirty seconds by the time he started.

"Oh wow," he said. "That was amazing." Joel quickly ran his thumb over each fillet, plucking a couple stray bones from the meat. After a full minute, each boneless fillet was ready. The two slobs didn't say anything, unwilling to admit their impressions. With a scoff, they walked away, much to Joel's approval. Tindell shook his head, annoyed.

"You know you can turn down reservations," Joel said to him.

"They're only here through the weekend," Tindell said. "Luckily, I don't think they'll bother you too much. Besides, it's a party of four." Joel knew that was code for "more money." Tindell turned to the customer. "Well, sir, that's a nice walleye."

"Thank you," the customer said. Joel sealed the fillets in a plastic bag and handed it to him.

"Here you go," he said. "If you need any more help, just let me know."

"Thank you," the customer said. He turned to leave, but stopped. "One quick question: what's the biggest fish in this lake? I mean, the biggest size you've heard of?" Joel thought for a moment.

"The biggest I'm aware of was someone who caught a forty-eight-inch pike," he said. Tindell nodded in agreement. The customer took his hat off and wiped some sweat off his brow, looking slightly puzzled.

"The reason I ask is because, while I was fishing, I saw this bird land in the water. It was a big stinking bird too, probably a swan. It was pretty far off from where I was. I look away, and suddenly I hear this splash. When I looked back, there was this huge wall of water, and when it settled, the bird was gone. Weirdest thing I ever did see."

"Maybe a fish tried to nab it, and the bird flew away."

"I didn't see it anywhere," the customer said.

"It'd be hard to miss. If it was a swan, those things can get up to over four feet," Joel said. He looked to the customer. "Honestly, I couldn't tell ya what it was."

"Oh, no big deal," the customer said with a small laugh. "I just thought it was strange. But hey, thanks for your help!" He held up his bag and started to leave. "Have a good day!"

"You too," Joel said. Knowing there was another check-in scheduled, Tindell left the room as well to go up front. Joel wiped down the counter and tossed away the fish remains into a gut bucket. His mind pondered the man's story. Nothing in the lake was as big as what he described. Perhaps the man was mistaken to the type of bird it was. It was probably something much smaller, and nabbed by a pike. His thoughts were interrupted by the sight of a few fishermen coming toward the station. Each carried a stringer or basket full of fish. Joel arranged his knives on the counter. The busy hours were about to begin.

CHAPTER 5

"He's still not answering his damn phone," Susan Jean complained, slipping her iPhone into the back pocket of her jean shorts. She sat on the top of a picnic table, looking down toward the beach at her college friend Robert Nash. Dressed in swim trunks and a white T-shirt, the thirty-two-year-old Navy veteran stretched his arms toward the sky, then down to his toes. It was a common routine for him to warm up his muscles before completing a big swim. They had already jogged over a mile to get to this little beach, but Robert liked to be as prepared as possible.

"Perhaps he's flirting with his neighbor," he said, bringing his hands to his hips, then to his knees. As he stretched back upward, he briefly waved his hand in front of his face to keep a mosquito from landing in his ginger goatee. "He let it slip that he had the hots for her."

"His neighbor?" Susan said with a laugh. "Isn't she like twenty years older than him?" Robert completed another couple rounds of stretching before kneeling to the ground for pushups. He glanced out at the water. During the evening hours, the lake appeared as flat as a mirror, and even seemed as reflective as one. Upside-down images of the tree line stretched out into the watery surface. Usually after *7:30* p.m., most boaters came in from the lake. Because of this, Robert chose the evening hours to train; as it was less likely he would encounter speeding boaters or paddleboats as he swam. He was preparing for the YMCA National Competitive Swimming event, which would take place in North Carolina the following week. He considered the midway point in the vertical slant on Ridgeway Lake to be a perfect training area. From one side to another, it was about a mile. Swimming that distance would be perfect endurance training for his upcoming event.

Susan was a co-worker from his job at a Red Cross center outside of town. She often would assist in his training by doing various tasks. Today, she would be standing by with a motorboat, docked in the water on public property. If Robert found himself in trouble while swimming, she would take the boat out to his location. On the other end of the lake, a second assistant named Don would also be waiting with a boat. But Don hadn't yet notified them of his arrival. Robert would have to wait until he did so before going out for his long swim.

Robert pumped out about twenty-five pushups, then stood back up. He looked up briefly at Susan, who gazed at him. There was no doubt she was checking him out. It was slightly awkward, being that they had been friends for a long time. Seeing her in those jean shorts and tight T-shirt did not help. He quickly looked away and tried to think of some more warm-ups. He was running out of them, and he didn't want to wear himself out before swimming a mile.

Finally, he heard the Blake Shelton ringtone coming from her phone. She dug it out of her pocket and read the caller ID.

"Yep, it's Don," she said. She touched the screen to answer. "Hey! What took you so long?"

"*Sorry, it took a while to get over here,*" Don replied. Susan rolled her eyes.

"I'm sure it did," she said. "So you're ready?"

"*Yep.*"

"Alright. I'll let Robert know," she said. "By the way, have you made any progress with what's-her-name?"

"*I don't know what you're talking about,*" he said. Susan wasn't convinced, but Don wasn't trying hard to begin with.

"Yeah, yeah," she said, chuckling. "See you on the other side." She hung up the phone and looked to Robert. "Looks like you're good to go."

****

Don hung up his phone and took a seat in his red fifteen-foot speedboat, which he kept tied to this dock. Dressed in a grey shirt and green shorts, he rested his elbow onto the upper edge of the starboard side and stared across the lake. The smooth surface of the water gave a peaceful feeling, and softened his mood a bit. He picked up a pair of binoculars and looked to the opposite shoreline. It took a moment, but he sighted Robert approaching the water. Behind him was Susan, attractive as ever, mounting into her boat.

Why he won't hook up with her, I'll never know, he thought. He figured Robert was just so focused on the competition that he didn't have women on the brain. Afterall, professional athletes were often instructed to refrain from sensuous activities during training periods. And in Don's mind, if Robert was able to resist Susan Jean, he deserved the gold medal.

He lit up a cigarette, fantasizing about making a move toward her. But he knew it would be a wasted effort. He kept his eyes on Robert through the glass of the binoculars. From the long distance, he appeared like a toy figure on a monopoly board, staring out into the lake. Don felt useless, seeing that there was no likely event Robert would need his help. But they were friends, and Don was happy to do this small favor. He watched as Robert stripped himself of the white T-shirt and began to wade into the water. Although they were far off, he could read Susan's expression as she watched him.

"Just make a move already," he said and snickered. His laugh turned into a cough as he accidentally took in too much smoke. "Fuck." He brushed his hand through the air to blow it away. "Make it quick, Rob. I'm bored."

****

The water felt nice and warm to Robert as he stepped in. The water came up to his waist as he waded twenty feet out. Susan sat in the boat, hanging on to his shirt.

"You sure you don't want me to row and keep pace with you?" she asked. She took the tie-off line from the dock and took a seat. The boat slowly began to float outward.

"You can row a little bit out, but there's no need for you to tire yourself out and keep pace the entire time," he said. "Just keep an eye on me with the binoculars. I'll meet Don on the other side."

"Alright," she said. "Just don't do anything stupid, like swimming underwater where we can't see you." Robert laughed.

"Don't worry about that," he said. He scanned the water one more time. It was as flat and undisturbed as before. The only thing he could see was a twelve-foot boat trolling his direction from the north. It was nothing that concerned him, as it was moving very slow. He'd be out of the way long before it'd pass by. He positioned his swimming goggles and took one more glance at Susan. "See you in a few!" He turned back and dove into the water, breaking the flat surface with several splashes. With several powerful strokes and kicks, he swam from shore at Olympian speed.

Susan rowed the boat out, keeping a distance behind him. Despite Robert being insistent that she didn't need to keep up, it was certainly the safer thing to do. A mile was a long swimming distance, with the record time being fifteen minutes and fourteen seconds. She was impressed with Robert's initial speed, which appeared to be on par with that timing. She rowed several more yards out and then grabbed her binoculars. She could see the water fizzing around Robert as he moved further out. She glanced down at her watch. It was getting late, and there was certainly limited sunlight, but he should have enough time to reach Don before it got dark.

We need to find an earlier time to do this, she vented in her mind.

****

Throughout the day, the large fish had nestled down among the thick weeds in the seabed. It was unaccustomed to the heat of the daytime, and the sunlight strained its eyes. Without eyelids to shield them from the brightness, the large fish went deep where it was dark and cool, an environment most familiar to it. There it remained for hours, pumping oxygen-rich water over its gills. Now, hunger was starting to set in. It had fed earlier in the day near the shoreline, shadowed by canopy. But its body was now demanding more sustenance, a need overwhelming its other instincts.

The sunlight coming through the surface was gradually subsiding, replaced by shadows from the trees along the shore. With the brightness levels down, the pain in its eyes receded. With a flick of its tail, the largemouth moved from its hiding spot at the lake bottom. In its search for food, it ingested two walleye, which were insufficient to its needs. It needed larger prey, which it could not locate in the depths.

Vibrations from the surface caused the largemouth to look upward. There was something moving; a lifeform considerably smaller than itself, but larger than anything else it had encountered. The fish moved closer and curiously watched its prey swimming in a straight line. Ready to strike, it moved in a semi-circular motion along the surface to intercept.

****

Robert stroked relentlessly, listening to the splashes in the water as he swam as if already in competition. The splashing sounds were almost always relaxing to him. He looked at it as a reminder that he was moving, and sometimes it even helped him gauge his speed.

But then he heard another splash, one that certainly did not come from him. His body did not feel relaxation from hearing it; rather, he tensed up. He heard another splash, and then he stopped.

"What the…?" he said to himself, catching his breath. He saw the water fizzing about forty feet away, with large swells of water rolling away from the disturbance. It was common for fish and birds to nibble at bugs, but this wasn't anything as small as that. It was as if a large anchor had been dropped in the point of origin. He was about to resume swimming when his eye briefly caught sight of something emerging from the water. It was like two small sails gliding along the surface, one directly behind the other. The one in the back was rounded in shape, a stark contrast to the other sail which appeared to be more triangular. It was more bizarre, as it appeared there were spines protruding from the top. It appeared to be attached to a large submerged body. Before he could look closer, the swells reached him. He dipped under and had to stroke his arms to remain afloat, and when he looked again, the strange object had submerged.

Robert's heart was already pounding in his chest from his exercise, but the new anxiety he was feeling was worsening it. Something inside him knew he wasn't alone in the water. He dipped beneath the water and looked through his goggles. After scanning for a moment, he saw the shape moving up ahead. Though the water clouded his vision, he could see the huge tail moving back and forth. The mouth opened and sucked in water, which was expelled through huge gill slits. From the mouth to the tail, the creature seemed to be well over twenty feet long. He saw it turn and look directly at him. Though the large circular eyes had no expression, they appeared to be fixated on him. He screamed in horror as the beast shot forward with a burst of speed. He broke the surface, uncertain of whether he was facing Don's or Susan's location.

"HEY! GET ME OUT—" The air went from his chest as the intense pressure of the jaws crushed his ribcage. The huge fish hoisted him a few feet into the air before it splashed down. Robert attempted to take a breath, but took in nothing but lake water. In a lightning-fast motion, the jaws suddenly opened and shut, creating a suction motion that drew Robert all the way into its gullet. The creature felt its prey struggle briefly inside of it, before the life slipped away.

As its eyes finally adjusted to the light level, the bass patrolled along the surface, the only place so far where it found sufficient food. Its eardrums quickly started picking up vibrations in the water. Something seemed to be approaching. The fish was still hungry, and it waited for the prey to come to it.

****

"Oh my God!" Susan yelled, after she watched Robert get lifted out of the water. She threw down the binoculars and switched on the motor. As soon as it started, she began speeding the boat out to his location, roughly seven hundred yards out. The propellers kicked up water as they pushed the boat forward. She dug her phone from her pocket, selecting Don's contact number. It rang twice before he picked up.

"Don! I don't see Robert!" she said in a panic. "Did you see what happened?"

"*I don't know!*" he said. His voice expressed alarm. "*I... I saw him waving, and then there was this huge splash! I'm trying to get this damn boat started.*"

"I'm heading out there now," she said, while fighting to keep back tears of fright. She heard Don cursing his motor as he attempted to start it. The starter cord made a loud screech with each tug. Finally, Susan heard the motor ignite.

"*Alright, I'm coming!*" he said. "*Any sign of Rob?*"

"No," Susan said. "I'm just about where he was at. I'm going to slow..." A solid impact at the bow caused the boat to briefly lurch upward. It smacked downward into the surface. The momentum caused Susan to fall forward, hitting her head on the metal edge of the boat. The motor stalled out, and the boat started to drift while slowly spinning.

****

The Carnobass instinctively shot downward after the boat made impact. The bow had struck it on the upper left side below the rear dorsal fin, popping off one of its scales. The exposed flesh bled and stung as the initial stages of infection started to set.

After creating a distance, the huge fish began to circle back. Its small brain registered the impact as a deliberate attack, and believed the boat to be a challenger. It turned toward the boat above, which appeared motionless in the water. The fish started fluttering its tail, gaining momentum for a retaliatory strike. Suddenly, it stopped, sensing new sound waves and vibration coming from another direction. Another potential enemy arrived, similar in size and shape as the one which struck it. Waving its pectoral fins back and forth, the Carnobass maintained position, watching its enemy above.

****

Don saw Susan's boat viciously bounce upward and then smack down into the water. He hurriedly drove his boat over to hers, which slowly drifted and spun about. He switched off his motor as he neared her, then stood to his feet to look over the side. Susan was on her hands and knees, completely in a daze.

"Hey, Susan!" Don called to her. "Jesus, are you okay?" Grabbing the starboard edge, she lifted herself to an upright seated position. She had a nasty cut on her brow, from which blood trickled down her face. She cupped her hand over her cut. It only hurt a little, numbed a bit by the adrenaline she was still experiencing. The hull under the bow was partly indented. "Jesus, what did you hit?" He scanned the water for any floating objects.

"I don't know," she said. Her voice sounded as shaken as she visibly was. His boat started to drift past hers. Don started looking around frantically. He was now looking for Robert, who was still nowhere to be seen.

"Rob!" he called out. He considered diving into the water, but there was a feeling of anxiety keeping him out. He replayed the huge splash that occurred before Robert disappeared. He didn't know what caused it, but that unknown struck enough fear into him to keep him in the boat. Susan ignored the pain while she scanned the water for Robert.

"Robert?" she called out. "Come on, babe! Where are you?" There was no reply, which worsened the dreadful feeling inside. She stood up and looked into the water, hoping he was just playing a prank on them.

****

The beast slowly moved in closer, preparing for an attack. As it neared, it caught the sight of smaller creatures on top of the inanimate objects above. Its insatiable hunger immediately went into overdrive. It remained deep and moved almost directly under the nearest boat. It could see its prey peering over the side, unaware of its presence: perfect for a surprise attack.

It waved its caudal fin, creating a strong burst of speed which propelled it upward. In less than a second, it closed the distance and hyperextended its jaws.

Susan didn't have any time to react. One moment, she was looking into a glassy lake surface. Then she saw something emerge; a gigantic circular white entry leading to a dark tunnel underneath. Water erupted upward and instantly she was caught by the jaws, which clamped down on her waist.

Don turned around just in time to witness the enormous fish breach the water. Green with a large black stripe down its side, it twisted and turned in mid-air. Susan's legs briefly kicked from the outside of its mouth. It came down on top of her boat, driving it under. The Carnobass was buried by an enormous splash, which sprayed Don who was screaming in horror. The natural instinct to flee took over. He twisted his motor key in the ignition. It revved for a moment, but stalled.

"Start, you fucker!" he cursed the machine. He tried again, only to have the same result.

The Carnobass sucked Susan's mangled corpse into its gullet. It quickly redirected itself to the remaining boat. It could hear the panicked actions of its remaining target. With a flick of its tail, it darted at an upward angle to launch another attack.

"Come on!" Don yelled at his boat. He turned the ignition with a hard jerk. Finally, the motor came to life. Don immediately pushed it to top speed. The boat shot forward, nearly throwing him over the stern. He grabbed the transom to support himself. He looked up, just as the fish breached where the boat had been a moment prior. The Carnobass splashed back down and immediately began pursuit, its spiny dorsal fin cutting along the surface like a great white shark. Each flutter of its tail created a fresh burst of speed that brought it nearer to its target.

Don's eyes widened with shock. The enormous beast was catching up to him, despite his boat going at top speed. He watched the long double-fin cut slowly closing the distance. He hoped for a miracle. He knew he had to be nearing the beach.

He turned his eyes to the bow. The shore was there, less than a hundred feet off and quickly closing. Between him and the shore was a boat with a trolling motor. On board was a man of forty, wearing a grey cap and red flannel shirt. He barely had time to react upon seeing Don's boat speeding toward his.

The bow slammed into the portside of the trolling vessel. The propellers still spun as the bow flipped upward, launching Don into mid-air. Screaming, he waved his arms wildly and kicked his legs. He landed a few feet from shore, bouncing off the sand beneath the shallow water. His boat completed two full flips before crashing down into the lake. The other boat had capsized completely and drifted toward shore, with the portside completely caved in.

The fisherman took a breath as he emerged alongside it. Pain flooded his side as he did so, as several broken ribs poked into his lungs. He tried to kick to shore, but only had use of one of his legs; the other was broken at the femur. He painfully paddled his arms. The overwhelming pain limited him to only gain a few inches with each stroke.

Disoriented and in pain, he didn't even notice the Carnobass approach from behind him. All he saw was the shadow from its huge bulk, and all he felt was the suction-like force which drew him backward into its mouth. He was in an upright position when the jaws shut downward, flattening his body into a fleshy pancake. His neck was forced downward between his shoulders, bending his spine into disproportionate positions which caused vertebrae to snap. Ribs were smashed together, and internal organs exploded from within. The ravaged corpse was then swallowed, and the Carnobass instantly swam back out to the deeper region of the lake. There it would take a short time to rest, but not too long, as its body was demanding it find more sustenance.

Don didn't yet feel the pain from the numerous fractures he suffered. He crawled a few feet further away from the shore and rolled onto his back. He stared straight up at the darkening sky for a few moments before slipping into unconsciousness.

CHAPTER 6

The time was *9:23 p.m.* as Morgan Sydney stared up at the ceiling in his bedroom. He was tired but unable to fall asleep. The pain in his leg throbbed, and the fact that his mind dwelled on it only made it worse. His eyes consistently went to his window. Sunset had occurred about twenty minutes ago, typical for this time of year. He felt himself grow frustrated and actually longing for his *Meperidine* pills. He hated them, but at least the drowsiness side effect came in handy for nights like these.

The thought of the medicine brought his ex-wife to mind again. And each thought of her seemed to worsen his leg pain. It brought back memories he regretted, and the torture of reminiscing the things he would've done differently.

His cell phone rang, breaking his train of thought. It was resting on his dresser, which was right next to his bed. He reached over, accidentally knocking it off the floor.

"Goddamnit," he cursed. He fumbled for the phone and finally answered it. "Chief Sydney."

"*Hey, Chief,*" answered Tim Marlow's voice. "*Sorry to call you this late.*"

"It's no problem, Tim," he said. He had forgotten the young officer had signed up for a double shift. "What can I do for you?"

"*Well, uh...we have a bit of a situation here over at 4351 Harrison Street. Somebody found somebody unconscious over by the water.*"

"Is EMS there?"

"*They're almost here. I can hear their sirens down the street. But here's the strange thing, Chief: It looks like this guy might have had some sort of boating accident. There's a boat here on the shore, all smashed up...and there's also another one submerged out in the lake. You can see the front of it sticking up. And there's nobody else out here.*"

"Oh shit," Sydney said. "Okay, just give me a couple minutes and I'll head out there. How many other officers are on scene?"

"*Me, and two others,*" Marlow said.

"Alright," Sydney said. "Keep your flashers on, and spot for the ambulance. Keep anybody else off the scene. Get a statement from the person who called it in. I'll be on the road in three minutes."

"*Yes, sir,*" Marlow said. Sydney hung up the phone and limped to his closet. He pulled out his uniform and began dressing himself. He clipped his duty belt on and holstered his Beretta M9. Being the RPD chief had a few perks, one of which being he could use whichever weapon he wanted. The M9 wasn't favored by most, but it served him well, and he usually hit what he shot at.

He made his way through the kitchen toward the front door. He twisted the handle to open it. He then stopped, looking at the orange prescription bottle on the table. Ibuprofen barely did anything for the pain, and usually made his stomach worse. However, it would be better than nothing.

"Fuck it," he said aloud to himself. He spilled an 800 mg pill into the palm of his hand and guzzled it down with a full glass of water. He then proceeded out the door.

****

The emergency flashers installed on the Jeep Rubicon created a red glow in the dark street as Sydney steered onto Harrison Street. He could see the flashes from EMS, Fire Rescue, and RPD up ahead. After arriving at the scene, he parked off the road, leaving the engine running as he stepped out.

Tim Marlow approached him. Sydney looked past him at the EMTs and paramedics grouped around the victim. It was the same group of people, mainly a volunteer unit. He recognized one of those volunteers as Joel Pobursky, whom he had met several times at the lodge. Joel was busy directing the workers in loading the victim onto a stretcher.

"Has there been any update?" Sydney asked Marlow.

"None so far, sir," Marlow replied. "It sounds like this guy's pretty busted up."

"Is he conscious?" Sydney asked.

"He's been in and out. He muttered something about a fish, and then slipped away again." Sydney started walking down to the beach area, keeping distance to give the first responders space to tend to the individual. One of the other officers had a spotlight fixated on the bow of a mostly submerged boat, roughly thirty feet from shore. From what he could see, the left side appeared to be caved inward. Washed up to the left was the other boat. The bow was an unrecognizable mess, crunched in entirely, and much of the underside was crumpled inward as well.

"Definitely a collision," Sydney said. He looked at the surrounding lake area near the partly submerged boat. "Plenty of open space. How in the hell did he manage to hit this other boat?" He grabbed his flashlight and scanned the shoreline. Fishing lures, hooks, and bits of bait were washing up, collecting in the sand. He looked to Marlow. "Do we have any idea what time this occurred?" Marlow shook his head.

"We got the call roughly ten minutes before I called you," he said. "This isn't really a residential road, so not many people pass through here."

"So God only knows how long that guy was lying there until someone saw him," Sydney said. "Is the person that found him still here?"

"No, he wanted to take off," Marlow said. "There wasn't anything he told us that we don't already know from looking at this. And there's no sign of the owner of that other boat."

"Damn it," Sydney cursed. "Something tells me we're looking for a body. We're probably gonna have to dredge this area if this other possible boater doesn't turn up." He looked back to the EMTs. They had the individual secured on the stretcher. Joel kneeled at the front with another at the back, grabbing the grips.

"One…two…three…lift," Joel said. They lifted up, elevating the stretcher three feet, and began rolling it toward the ambulance. He stepped into the ambulance bed and then lifted the stretcher to move it inside. Sydney started to jog over to them, which caused the pain in his leg to flare up. He quietly cursed and reduced his speed to a fast walk.

"Joel!" he called out. Joel looked up at him.

"Howdy, Chief," he said.

"Is he conscious? Has he said anything about what happened?"

"He's been slipping in and out," Joel said. "But we need to get him to the hospital. He's got multiple contusions, likely several fractures, a concussion, and I think he might have internal bleeding."

"Alright," Sydney said. "I'll follow you guys to the hospital." The other EMT climbed into the ambulance and shut the door. The siren started blaring as the driver steered the ambulance onto the road. Sydney started walking toward his Jeep. Marlow kept pace with him.

"What do you want us to do, Chief?" he asked.

"Stay here and preserve the scene," Sydney said. He then took in a slow breath and continued. "Also, take a walk along the shoreline…in case another body washes up." Even in the dark, Sydney could see Marlow turn pale. The young officer was clearly unconditioned for seeing such a thing.

"Y-yes sir," he said. Sydney climbed into his Jeep and blared the siren as he took off.

****

The ambulance was stopped at the Readfield Hospital's emergency entrance as Sydney drove into the lot. He drove up and parked his jeep twenty feet behind the ambulance. Joel and his fellow EMTs had already unloaded the patient and were wheeling him into the ER. Sydney followed them in.

The ER lobby was wide open and brightly lit. Two nurses immediately approached the stretcher. Sydney stayed back and allowed them to do their work. While waiting, he could overhear the conversation between the EMTs and nurses.

"He's been in and out since we found him," Joel explained. "He has not been coherent; clearly a concussion. Blood pressure's 87 over 52. It looks like he's got a bit of swelling going on. Possibly internal bleeding, judging from the low blood pressure…" He paused for a moment and looked around the room. "Don't you guys have an ER doctor?"

"I'm here," a voice called out from the rear hallway. Sydney looked past the gathering, seeing the doctor stepping out into the lobby, tying her hair back behind her head. Sydney swallowed hard, recognizing the doctor to be Meya.

"Oh you've got to be kidding me," he said to himself. Dressed in blue scrubs, his ex-wife put on some latex gloves and walked to the stretcher. Joel directed his attention toward her.

"I was telling the nurses that this guy might have…"

"I heard you from back there," she cut him off. She put on her stethoscope and pressed the diaphragm to the patient's chest. "I need a line on this guy and a bag of saline, wide open. Let's get a new blood pressure reading," she then said. The nurses placed a cuff on his upper arm, and Meya placed the diaphragm of the stethoscope over the brachial artery. The nurse inflated the cuff then released the air. Another nurse began tapping at his other arm to make a vein stand out so she could start an IV.

Joel moved away from them and stood beside the chief. "Yeah, not like we didn't just take his blood pressure," he griped. He noticed Sydney's sour expression. "What's up with you?" he questioned with a grin. "Swallow a pigeon?"

"Nothing you'll want to hear," Sydney said. Joel looked over at the doctor.

"You have a crush on the lady-doc, do ya?" he cackled. Sydney bit his lip.

"No… I was married to her for nine years," Sydney said. Joel's grin transformed into a surprised expression.

"Oh…wow," he said. "Small world."

"Too small," Sydney said. "Did you get a name for the individual? Was there any identification?"

"No," Joel said. "His shorts pockets were empty. And he wasn't even lucid enough to tell us his name." Meya's commanding voice caught both their attention as she barked orders at her nurses. The patient had woken up suddenly, as if hit by a shot of adrenaline. He panicked and started squirming in his stretcher, rocking it back and forth.

"Sir, sir! You're all right! You're in a hospital," Meya said to him. The panicking patient did not relent. He kept trying to look back, as if he thought something was behind him. His eyes were wide open, nearly bulging out of their sockets. Meya grabbed his arm to keep his IV line in. She knew she had to get him under control, or else his blood pressure would drop even further. "One milligram of Ativan!" she yelled to one of the nurses. Joel hurried over and helped hold the patient down as a nurse filled a syringe with the dosage and injected it into his IV. After about thirty seconds, the patient stopped struggling and laid back, appearing to be in a trance.

"Alright, we need to get him into the operating room," Meya said. They started wheeling the stretcher down the hallway. Sydney stepped forward and raised his hand.

"Whoa, one quick sec!" he said. "I need to get a quick statement from him." Meya looked back at him, visibly irritated. The nurses continued wheeling the stretcher while she hung back.

"Listen, *Chief,*" she said, "I don't know if you've gone blind in the last couple years, but it's obvious this man's not in any condition to be interrogated."

"It's not an interrogation," Sydney said. "There's important info I need to get from him regarding the accident. There might be another—"

"I'm sorry, it's not happening," Meya said. "Take your damn ibuprofen and let me do my job." She turned and marched down the hallway. Joel could hear Sydney curse under his breath.

"Anything I can do to help out?" he asked.

"No, thanks," Sydney said. "I need to head back. We might need to get divers in the water if we can't find the owner of that second boat." He exited the ER lobby and boarded his Jeep. He drove through the turnaround and sped through the lots, lights still flashing.

Joel's volunteer work was done for the night. He and the other EMT boarded the ambulance to go home. All he could do at this point was to go home, reheat his chili dinner, and hope for good news on the victim.

****

Tim Marlow could see the emergency flashers on the chief's approaching Jeep light up the street in strobes of red. He had just returned from patrolling the shore north of the accident scene, with no luck of locating the other boat owner or any witnesses. His boots and bottom of his pants were now wet from checking the shoreline, and he was exhausted from the long day. His watch read *10:13*, forty-seven minutes away from the conclusion of his double-shift.

Chief Sydney parked his jeep off the side of the road. He stepped out and saw Marlow approaching.

"Did you find anything?" he asked the young officer.

"Nothing, sir," Marlow said. "How's the guy? Did he ever wake up?" Seeing the chief's agitated facial expression, he somewhat regretted asking.

"He did, but they had to sedate him," Sydney said. "I wanted to attempt to ask about the accident, but Meya had to stick it to me. '*This man's not in any condition to be interrogated,*'" he mimicked a woman's voice.

"Meya?" Marlow asked, confused.

"My ex… uhh, the doctor at the hospital," Sydney said quickly. He walked down to the shore. The scene remained undisturbed, with each boat untouched. There were two more officers on scene. One was poking a branch into a collection of cattails. He expressed a nervous grin when he noticed the chief staring at him. "What are you doing?" "Just…uh…just trying to see if anyone possibly washed up over here," he stuttered.

"We're not looking for a bullfrog," Sydney said. He then looked at his manpower. There were four officers on scene, with a fifth patrolling the town. "Alright, I want one person to remain here. Call dispatch and have them get somebody out here to tow these boats away. Have you guys been taking photographs of the scene?" He watched the three officers look at each other timorously. *What police academy have these guys been to?* Sydney thought.

"I took some on my phone," Marlow raised his hand. Sydney barely hid his surprised reaction.

"Alright," Sydney looked at the other officers. "Two of you keep patrolling the shore. Marlow and I are gonna get a boat and check the other side." One of the officers glanced down at his watch. Sydney knew what was on his mind. "Got a date?" Sydney said to him.

"Wha…no. Just, uhh…"

"Don't even mention shift change," Sydney cut him off. "Alright, get to it guys. Radio in if you find anything." He turned and went to his Jeep, followed by Marlow.

****

The police docking station was only a seven-minute drive from the accident. It was composed of two small decks that protruded twenty feet into the water, each with a twenty-foot police vessel tied alongside. Sydney and Marlow boarded one and began patrolling the water. Sydney asked dispatch to phone the hospital to check if anyone else had been checked-in for injuries related to the situation. So far, nobody had been admitted, which made Sydney dread the situation more. Missing person cases were no picnic, and they were even worse when he didn't know who the missing person was…or even if there was one.

Sydney operated the boat from the cockpit, while Marlow aimed a spotlight attached to the starboard railing. He moved the beam of light over the water. A light fog had formed over the water, making it harder to see anything. Sydney had pointed out that the person was likely wearing a life vest, so finding him afloat would be no problem.

"There was a dock over there," Marlow said. "Could it be possible the missing guy's boat was docked there, came loose, and then the other guy hit it?" He realized almost instantly how unrealistic it sounded. "Actually, nevermind."

"At least you're attempting to use your brain," Sydney said.

"Are you gonna go to the hospital tomorrow to try and speak to that guy?"

"Yeah, but by then we'll probably have found the other individual," Sydney said. "But we still need his details for our report." Marlow continued guiding the light over the water.

"Have you had a lot of cases like this when you were with the state?" he asked. Plain dumb conversation was better than silence.

"I've dealt with more than my fair share of missing persons," Sydney said. "But usually they were kidnappings, murders, or runaways. Something like this, they usually turned up quick. Honestly, I'm surprised we haven't found this person yet."

"I heard of this one case down in Florida," Marlow said. "They made this big drug bust, and one of the suspects made this run into the marshes. Apparently, this guy wore this red crystal ring on his middle finger. They could not find the guy. And he never turned up anywhere. Even associates reported they couldn't find him. Then some gator hunter shot himself a twelve footer. Then he gutted the thing, found this red crystal ring lodged in its stomach." Sydney allowed a small grin to show through. It quickly went away as he winced in pain and put his hand over his leg. After a moment, he saw Marlow looking at him with concern.

"I know you've been wanting career advice from me. Well, I got some here; don't get shot," he said.

"How'd you know I wanted advice?" Marlow said.

"Kid, I can read you like a book," Sydney said.

"I can read you too, sir," Marlow said. "I know you miss working for the state, and you don't want to be here. Getting your leg nearly blown off changed things. I can tell you don't think you're living up to your full potential here, and in a way that hurts more than the leg." Sydney stayed quiet for a few moments. He wasn't sure whether Marlow was as intuitive as he seemed, or if his misery was simply that obvious. Either way, the young officer was right, though Sydney would never admit it.

"Most rookies aren't so straightforward," he said.

"Like I said before, I hope to be running my own department one day," Marlow said. "I figured straightforwardness is a quality in a leader."

"You know another quality in a leader?" Sydney turned toward him. "Not doing shit like going to school while on duty." Marlow didn't say anything. Sydney knew he was still embarrassed about that, as he should have been. A rare feeling of sympathy swept over the chief. He knew the kid meant well, and overall had a really good work ethic. "So you mentioned wanting to try out other units to work your way up?"

"Yes," Marlow said, continuing to look out into the lake. Sydney took a breath. In the past few years, kindness hadn't been his suit.

"Most of those specialties demand at least two years of road patrol service," he said. "You've been with me for about six months now, right? Tell you what…get through the next eighteen months without doing anything stupid, and I'll get you in somewhere. I've gotten to know a bunch of chiefs and sheriffs very well over the years and most of them will still be in office by then. I still have a lot of pull." Marlow looked at him. His face initially expressed shock at the chief's officer, but quickly lit up with excitement and gratitude.

"Holy crap…Chief…are you serious?" Marlow asked. "No…nevermind. Thanks… I don't know what to say."

"Oh God," Sydney said, feeling slightly uncomfortable with the poignant moment. "Yes, I'm serious. Just don't do anything stu—" His voice trailed off and his eyes went down to a reflection in the water. "Turn that light back." He turned and went for the console to swing the boat to starboard. Marlow grabbed the spotlight again and swept it over the water. At first, he wasn't sure what he was looking for, but then he saw the flashy reflection. Something was floating in the water. As the boat passed by it, he was able to scoop it out of the water with a scoop net. Sydney stopped the boat and joined him on the deck.

"What the hell is that?" he asked. Marlow freed the item from the net. It was fan-shaped, flat, and very solid. The lights on the bridge illuminated it fairly well. It had a greenish tinge to it, but also appeared pale. Marlow flicked the top of it, bruising the tip of his finger on its hard surface.

"Damn! It's pretty hard. Could it be part of a turtle shell?"

"Turtle shells are more rounded than this," Sydney said. He took it from Marlow. As he did, he felt something soft and squishy on the bottom. He flipped it around. A soft, grayish pink substance stuck to the underside of the plate. Sydney removed a pen from his shirt pocket and prodded the substance. It was meaty and had a very soft reddish tinge to it. "That's odd." He took it to the console and pulled out a clear plastic bag.

"You're taking that in as evidence?" Marlow asked.

"This area is considered the scene of an investigation," Sydney said as he started stuffing the item into the plastic. "So, yes, I am. Or rather; you're taking it in."

"Me?" Marlow said.

"Yeah you," Sydney said. "Don't forget it's almost shift change."

"But, sir, don't worry about that," Marlow said. "I'd like to stick around and help with the search."

"Unfortunately, it's illegal for you to work more than sixteen hours," Sydney said. "I'll drop you off and you can take your patrol vehicle back to the station. Make sure this thing is refrigerated. And tell the midnight guys to get out here as soon as possible." Marlow nodded. Sydney took to the controls and started steering the patrol boat toward shore. He knew that Marlow was disappointed. It was the first truly interesting case the department has had since its foundation, and he wanted to be a part of it. "Hey, kid," he said. Marlow looked at him. "You've done good."

The words were very encouraging. This time, it didn't feel awkward or uncomfortable for Sydney to say them. Rather, it felt refreshing.

CHAPTER 7

The distant glow of emergency lights across the lake reflected off the yellow taxi's windshield as it pulled into the large driveway of a lake house. For the husky forty-year-old driver, it provided a nice distraction from the impassioned spectacle in his rearview mirror. He put the taxi in park, and awkwardly glanced back. The man and woman grabbed at each other vigorously. Hands were all over each other as they each dug their tongue deeper into the other's mouth.

"Ah-hem," the driver uncomfortably cleared his throat in an attempt to get their attention. "We have arrived. That'll be *$22.30*." The man in the back, dressed in blue jeans and a navy blue shirt, reached toward him with cash in hand.

"Keep it," he said, hardly severing contact from the brunette's face. The driver unfolded the cash, revealing two twenties. The generous tip certainly brightened his mood. He looked up from the money to see that the dark-haired male exited out the passenger side, pulling the well-endowed lady out with him. He enthusiastically began kissing her neck and shoulders. "Have a great night," the driver said with a wave. He put the car in reverse and steered out the driveway.

Amanda Stanton tilted her head far back, allowing the athletically built Jack Penn further access to her neck and cleavage. He took advantage, nuzzling his lips down to the straps of her red dress. That dress, which displayed her well-endowed cleavage, was the very thing that initially drew him toward her when they met at the bar. His logic was: *any single woman wearing something like that is looking for something.* Her gaze toward him supported that theory. Several beers later, they found themselves calling a cab, while other patrons complained for them to "get a room."

Jack felt himself getting more worked up by the second. That red dress was barely hanging on Amanda's shoulders. It looked as if barely any motion would drop it off her, which was what he longed for. The two drunken lovers started stumbling up a small hill to the front porch. Had he been sober, and thinking straight, Jack would've noticed the size of the house they were approaching, which would bring him to ask what she did for a living to afford such a place. They struggled to the front porch stairway, laughing in a drunken, passionate fit.

"I'm still maintaining that your assumption of me is wrong," she said through her laughter.

"You can say that, but I'm still not convinced," Jack said.

"I can convince you," she replied, still laughing. She started her way up the steps. She instantly started wobbling. "Whoa," she said, exaggeratedly.

"Damn, girl," Jack snickered. "You gonna make it?"

"Oh bite me," she retorted. She took another drunken step. This time, she lost her balance completely. Laughing obnoxiously, she fell backward onto Jack who managed to catch her. The laughing continued as they both fell to the ground. They rolled over on one another, fumbling with each other's clothes. Panting heavily, Jack went for Amanda's dress straps. She lightly smacked his hand and then stood up, much to his surprise.

"Nah-ah-ah," she said, waving her finger back and forth. "You're gonna have to work for it."

"Work for it?" Jack asked, grinning lustfully. "Haven't I already been doing that? I figured buying you those beers and taking you onto the dance floor counts as working for it."

"Not enough," she said. She started strolling toward the sandy shore. She kicked off her sandals and splashed her feet into the water, a few feet out from the dock. After being knee deep, she turned back toward Jack, who had already removed his belt from his jeans. "Whoa, slow down, cowboy," she said. She toyed with her dress strap with her thumb, taunting her one-night stand. "You want this, come get it." With a flick of her thumb, the dress peeled off. Jack gazed at her athletic body, covered only by a red off-the-shoulders bra and matching panties. With a laugh, she backed out further. Jack removed his shirt, jeans, and boots and started toward the water. As he waded in, Amanda had backstroked out past the end of the dock, where the large pontoon boat was tied up. She smiled and waited as he approached. Jack swam toward her, quickly closing the distance.

"Gotcha!" he exclaimed, reaching out to grab her. His arms snatched up nothing but water, and the next thing he noticed was Amanda laughing victoriously after paddling out of his reach. A chase began, and both of them kicked up water as they played their game. Their drunken laughter echoed through the air, mixed with amused shouts and screams as Jack nearly caught up with her.

****

The fish glided gently under the surface, conserving energy as it studied the red flashing lights above. Hunger was setting in again, and it considered making a strike on the large mechanical organism above. Its brain could not yet comprehend that the police boat was inorganic. However, the target was only a little smaller than itself; not ideal for a food source. The prey it had consumed earlier was softer than prey it had consumed in its previous environment. Because of this, its metabolism worked much faster, increasing its appetite. Due to the lack of sufficient prey in its current habitat, the bass was forced to feed on whatever it could find.

As it stalked the boat, its eardrums picked up on vibrations from further up the lake. Although faint, it was able to detect that the movements in the water were erratic, indicative of prey like it had fed on prior. It gave up on stalking the vessel and turned around to investigate. With a flutter of its wide tail, it moved toward the vibrations.

As it got closer, it was able to detect two sources of motion. Both lifeforms were of a size suitable for sustenance. It moved in close enough to visibly inspect its prey. They were gradually moving out into deeper water, straight toward it.

****

"What? Is this too much for you?" Amanda continued to tease her zealous pursuer. She continued to backstroke, keeping a few feet of distance between her and Jack. He watched her intently, feeling more lustful with each passing moment. He kicked his legs and paddled his arms, quickly coming within reach. He wrapped his arms around Amanda's bare waist.

"Gotcha!" he proclaimed. He didn't waste any time before kissing her neck and shoulders, nibbling slightly with his teeth. The make-out persisted for a couple minutes, during which Jack began to slip his fingers beneath her undergarments. Naturally, Amanda took notice, and now she was willing to submit. "How 'bout we swim back and finish this inside?"

"I think that sounds good," Jack said. Amanda gave him one more kiss on the lips before swimming around him. Facing him, she backstroked toward the dock, and Jack kept pace, trailing only a few feet behind her.

The Carnobass watched its prey change direction. It decided not to wait any longer. It shot upward, with jaws protruding.

Amanda shrieked as the water around Jack erupted before her very eyes. As fast as the water rose, so did Jack…inside the mouth of a huge fish that breached the water. The huge scaly body reflected the porch light during the brief moment the creature was twisting about in mid-air. Shock, fear, and confusion didn't have time to register in his brain before he and the fish crashed down into the water. As soon as they went under, the Carnobass turned and ran, sucking its prey down its throat. Its tiny teeth, like sandpaper, shredded Jack's torso as he passed over them. The passage down the throat crushed ribs, until he landed in the dark acidic dungeon of the bass's stomach.

Panic and shock took a few moments to overtake Amanda's drunken bewilderment. When it did, it was manifested with a high-pitched scream. She turned and paddled harder. The water in her eyes, along with the consumed booze, had clouded her vision, but she knew she was moving toward shore. Almost blind, she continued forward.

The Carnobass detected the rapid movements from its remaining meal. It turned around and immediately began pursuit. Its prey was moving into shallower waters, stimulating a sense of urgency in its resolve. A powerful flap of its tail launched it forward like a torpedo.

A sixth sense in Amanda's mind alerted her that the terrible beast was approaching. Adrenaline and desperation put her racing heart into overdrive. Various expressions were shouted, each one cut off by water splashing into her face. One moment she'd be begging God for mercy, next she'd be cursing Him for this predicament. She paddled forward, eyes shut from the splashing water. After several long moments, she finally opened them, and screamed at the sight of something enormous in front of her. She bounced off the side of it and began to kick away until she realized it was the pontoon boat.

There was no time for relief. The churning sound of water behind her caused Amanda to look back. The narrow, spiny fin emerged and was slicing its way toward her. Shrieking in terror, Amanda turned to grab at the edge of the deck. She moved around the pontoon boat, reaching up to the dock. Her fingers barely touched the side of the plank before she slipped down and bumped into the pontoon.

The fish lined up for a linear attack on the surface, with the water being too deep for it to come up from underneath. Amanda saw the creature speeding her way, and let out a bloodcurdling scream. As it shot forward, its eyes caught sight of the pontoon boat rocking in the water. Its brain registered the moving object to be another predator moving in for its meal. It banked suddenly to the right, crashing into the boat. Bits of fiberglass broke from the bottom, causing water to leak into the hull. The impact pushed the boat away from the dock, tightening the slack in its tie-off line.

Clinging to the leg of the dock, Amanda felt an intense tightening around her stomach. She looked down and realized she was in the middle of a loop in the tie-off cable. As it began to tighten, the loop constricted her midsection. She gagged and cursed as she struggled to free herself.

The Carnobass shuttered its body to spit the inorganic bits of boat from its mouth. No longer concerned about the perceived competition, it turned once again toward its prey. Its jaws extended, with bits of Jack's flesh still caught within its small teeth.

"No!" Amanda screamed, failing to remove the cord. Seeing the huge swells of water coming her way, she started kicking backward desperately. The Carnobass closed its jaws, engulfing her all the way up to her abdomen. As soon as it had a hold, it drove itself under and ran with its prey. Amanda attempted to scream both from terror and intense pain, but was muffled by the suffocating water.

The line, snagged around Amanda's midsection, became fully stretched out. The pressure snapped several ribs and squeezed her lungs. Bubbly blood spat from her mouth, and her eyes bulged from their sockets. Unaware of why it was hung up, the Carnobass tugged harder and harder to free itself from the unforeseen force holding it back. Each tug tightened the loop even more. The fish swung its tail in huge motions to gain extra force, keeping Amanda firm in its jaws.

Amanda's last sensation was that of her vertebrae detaching in the lumbar region. Tendons snapped and internal organs ruptured as she was torn in half. Skin and muscle tissue pulled apart, spilling bodily fluids into the open water. Swallowing the bottom half of its prey, the Carnobass swam free into the depths of the lake, leaving Amanda's ravaged torso. Torn away at the stomach region, she floated back toward the deck, with a strand of bloody intestines trailing behind.

CHAPTER 8

Sydney walked like a zombie from his office to the lobby, straight for the coffee pot. It was nearly empty, down to its last measurement. He filled his cup with what remained and started a fresh pot. After adding two scoops of sugar to it, he limped back to his office and shut his door behind him. Leaning back in his chair, he fought against droopy eyes.

The time was *8:43 a.m.*, and he was already on his third cup. He had been up most of the night assisting his staff in the search for any possible victims. Around *3:30 a.m.,* he returned home to catch a quick snooze while the midnight staff continued searching. He returned by *6:00 a.m.* in time to meet the divers sent in by the state police. With no current in the lake, any bodies in the surrounding area should have been relatively easy to locate. But after two hours of looking and moving further out, there was nothing. Not a trace.

Most of the staff in the department was convinced it was a wild goose chase. Sydney, however, remained apprehensive about the situation. He had mandated the afternoon staff to remain on duty for four hours, and mandated midnights for an hour-and-a-half. Before returning to the office, Sydney ordered the day-shift officers to keep patrolling the lake. Rumors were already starting to circulate that Sydney was looking for an excuse to demonstrate authority. Some of the officers also doubted the chief's judgment, thinking his prime days were behind him. Sydney was well aware of the gossip. He had been a cop long enough to quickly pick up on the buzz regarding leadership.

Even Mayor Greene seemed a bit uneasy about the situation. His reasoning was regarding appearances. During a fifteen-minute phone conversation, Sydney was grilled with questions about patrol boats cruising along the shore. While Greene understood the initial investigation, he wasn't too pleased that the case wasn't closed after the state failed to find evidence of another victim.

"There was evidence," Sydney had explained. "There were fishing lures and bait everywhere."

"*Haven't you considered that belonged to the guy in the hospital*?" Greene retorted.

"I've considered everything. But I'm not giving up on the possibility that there might be another victim in this accident."

"*My office has been blowing up with calls about whether the lake is safe,*" Greene said. "*People saw the state vehicles entering and leaving, and now they see your patrol vessels out there. People are here to fish and have a good time.*"

"I understand that, sir. But I believe we may have a possible missing person and—"

"*Has anyone been reported missing since last night?*"

"No, but—"

"*Has anyone else been checked into the hospital pertaining to this incident?*"

"No… BUT—"

"*Then the matter is closed until further notice. You may keep an officer patrolling the lake, as long as it appears routine. Otherwise, get your men back to their normal duties.*"

At least Greene didn't question him on why he called the state and not the County. Despite this, it almost seemed as if Greene had forgotten why they created this police force. The town seemed to have elapsed back into the comfortable status of having hardly any crime. It was as if everyone expected the police to be just a deterrent, rather than actually performing investigations and other police duties.

"Here's to my legacy," Sydney said aloud to himself, lifting his coffee cup. As he nearly touched it to his lips, his office phone started ringing. He recognized the listed extension as being from the front desk. He placed his coffee down and picked up the phone.

"Chief Sydney," he answered.

"*Hi, Chief,*" he recognized Abby's voice from the dispatch desk, "*are you available? I have someone up here who's requesting a meeting with you.*"

"Yeah, I'm available," Sydney said.

"*Okay. Do you want to meet her up here, or do you want one of us to escort her to your office?*"

"My office will be good. Thanks," Sydney said.

"*Okay, just a moment,*" Abby said and hung up. Sydney leaned back and stretched. Normally, he would meet people up front, but today he was feeling hardly any motivation. However, he had to get up and open the door. Hearing the footsteps coming down the hallway, Sydney pulled himself to his feet and opened the door.

"Good morning, what can I do for—?" he paused, recognizing Meya standing in the hallway. "Oh…"

"Good morning, Chief," she said. Dressed in black slacks and a navy blue blouse, she stood there with her hands on her hips. Sydney felt himself grow tense and even more irritable.

"Hi…uh, come on in," he said. He stood aside to let her enter his office. *This is just what I needed. What's next, liver cancer?* "Feel free to take a seat," he said while faking a smile.

"That's alright, but thank you," Meya said.

"Okay…well, what can I do for you?" he asked. He made a particular point not to speak to her as if he'd known her for years.

"Listen, I came by to give you this," Meya said. She pulled out a folded sheet of paper from her shirt pocket and handed it to Sydney. He examined it. It was the information file on the victim; Don Baker. "It has his personal info on it, which I know you needed for your police report."

"How'd you get this?" Sydney asked.

"We stabilized him, and he was coherent for a short bit," she said. "He told us his info."

"He's stable? Did he say what happened? Did he mention anyone else?"

"He mentioned something about some friends, but didn't give details. He started babbling about some big fish in the lake. Almost as soon as he started explaining, he slipped into another panic episode. I had to sedate him again. He'll have to be transferred to another hospital, since we don't do psych at ours." Sydney wrote down her statement and looked over his notes.

"I don't think 'sea monster' will look good in the report," he remarked. To his amazement, Meya cracked a smile. He figured it was unintentional, because she looked away for a brief moment.

"Listen," she now sounded slightly uncomfortable, "I also wanted to apologize. I was a bit…well, quite rude to you yesterday both times I saw you. It was uncalled for. And I'm particularly sorry about how I was at the ER. I didn't realize you thought there might have been a second victim."

"Nah, don't beat yourself up over it," Sydney said. Behind his casual demeanor was a feeling of astonishment. He assumed she was going to be even more callous than before; he certainly didn't expect an apology, and especially not a smile.

"I must say, seeing you here was very unexpected," she explained. "I guess I was caught a little off guard." Sydney chuckled.

"You and me both," he said.

"Yeah, but you handled it better," Meya said. "At least you attempted to be polite. I wish I could chalk it up to working a long day, but I'm not one to make excuses."

"I wouldn't worry about it," he said. "By the way, how come you were working the ER last night? Don't you have doctors for that?"

"The scheduled doctor caught the stomach flu, and I couldn't get anyone to pick up the shift. Naturally, being the one in charge of the hospital, I had to cover," she said with a sigh. "You remember those days." Sydney nodded. Of course, she was referring to their years of marriage, when their time together was plagued with mandated overtime.

"I do," he said and then laughed. "That's what I like about my job now. I get to mandate others instead." Meya smiled again. He was still getting used to that sight.

"You were working last night," she pointed out. Sydney thought about it.

"Yes…yes, I was," he said. A quiet moment naturally occurred as they looked at each other smiling. Such a moment hadn't happened in years, and at once, they both realized it and wanted to change the subject.

"Well, uhh, I guess that's it," Meya said.

"Okay. Off to work?"

"No, home," she said. "I stayed at the hospital all night to keep an eye on the patient."

"How did you get today off? You used to work several days in a row, back when we were…" Sydney started.

"Dr. Masood is covering for me today, since I was there all night," she cut in quickly. She then started toward the door. "Were you guys able to find anyone last night?"

"No," Sydney said, standing up to get the door. "Nobody found anything. Not even the divers. All I found was this weird shell floating in the water."

"A shell?" Meya asked.

"Yeah, with what appears to be a strand of flesh attached to it. We took it in, but I'm not sure it's connected to what happened. I'm more curious to know what it is at this point." Meya appeared genuinely interested.

"I've got time," she said. "Mind if I take a look?" Sydney thought about it for a moment. He had plenty of time to kill.

"Yeah, what the hell," he said.

He led her to the storage room. During their marriage, Meya had been in police stations before, but had never seen evidence storage. The room was a little more than two hundred square feet in size. Several shelves lined the walls, carrying containers for properly storing items. Most of these containers were empty. On the right was a large metal refrigeration unit, with an electric thermometer reading 35 degrees. Because of the internal pressure, Sydney had to pull on the large grey door. It opened with a slight hiss, revealing a white mostly empty compartment with a few metal shelves. Sydney stepped in and grabbed the item he found in the lake. After shutting the door, he took the thing out of the bag and handed it to Meya. It was cold, but not frozen.

They stepped out of the room and went to another room with a large table. She eyeballed the meaty substance and touched it with her finger.

Looking closer, she could see something in the substance resembling a red sewing thread. She looked closer.

"Do you have a magnifying glass?" she asked. Sydney reached into a pocket on his duty belt and pulled one out. "Thank you." She took it and examined the flesh. "I think what I'm looking at is a superficial blood vessel. Whatever this is, it was part of something living," she said.

"Really?" Sydney said. "I mean, what could it belong to?" Meya stared at the object and shook her head.

"The closest thing I'd say is a turtle shell, but this doesn't look like the right shape," she said. "But I'm no expert in that department." She handed the item back to Sydney, who placed it back into its storage bag.

"I guess we'll never know," he said. He started to take it back to the storage area. Meya stood up from her chair.

"I do know of someone who might know," she said. Sydney stopped and looked back, waiting on her to clarify. "Have you ever been to Florence University? There's a guy who works there named Dr. Nevers. He was one of my instructors during medical school. We've kept in touch, and I remember him mentioning some biologist that works there. They might know what it is."

"I don't think it's that important," Sydney said. "It's probably nothing anyway. There was probably no need for me to bring it in."

"Perhaps," Meya said. "Although, I am curious what it is. I'd offer to take it, but I know it's been logged and needs to remain in police custody." Sydney thought about it for a moment. If he could determine what the item was, he could create a proper disposition for it.

Suddenly, he realized he was committing to a trip with his ex-wife. He felt the butterflies starting to swirl in his stomach. He wasn't sure if they were good or bad. His mind warned him of what he was about to do, but the words came out of his mouth instinctively. "Okay. Let's go. On our way out, I'll just need to step into my office real quick."

"Alright," Meya said. As they proceeded into the hallway, she took new notice of his limp. She peeked inside as Sydney stepped into his office to grab his coffee mug. Near the computer was the orange prescription bottle. Instinctively, she felt the urge to give some medical advice, particularly to remind the chief to use his cane. She wasn't sure if this coming from a medical standpoint, or somewhere deeper. She forced the thought from her mind.

"All ready," Sydney said. He had transferred his coffee into a travel mug. He led Meya out the front entrance and informed dispatch he'd be out. The sight of his Jeep brought memories back to Meya. Just like with Sydney, she hadn't seen it in over two years. Strangely, she missed it. They boarded the vehicle and exited the lot. "You know the way, right?"

"Yes, I'll guide you there," she said.

CHAPTER 9

"YEEEAAAHHH GIRL! WORK THAT POLE!" Mike Wilkow shouted with his fist raised victoriously in the air. His shouts were followed by cheers from the twenty people gathered around them, most of whom were in their twenties. Standing near Wilkow in the center of the group was a twenty-year-old female student, dressed in cut-off jean shorts and a blue tank top, tugging on a fishing pole as she fought against the struggles of a largemouth bass.

"You see that, everybody?" Wilkow turned to the group. "See how it hit while she was bringing the spinner in?" A couple of the students nodded yes, but most were fixated on the attractive female reeling in the bass. She pulled the pole back and quickly reeled in the slack, then held it firm as the fish attempted to run. "Don't reel yet. Let it wear itself out," Wilkow said to her.

"I know how to do this, Doc," she said.

"You most certainly do!" he said, triumphantly. After a few moments, the fish turned in a more favorable direction, allowing the student to continue reeling. Finally, with only a little bit of line left, she lifted up on the pole. The fish was hoisted out of the water, flopping in mid-air as it dangled from the hook in its mouth. The students clapped in her honor. "Yeah!" Wilkow shouted. "BABY GOT BASS!" He took the sixteen-inch bass off the spinner and held it by its lower jaw. "You guys see how that worked?" Naturally, nobody spoke up. "Can anyone explain how this fish was able to detect this little thing?" He shook the spinner, which rattled a bit.

"It smelled it?" one of the students said. As usual, it was an answer in the form of a question.

"These guys can smell, but that's not how he knew lunch was here. Anyone else?" Wilkow waited. "Oh come on! It's easy!"

"Water displacement," the female student said.

"We have a winner!" Wilkow called out. "You see, anything that moves into the water creates displacement. This guy uses his lateral line," he ran his ringer along the upper side of the bass, "and some canals on his head to detect vibrations in the water." He pointed to areas near the fish's lower jaw and eyes. "When the spinner twisted around, the fish could hone in because of the displacement. Then it could see the flashes on the metal tab. But it wouldn't have noticed if it didn't feel the vibrations caused by the movement in the water." He held up the fish with both hands and turned it toward his face. "Sir, I appreciate your help with today's lesson." He tossed the bass back into the water. As soon as it broke the surface, it shot deep into the weed beds. Wilkow took the pole from his student. "Please tell me one of you guys remembers what the lateral line is." One nervous student raised his hand.

"It's a…uhh…organs that can sense things that, uhhh, vibrate," he stuttered.

"Luckily, the exam will be multiple-choice," Wilkow commented. "He's correct in the general sense. It's a *system* of sense organs. Yeah, they detect vibrations, as well as pressure gradients and general movement. It can detect movement in the water, because movement creates…" he waited for one of the students to fill in the sentence. For a moment, it seemed hopeless, until one of them raised her hand from the back.

"Water displacement," she said.

"YEEEAAAHH!" the animated Mike Wilkow called out and pointed at the student. "You get an 'A' for the day!" Many of the students laughed. Summer classes were usually very boring. Nevertheless, Wilkow contained such an oddball energy that the four-hour class went by quickly. As if out of pure joy, the instructor took the pole from the student and launched a cast into the water. He steadily reeled it in. "Look at that motion…that's gotta be tempting for some big boy down there!" Finally, a big splash overtook the spinner, right before an eighteen-inch largemouth leapt out of the water with its catch.

"WOOHOO!" Wilkow called out. The students cheered and applauded him. He fought the fish, allowing it to spend its energy tugging on the line. "Not today, my friend! I'm gonna get me some BASS!" The students laughed and cheered him on.

****

As Sydney steered the Jeep onto the campus's lot, he and Meya could hear the echoes coming from across the lot. They looked toward a crowd standing near a large pond. In the middle was a man in his mid-thirties, dressed in what appeared to be grey cargo pants and a black shirt, holding a fishing pole. They could hear his exultant shouts as he lifted a large fish from the water. He held it up to the people surrounding him. His shouts traveled far and long.

"Yeah! Kiss my bass!" Laughter followed the quip.

Meya and Sydney looked at each other, both finding the sight both amusing and odd at once.

"Somebody's got a little too much energy," Meya said. On her lap was the item, stored in a container filled with a Transeau solution which she took from the hospital.

"Yeah, I'll say," Sydney said. He drove along the service drive, looking at the large buildings which bridged together in the center of campus. "Okay, which building are we looking for?"

"The Liberal Arts building," Meya said. "The names are listed on the front of the buildings. The biology department is on the second floor." The first building read *Blake Webb Building*. He drove past it and approached the next one. *Liberal Arts Building*. "Here it is," Meya said. Sydney parked his Jeep into the nearest lot and they stepped out.

After walking the long pathway to the building, they entered the lobby where a few students were studying in assorted tables. Naturally, their attention was drawn to the law enforcement officer entering the building. Sydney was used to this, and ignored the gazes as he and Meya walked to an elevator at the end of the room. It took them to the second floor.

"Where would this guy be?" Sydney asked.

"Either in his lab, or in his office," Meya said. As they started to walk toward a hallway, she stopped and noticed a door entry to a large core area. She peeked through the window and saw various sorts of lab equipment. Vials, microscopes, measuring cups, and many types of solution were organized on the side tables, and a couple lab techs were moving about. "Here's the lab," she said.

"Is he in it?" Sydney asked. Meya couldn't open the door, as it was secured via electronic locking system. She knocked on it, getting the attention of one of the lab techs. The tech opened up the door, appearing almost nervous at the sight of Chief Sydney.

"Hi," she said. "Can I help you?"

"Hi. We're looking for Dean Nevers," Meya said.

"Oh," the tech said. "He's in his office. It's right around the corner over that way." She pointed to the bend in the hallway. "It'll be the first door on the right when you head over that way."

"Thanks," Meya said. They followed the tech's directions and found the door. The post read *Dr. Richard Nevers, Dean of Biological Science.* Before she knocked, the door swung open. A balding man of sixty-three opened the door, dressed in a grey blazer and pants. He looked to Meya and smiled from ear to ear.

"Dr. Nasr!" he exclaimed, holding his arms out for a hug. Meya did the same, and they shared a friendly hug.

"Dr. Nevers," she said. "I'm sorry to just drop in like this."

"Oh, don't be ridiculous," Dr. Nevers said. He looked at Chief Sydney. "What can I do for you? Tracking down a suspect?" He chuckled at his own joke.

"No, no," Meya said. "This is Chief Sydney of Rodney Police Department. We were just hoping you could help us identify something we found."

"Sydney?" Dr. Nevers said, thinking for a moment. He recalled Meya's married name. "Morgan Sydney?"

"Yes, sir," the chief said.

"Oh wow," Dr. Nevers said. He recalled some of the details of the divorce, and how Meya had seemed bitter. But now, she clearly seemed more at ease. "You guys back together?" The question slipped out.

"No!" Sydney and Meya simultaneously answered at once. They both glanced to each other, as if surprised to hear the other's reaction.

"Forgive me," Dr. Nevers said, barely concealing his amusement. "You said you wanted me to take a look at something?" Meya held up the container and Nevers took it. He looked through the glass at the shell. He placed it on his desk and put on some rubber gloves. After carefully removing the lid, he lifted the item and held it just a couple inches over the container.

"I found it last night floating in Ridgeway Lake," Sydney said. "It looks like it was part of something, but I don't have the first clue."

"Hmmm," Nevers said as he examined it. "I'm not too sure myself. It might be a solidification of jelly and plankton that was on the surface for too long and dried up." Nevers was just guessing, and knew that theory was not likely correct.

"Of course that wouldn't account for the flesh attached to it," Meya said.

"There is that," Nevers said. "I'm honestly not sure."

"What about the other biologist who works here," Sydney said. "Is he available to take a look?"

"Oh, that's Dr. Wilkow," Nevers said with a laugh. "I won't waste your time with him. I doubt he'll be able to tell us what it is. Besides, he should be in the middle of a class right now."

"Not the class fishing in the pond outside?" Sydney said. Nevers looked straight at him. His expression was now very serious.

"I beg your pardon?"

"There's this group outside…I'm presuming it's a class…over at the pond. There's this really enthusiastic guy over there leading the thing, with a fishing pole." Dr. Nevers' face tensed up for a moment.

"Oh, you've got to be kidding me!" He placed the shell back in the solution and removed his gloves. He hurried to a window in the back of his office and looked outside. He could see the class across the parking lot, huddled by the pond. He grabbed his cell phone from his pocket and dialed a number.

****

Wilkow felt his phone buzzing in his cargo pocket. He dug it out, seeing Dr. Nevers' name in the caller ID. He tapped the button to answer the call.

"I knew to never say Never!" he quipped.

"*You're hilarious,*" Dr. Nevers said. "*When you're done with your class, I expect to see you in my office.*" His voice was stern.

"Grades aren't due until August," Wilkow joked. He could hear the dean sigh through the phone.

"*I think you already know what I'm about to chew you out for,*" he said.

"Looking forward to it, Doc," Wilkow sarcastically remarked. "Be there soon!"

"*After your class is over,*" Nevers emphasized. He understood summer classes were expensive, and wasn't about to interrupt the lesson, despite how ludicrous it was.

"As you wish," Wilkow said before hanging up the phone. He turned to his class. "Alright everyone; that'll be it for today. Read chapters six through ten over the weekend. Remember, the stuff in bold is important. See you on Monday!" The group broke up, with some students going straight for their vehicles, and others returning to the building to collect their belongings. Wilkow secured the line on his fishing pole and started walking to the *Liberal Arts Building*.

****

Dr. Nevers had led Sydney and Meya into the lab, where he carefully removed a bit of flesh closest to the attachment on the shell. He then placed the meat on a slide and placed it under a microscope. The images he saw were a series of greenish squiggly shapes all conjoined.

"Well, it's definitely organic," he said. "The greenish bit of flesh here is definitely skin. Although, it's surprisingly thin."

"That's weird?" Sydney asked.

"Even in small species, you'd be surprised how thick skin can be. This stuff is thin…characteristic of bony fish."

Just as he spoke, the lab door swung open. Dr. Wilkow entered and removed his fishing hat. Dr. Nevers felt his blood pressure increase at the sight of him, and he carefully placed the specimen down.

"You said you wanted to see me?" Wilkow said in a loud booming voice.

"In my office!" Nevers nearly yelled. "And after your class is finished."

"Done!" Wilkow said, holding out a thumbs up.

"You've already dismissed your class?" Nevers said.

"Sure did!" Wilkow said. Nevers looked at his watch.

"You had at least another hour!"

"Yeah, but it was a great lesson!" Wilkow said, lifting up the pole. The tip scratched the ceiling, irritating Nevers' further.

"Yeah? What'd they learn? How to bag the big one?"

"Oh come on, Doctor," Wilkow said.

"Address me as Dean," Nevers said, imposing his authority.

"Okay, Doctor Dean," Wilkow said. Nevers' face tensed up. "These guys are bored as hell with these summer courses. They learned about sound travel in water, digestive enzymes, along with other cool things. They retain more this way."

"I wish you'd retained the fact that you're not allowed to fish in those ponds. If the vice-presidents...or the president herself saw that, they'd be on my ass," Nevers said. Wilkow looked over at the two guests, particularly at Sydney.

"You under arrest, Doctor Dean?" he asked. Nevers looked at them. For a moment, he almost forgot they were there. Sydney and Meya didn't know whether to feel awkward or amused at the exchange they witnessed. It was hard for them to believe that Dr. Wilkow was even a scientist, much less a professor.

"I'm helping them out with something," Nevers said. He turned to face them. "Tell you what, if you let me, I'll keep this for a while. I'm sure I'll figure out what it is."

"That's perfectly fine," Sydney said. "Either way, I think I can discontinue its status as evidence."

"Thank you," Meya said. Dr. Nevers led them out of the lab, leaving Dr. Wilkow alone. He approached the large shell to look at it. Upon seeing it, his heart began to beat hard in his chest. He felt a wave of excitement start to blast through him. It was as if he injected himself with adrenaline.

"Holy shit!" he called out. He saw one of the lab techs coming in. "Do you have any idea where this came from?!" She stopped after seeing his energized demeanor.

"Uhhh...I think I heard them say it was Ridgeway Lake," she said. Wilkow looked closer at the shell, and the sample Nevers took. He saw the skin cell structure, and took a closer look at the underside of the solid object. The inner layer seemed to be made of lamellar bone. He felt the surface, believing it to be keratin. He looked at the tech, who stared at him, concerned.

"Babe! You know what we have here?!" The tech slowly shook her head. "This is a fish scale! We got ourselves a giant prehistoric fish!"

The tech suddenly recalled the notorious history of Doctor Mike Wilkow. It was so well known and infamous, it was practically part of the orientation for new employment. After obtaining his doctorate, Wilkow obtained funding to explore his theory of underground lakes and the ecosystems they contained. He was fascinated with lake fish, and developed theories that some of the species evolved to be giant-sized over the course of time. During his studies, he discovered partial skeletons of unidentified aquatic species in caves of Lockport Cave in New York. He used part of his funding to investigate random flooding in a rural area in Illinois, when an area of farmland became flooded without explanation. He stated in a thesis that a massive underground lake rested beneath the area, and that pressures caused by a recent earthquake caused some of the water to seep up through the earth.

When examining samples of the water, he reported that he found trace elements of fish slime. His sponsors scoffed at his claims, as did several other scientists. They believed it was simply rainwater stored deep in the ground, brought up by the pressures created by the quake. Additionally, Wilkow's eccentric personality helped push the belief that he was simply a crazy playboy using university funds to simply gain fame.

His wide joker-like smile only perpetuated that image to her. With an uneasy chuckle, she collected what she needed and returned to the next room. Wilkow looked once again at the scale. Further tests would be needed for his thesis. He knew he only had limited time before Nevers would return, so he quickly started gathering samples from the specimen.

CHAPTER 10

"That'll be twenty-four fifty," the scrawny taxi driver said to his customer. Jimmie Stanton handed him a company VISA card, labeled CAMPIONE on the top. After the transaction was completed, Stanton stepped out of the back seat. The taxi backed out of the driveway. Stanton started walking toward up the small hill to the porch steps, with his grey suit jacket hung over one arm. The sight of his lakeview home was gratifying after being gone for a week.

Being a vice president for an Italian food distributor known as Campione Foods, he often had to travel to locations across the country for inspections. It was a rewarding career where his hard work paid off with him moving up in the company. As he climbed the ladder, his bank account inflated along with his midsection…a result of corporate lunches. This recent trip was to inspect a restaurant in Louisiana. There, he spent six days and seven nights tasting foods and inspecting conditions of the warehouses.

After returning from his flight, he had to stop at the office to file some paperwork. He rushed the work and took a cab home, at Campione's expense. With only a couple hours sleep, he was ready to get out of his business suit and get into more comfortable attire. His blue tie was already loosened at the collar, and the top three buttons of his dress shirt were undone.

"Amanda," he called as he walked up the steps. "I'm home." His wife didn't respond, which was sometimes typical. She seemed to resent the demands of his jobs, particularly his traveling. Or maybe it was envy. He was never sure. All he was sure of was how irritated she felt each time he had to leave. Of course, she didn't mind the income it brought. Every time he returned, he'd find tags for dresses or shoes.

He grabbed the doorknob, only to find that it was locked. Considering the time of day, it was a bit unusual. *Where is she?* he thought. As he dug into his pocket for his house keys, he thought she may have gone out shopping. However, her car was still in the driveway.

"What's up, babe?" he called out. "Having an indoor party?" As he prepared to insert the key into its slot, he noticed something in the reflection of the door window…something in the sand near the dock. He turned around, seeing the pile of clothes bunched up. "What the…?" he mumbled to himself. He went down to inspect. Scrunched up in the sand were a pair of jeans and a navy blue shirt, damp and peppered with sand, next to a pair of brown boots. All of which were men's size.

All of a sudden, Stanton found himself wide awake. The drowsiness had been overtaken by a swell of anger and distress. His mind fought for any other explanation for why these men's clothes were here on his property. Finally, he had to surrender to the obvious after seeing the red dress washing up in the water. He took a quick look at it. It was definitely Amanda's size, and new. She never wore it for him, and it was certainly designed to attract attention. Tunnel vision set in. Both of his hands clenched into fists. Confusion and despair overwhelmed him. Stanton twisted and turned, walking several steps in multiple different directions, kicking up sand with each thunderous stomp.

With bloodshot eyes, he looked up to the door. No wonder it was locked; his wife was screwing somebody inside! Probably in his own bed. He charged up to the porch, nearly tripping over a step in his blind rage. At the door, he started fumbling for his house key, only to throw them down in a fit of anger. With a heavy kick, he busted the door off its hinges, sending it crashing down into the living room. He marched inside and saw the empty living room. He started to stomp his way upstairs, knocking over a tray table in his path.

"You having a good time?!" he yelled as he ascended. He entered the small hallway, seeing his bedroom door closed. He didn't bother with the door handle. He body slammed it, breaking the latch with his hefty weight. "Am I interrupting?" he shouted as he lifted the covers, only to find nobody there. He hurriedly explored the closets before checking the bathroom, believing his wife and her lover to be hiding. His rage increased with each failed attempt to locate them. He checked all of the rooms but they weren't there.

He looked out the window for any more clues. His eyes went straight to the pontoon boat floating about ten feet from the dock. There was a cover on it; the only rational spot to hide from him. Stanton charged outside, grabbing a baseball bat from the living room on his way out. On the dock, he stomped hard on the wooden planks as if to signal his arrival. He grabbed the tie-off line and pulled the heavy boat closer. It took a lot of effort, but the adrenaline coursing through his veins added strength to the outraged husband.

"Okay, you ungrateful bitch!" he yelled. Before he could leap into the boat, he saw that it was empty. Now he was getting frustrated. He wanted so badly to viciously beat the man who was with her. "Where the hell are you?" he roared at the top of his lungs.

A slight banging on the dock posts caught his attention. He looked down below and saw a rope-like object in the water beneath him. It was red and white in color, unlike any plant, and it definitely wasn't a snake. Through the cracks in the deck, he could see that it was attached to something else, which was bumping into the deck leg with each swell of water. He knelt down and reached beneath with his baseball bat to prod the object out from beneath the dock. It floated into view, a white, shrunken upper torso. Stanton stood up, struggling to comprehend what he was seeing. Although pale and drained of blood, he recognized Amanda's face. Her jaw was agape and her eyes stuck wide open, as if still experiencing the terror that took her life. Her lower body had been torn away at the abdomen, causing her intestines to come unwound. The edges of the large wound flapped in the water as little fish swam up to nibble on the loose bits of flesh.

His frustration was now replaced by a combination of despair and nausea. Feeling the blood drain from his face, he started to stagger. He put his hands on top of his head, as if somehow that would stop the spinning sensation he was now experiencing.

"I…I…oh my God…" he muttered and repeated. Each word was louder than the last, and soon he was screaming at the top of his lungs. He stumbled down the dock toward shore, eventually collapsing to his knees to vomit into a bed of cattails.

CHAPTER 11

"…So yeah, ever since then he's been obsessed with his ridiculous theories," Dr. Nevers said to Sydney and Meya, explaining Dr. Wilkow. He led them through the building's main lobby to the exit. "Once again, I apologize for that display."

"Oh, don't worry about it," Meya said. She and Sydney took turns shaking hands with the Dean. "Thanks again for your help."

"Yes, thank you," Sydney said.

"Not a problem," Nevers said. Sydney and Meya left through the front doors and returned to his Jeep. They buckled in and Sydney started driving off campus.

"So *that* was the great biologist they have?" he said, steering onto the main road.

"I never said he was great," Meya said. "Nevers just told me there was a biology professor working there. I didn't know he was some sports star wannabe."

"He's something," Sydney remarked. After a couple minutes, they came to a stop at a red light. While they waited, a loud thundering bang echoed from the south. The ground briefly shook beneath them as a shockwave traveled outward. Meya naturally grabbed her seat, despite knowing there was no danger.

"Good God," she said.

"They're blasting at Corey Mine again," Sydney said.

"They've been doing that quite a bit lately," Meya said. "What's the deal? Do they just have a quota of how much dynamite they have to blow up? Good lord, even at the hospital, we feel the aftershocks."

"Don't even get me started," Sydney said. "We've received several complaints over the past week. Even the mayor has bitched to me about it. But what can I do? They have the permits, and apparently, they've struck a thick layer of granite. There's no other way to get through it."

The light turned green, and Sydney resumed driving on the street. It led them onto an overpass, where they had a decent view of the large Corey Mine. The dark brown abyss contrasted strongly with the vast circle of trees that surrounded the sight. Enormous cranes elevated their arms at sixty-degree angles, some towering over two-hundred-and-fifty feet into the air. Dump trucks were parked all around the site, and several workers moved about in pathways carved into the enormous pit. A cloud of smoke billowed from the opening, and cranes started swinging their large crates, which contained more dynamite. The view disappeared as they descended down the other side of the overpass.

"I'm shocked your ER isn't flooded with workers coming in with black tar in their lungs," Sydney said.

"They'd be transferred to other hospitals," Meya said. At that moment, the police radio installed on the dashboard blared.

"*RPD Dispatch. Chief, you there?*" Sydney picked up the radio speaker and clicked the transmitter.

"Chief Sydney. What's going on, Dispatch?"

"*Chief, we just got a call regarding a homicide. Resident's area; 4619 Hogback road. Caller called in a panic.*"

"Is there a suspect on the premises?"

"*He says he found the victim when he got home,*" Dispatch said. "*Emergency services have already been notified.*"

"Okay, all units, head over to that address right now," Sydney said, knowing the other officers were listening. Each officer responded over the radio. Sydney looked at Meya, quickly trying to figure out what to do. "Uhh…do you want me to drop you off at the hospital, or…"

"Just go," she insisted. "I'll stay out of the way." There wasn't any time to argue. Sydney blared the siren and switched on the emergency flashers.

****

Upon arriving at the address, Sydney saw no choice but to park the Jeep off to the side of the street. The driveway was packed with police vehicles and two ambulances. Sydney quickly walked across the street into the driveway. Meya stayed behind, standing outside the jeep, observing the scene.

Two police cars were parked in a line, almost directly behind one of the ambulances. Sydney noticed their drivers standing by them, looking as if they'd seen a ghost. Another police cruiser was parked off to the left. Leaning on the hood was another officer, breathing long deep breathes as if trying to regain his composure. Sydney looked at him and saw his sickly greenish complexion. He was barely holding it together. Sydney looked ahead toward the beach area. Police and EMS personnel were gathered at the dock, with the paramedics kneeling down at the far end to observe the reported body.

An officer stumbled back from the dock. His eyes were watery, and his complexion was growing pale with each shallow breath. Sydney heard a gulping noise, and immediately the officer made a dash for the nearest grassy area. Putting his hands on his knees, he hunched down and vomited. The other ailing officer caught sight of his coworker losing his lunch, which triggered a reactionary reflex. He grabbed his stomach and joined his comrade.

Sydney ignored his hurling staff as he walked up to the dock. Standing at the front steps was Tim Marlow. He too, looked slightly pale, though he appeared to retain control of his gag reflexes. He stood there, staring down at the sandy ground by the foot of the dock, not even noticing the chief standing in front of him.

"Marlow…Tim!" Sydney snapped his fingers in front of the young officer's face. Marlow flinched and blinked several times before regaining his focus.

"Ahh… Boss, errr… I mean, Chief," he muttered.

"You alright, kid?" Sydney asked.

"Yeah…I think so," Marlow said. "She's back there…in the water." He gestured toward the far end of the dock with his elbow. Sydney looked past him, seeing the paramedics knelt down trying to move the body. The chief approached them.

"Hold it," he instructed, "don't move the body yet." The paramedics stopped and looked his way, puzzled. Sydney moved in between them and knelt down to look, while Marlow stayed back several steps. The body bobbed in the water, tangled in the lily pads. Her face was shrunken, with strands of hair stretched out in all directions. The skin was shriveled, and the loose bits of flesh rippled with the tiny swells of water.

Sydney took one deep breath and stood up. He looked at the corpse once more. He had seen more than his fair share of mangled bodies over time. As he observed the severed torso, his thoughts went to how she was torn in half.

Propeller, maybe, he thought. Though, where was the rest of her? He looked to Marlow.

"Do we have photographs of this?" he asked him. Marlow slowly nodded. Sydney scanned the area with his eyes, looking for anything else unusual. That's when he saw Jimmie Stanton seated on the porch steps, staring down at the grass. His shirt was wrinkled and untucked. "Is that the homeowner?"

"This was his wife," Marlow said. "He apparently just got back into town. He found her like this." Sydney informed the paramedics to resume their duties and started walking back. He noticed the pile of clothes bunched up in the sand. Jeans, boots, and a T-shirt. Looking at Mr. Stanton, he knew these didn't fit his unfortunate girth. Clearly, they weren't his. Looking at the water, he saw the dress.

"Oh shit," he said. His fears were worsened when he observed the open doorframe. He went over to Stanton. "You mind if I take a look in your house?" Stanton appeared as if in a trance, staring down at the ground. He gave a very small nod. Sydney investigated the interior, seeing the wreckage caused during Stanton's outrage. He knew Stanton was in some sort of shock, but began to worry if it was simply from finding his wife…or something worse. Marlow followed him inside.

"Where's the other guy?" Sydney said to himself. "I highly doubt he's running around without his clothes on."

"Maybe he brought a change," Marlow said. "Took off when he knew the husband was here. There's no visiting vehicle here."

"You're thinking," Sydney said. He looked at the destruction within the living room. "I still don't like it. A dead woman, and possibly a missing date…all right when the husband comes back into town." They went back outside and walked up the driveway. "Make sure somebody gets a full statement from this guy," he told Marlow. "You said he was out of town, I'm gonna want to verify that. Until we know for sure, this is a possible murder. And I also want any reports of any missing persons." He turned around and watched the paramedics remove the body. "Crap. I'm gonna need a medical examiner."

"That's something I'm good for," Meya's voice called out. Sydney spun around as she approached. "Sorry, I guess I got too bored waiting. What happened?" Sydney sighed, reluctant to give her any information. But unfortunately, she was correct.

"We have a female floating in the water…at least half of her is," he said.

"Jesus," she said.

"Right now, I'm focusing on the husband," Sydney said. "I think it's a little strange that…" he paused and looked at Marlow. "Didn't I give you instructions?"

"Oh…right," he said before taking off. Sydney turned back toward Meya, only to see a glare. He'd seen it many times before.

"What?"

"This guy lost his wife, and you're gonna treat him like a suspect?"

"Only until I'm convinced otherwise," Sydney said. "There's evidence she was likely seeing somebody. I'm worried hubby got home and caught them in the act."

"You don't think that's a little extreme?" Meya asked.

"I've learned there's no such thing as extreme," Sydney said. The sound of more police sirens drew his attention to the road. Three Ford Explorers pulled up, black in color with blue stripes. Text within the stripes read Claire County Sheriff's Department. "Oh, come on!" Sydney said, kicking up a bit of gravel. "Who invited these guys?"

The vehicles parked along the side of the road, and the deputies started coming toward the driveway. The man leading them was a tall individual with dark skin, a black cap covering his bald head, with a tattoo on his left forearm of an eagle, globe, and anchor.

"That's Sheriff Logan?" Meya asked.

"Yes," Sydney said through gritted teeth. "Ever since our department has formed, he's had a stick up his ass. Of course, he can't accept he's the reason we're even here. The guy doesn't have the brains God gave an oyster."

"Alright, guys," Logan called out in a deep booming voice to his deputies, "I want someone checking for prints in the house, someone get photos of the body. I'll get a statement from the homeowner." He approached Sydney. "Hey, Chief. Have you set up road blocks yet?" Sydney went over a list of curse words in his mind he wanted to hurl at the sheriff.

"Road blocks for what?"

"Well, we might have a murder here," Logan said, in a matter-of-fact tone. Sydney let a small scoff slip through.

"This body's been in the water at least all night," Sydney said. "Plus, we have a possible suspect here," he pointed to Stanton, still on the porch steps. "By the way, we're in the middle of getting a statement. And we have photos." *Of course, if you weren't late as usual, you'd know all this.* Logan continued directing his deputies, as if actively ignoring Sydney. Two deputies went to speak with the paramedics, while two more went to the house. They started snapping photographs of the scene and examining the damage.

"I need two more units to set up road blocks," Logan spoke into his radio. Sydney turned away for a moment to hide his irritated expression. The sheriff was actively ignoring him, as if his findings weren't sufficient. As usual, Logan was trying to show him up. "Do you have a coroner?" Logan asked him. Sydney waited a moment before answering. He didn't, but he didn't want to admit that to Logan, who would treat it like a sign that RPD isn't a sufficient police force.

"I'll be examining the body," Meya cut in. She extended her hand. "Dr. Meya Nasr," she introduced herself.

"Well...okay then," Logan said, looking somewhat surprised. "Well, Chief, I'd like to know the details after the examination." Without saying anything, Sydney started walking off. "Oh! How's it going with that missing individual?" he called after Sydney, referring to the boat accident. Sydney knew it was a subtle taunt. Sydney didn't say anything and just kept walking to the paramedics, who were talking to the deputies. The body, or what was left of it, was loaded into a large plastic bag and loaded onto a stretcher.

"Excuse me," Sydney interrupted the deputies. He moved in close to the paramedic, speaking almost in a whisper. "Take the body to Readfield Hospital." He then approached Marlow, again speaking in a whisper. "I want someone to wait here with this guy until we check his story." Marlow nodded. Meya overheard and gave Sydney a disapproving look. He ignored it and started walking to his Jeep. "You coming?" he said to her. She gave a mock salute and started coming along.

Yeah, don't say thanks or anything, she thought.

CHAPTER 12

With his back pressed against the wall, Dr. Wilkow repeatedly glanced at his watch. *3:02*. Any moment now, Dr. Nevers was due to leave for the day. Wilkow grew impatient as he waited. He peeked around the vending machines he stood behind, listening for the sound of the office door. Dr. Nevers was very strict on use of the laboratory specimens, even for college professors. The only way for Wilkow to get a good look at the scale would be to wait for Nevers to leave.

A closer look at the samples he obtained revealed the specimen to be composed of keratin, with a layer of cosmine beneath it. The sample of the inner surface revealed lamellar bone, reminiscent of fish scales. Everything pointed toward to evidence concerning his theory of a subspecies of freshwater fish. The answer was possibly stored in a glass container inside that lab.

He strategically leaned against the wall, biding his time. A student walked by, confusedly looking at the bizarre sight of the college professor hiding behind vending machines. Wilkow gave an awkward smile as he passed by. The student raised his eyebrows and left.

Finally, he heard the sound of a door opening. Initially, he was unsure whether it was Nevers' office until he heard the sound of approaching footsteps from that direction. He heard the bell of the elevator and the mechanical opening of the doors. He took a very brief glance around the corner of the vending machine and saw Dr. Nevers entering the elevator, and then ducked back. After hearing the doors shut, Wilkow emerged from his hiding spot and went straight into the lab.

The lights were still on, although no techs were inside. He went to the storage and found the scale on the top shelf. Placing the glass container on a lab table, he removed the scale and set it on a sterile sheet. He quickly observed the shape and measured the size. It was roughly eleven inches in length and nine in width. The scale was solid, with the cell structure being highly concentrated. But it contained a feature that gave Wilkow conviction it was a fish scale: Growth rings.

Similar to the rings on a tree, scales show the history of the fish. Under normal circumstances, Wilkow would need a computer or microscope to examine the specimen. However, this one was large enough to only require a magnifying glass. Any normal fish would grow as many as twenty rings in a year. However, as fish are coldblooded and don't grow as much during the winter, they form a thicker ring known as a year mark. In addition to age, they can help determine the size. Space between year marks are proportionate to the size of the fish.

Measuring year marks can help estimate the size and age of a fish. However, the process can underestimate the age of older fish, as they do not grow as much. This was the case with this extraordinary large scale in front of Wilkow. He counted as many as eight year marks, with approximately twenty rings between them.

"You're one big son of a bitch," Wilkow said out loud, as if speaking to the fish. He measured the space between the marks. "Damn…with this count, this guy's gotta be…" he mumbled a few figures to himself, "…twenty-five friggin feet, roughly. Good God!" He examined the flesh, and determined the injury to the creature had to be very minimal. Wherever it was, it was alive and thriving.

Where is this thing? He looked around for any lab techs, hoping one of them would know. None were in the connecting lab and lecture rooms. Thinking one might be in the hallway, he went to the core entrance. He opened the door and immediately saw Dr. Nevers standing behind it. The angered expression was unmistakable, as Wilkow had seen it a hundred times before.

"What's up, Doc?" Wilkow said.

"What are you doing?" Nevers asked.

"Oh, catching up on some lab prep for my next class," Wilkow lied.

"You don't have a next class," Nevers said. He stepped into the core. Wilkow awkwardly scratched his head.

"Oh really…oh, right! Ha!" He played it off. "I was thinking of spring semester." Nevers walked to a table and picked up the notepad he had forgotten. He saw the scale on the table.

"Oh, for crying out loud, Mike," he said. "What are you doing with that?"

"Well…" Wilkow thought of what to say, "do you know what that is?"

"I've been busy," Nevers said. "I was planning on…"

"It's a fish scale," Wilkow exclaimed excitedly. Dr. Nevers sighed, realizing Wilkow was back onto his theories again.

"No," Nevers simply said. He went and placed the scale back in the water. "I'm not entertaining your theories."

"No, that's what it is!" Wilkow said. "It's got growth rings, and its components are made up of keratin and cosmine, and…just look at the shape!" Dr. Nevers placed it back up on the shelf.

"I'm not gonna be held responsible for endorsing a lunatic's theory about giant fish. Besides, where have they been and why has one suddenly shown up?" He meant it as a rhetorical question, but still regretted asking after he saw Wilkow's expression light up.

"I've found evidence of underground lakes in the past," he said.

"Water coming up from the ground is not evident of a lake," Nevers said.

"And there have been fragments of skeletons found!" Wilkow said, ignoring the dean's argument. "If a passageway was formed to one of the lakes around here, a fish could've gotten through. You saw the scale! It belongs to something huge! The measurements I took predict it might be as big as twenty-five feet! The scale is just like that of a bass. Doc, we might have a twenty-five foot, prehistoric carnivorous largemouth bass…a CARNOBASS!"

Every fiber in Nevers' being wanted to tell Wilkow how insane he thought he was. He actually sounded like a mad scientist. But Nevers realized Wilkow would never drop the subject. But the scale was a bizarre anomaly, and didn't fit any known lifeform in the area. Still, he wasn't buying the thought that it belonged to a giant fish.

"Get this mess cleaned up," he said to Wilkow. "You still have grades to turn in from last semester. Get to it, or you're fired." He turned and walked out, leaving Wilkow alone.

Wilkow had no doubt there wasn't going to be any support for him to pursue any research. This meant he would have to do it himself. He marched out of the lab and took a seat in the faculty office. He switched on the computer, trying to look for any other clues to determine where the scale was located.

He remembered seeing Chief Sydney earlier in the day. *Rodney Police Department* was listed on his uniform. He knew of Ridgeway Lake.

A lake that size would definitely contain such a fish. He googled for any news reports concerning the town of Rodney. To his surprise, it didn't take long to find any clues. The first article to pop up was one concerning a recent homicide in the lake.

Local woman found mutilated off the shore of her lake home this morning. Police are currently investigating the scene. Reports indicate that the victim was found by her husband. Police are not yet releasing any more details of the crime.

For the next hour, he continued searching for any more related events concerning the town and its lake. He read of a recent boating accident, in which police are unable to identify the cause.

"It seems there's been a lot of activity," he said to himself. As he scrolled down the list of articles, he found one that piqued his interest. *Complaints of blasting of Corey Mine.* The article expressed residential frustration concerning the daily tremors caused by the consistent use of explosives used at the mine. Wilkow's jaw dropped open as a thought came to mind. He leaned back in his seat, feeling the adrenaline starting to pump away.

"If those quakes created a rift in the lakebed...perhaps it opened up a passageway..." he said to himself. He jumped up out of his seat. "If I can find it..." *...everyone will finally believe my theory,* his thoughts finished the statement. His mind continued to ponder the possibilities if he was proven right. He thought of the exploration attempts, the new discoveries, the simple fascination that there was a whole world beneath them.

Wilkow knew it would be up to him to find that newly formed passageway if it existed. He sat back down and began researching equipment he would need to explore the lake.

CHAPTER 13

"Yes, yes, I understand that," Sydney said into his phone. He struggled to keep his voice down as he paced in the hallway. He listened to the angry chatter from the president of *Campione Foods*, who confirmed Jimmie Stanton's alibi. With an exasperated sigh, he held the phone down by his leg, still able to hear the echoes from the president yelling about how he's such a dick for even suspecting Stanton. Once the chatter subsided, Sydney returned the phone to his ear, just at the president ended his rant with "*...you cops.*" Sydney had no interest in knowing what came before that.

"Thank you, sir," he said. "I appreciate your help. Have a good day." He hung up the phone as another rant was starting. The only good thing from the conversation was that he now was able to rule out Jimmie Stanton as a murder suspect. However, the question still remained of where the other guy was. The next step was to find out exactly how Amanda Stanton died.

Sydney went into a small observation room, separated from the Autopsy Room by a wall of glass. He saw Meya and a nurse, both dressed in blue scrubs, in the middle of an examination of the body. He saw the victim laid out on an operating table, and an assortment of medical tools he couldn't name. On a nearby table was an audio recorder, and Meya spoke of each step to make sure it was documented.

Meya lifted her arm to wipe her eyes with her upper sleeve. Her vision felt slightly cloudy. Working all night was finally catching up with her. She had not planned on doing this examination, but it was a favor to Sydney and he insisted that it'd be done quickly. They had stopped at the police station for her to get her vehicle, and came straight to Readfield Hospital.The chill in the room only worsened her drowsiness, and she had to resist the urge to rush the examination.

"Upper fixed rips have been severely cracked at the point of contusion beneath chest area," she said. "Along with the stretching and tearing at the latissimus dorsi and serratus posterior, there are multiple tendons that have been...snapped at those regions." She began examining the wound where the lower body had detached. "The remainder of the abdominal muscles show signs of thinning. Most of the intestines are no longer intact. Kidneys and bladder also appear to be missing, and a portion of the stomach has been torn away." She looked up at her nurse, who had taken a step back. Meya could hear her taking deep breaths. "You okay?" she asked.

"Y-yeah." The nurse nodded her head affirmative, even while appearing to be a little green around the gills. "Sorry…just needed to…"

"Not used to seeing this kind of thing?"

"It's more the smell," the nurse commented. Meya nodded her head, understanding. She sometimes forgot she was in a very small area that wasn't used to such incidents. She returned her attention to the corpse.

"Uhh…spinal column has been separated at…between lumbar and thoracic regions. Swellings in upper areas of spine indicate herniation due to trauma. There are no signs of…" she stopped as an uncontrollable yawn came out. "Excuse me…uhh…conditions of severed region indicate no signs of cutting or sawing. The…uhh…muscular and skin conditions…" she shook her head, tired and frustrated. She looked at the nurse. "Sew her back up," she said, practically whispered in exhaustion, and went back to the prep room. Sydney exited the observation room and went around a small hallway to join up with her.

"So…" he impatiently waited for her analysis, "what happened? So we know somebody didn't take a chainsaw to her. Why is she in two pieces?" Meya ripped off her mask and gloves and tossed them into a biohazard trash bin. Then she pulled on the hair tie that had held her hair back in a ponytail and gently shook out the waves.

"She was pulled apart," she said finally.

"Pulled apart?" Sydney questioned, as if waiting for her to clarify. "I mean, did somebody go medieval on her? What does that mean?"

"I don't know," Meya said. "She was clearly caught in the tie-off line for the pontoon boat. Something had a hold of her legs and just…" She made a creaking noise to mimic bones snapping. She scrubbed her hands and went into a changing room to remove her scrubs. She quickly came out in her regular clothes and walked out. Sydney followed her to a staff room, where she went straight for the coffee.

"What the hell is going on here?" he asked. "First, we had that boat accident, then this…in two consecutive days. Each one with unexplained circumstances." Meya loaded her coffee with sugar and downed half her cup. While she waited for the caffeine to settle, she thought of Sydney's mention of the accident. She thought of Don and his freak-out that morning, specifically his mention of a monster in the lake. Initially, she figured it was a confused, injured man babbling. Now, she wondered if there was something to it.

"What if there is something in the lake?" she said. Sydney gave her a blank stare. "Remember I mentioned the victim babbled something about a monster in a lake?" He nodded, warily. "With these disappearances, maybe there's an animal loose in this lake."

"You think an animal caused that accident, and tore that lady in half?" Sydney said. He spoke as if he was interrogating Meya, which irritated the exhausted physician. "There's no wildlife around here that could do that."

"But think of it," she insisted. "We found that shell. And already have a report of something in the water…"

"From someone with a concussion, high on meds," Sydney interrupted. Meya exhaled sharply.

"I'm just saying, what if…."

"What would it be? An escaped crocodile? There were no tooth marks found on that body," Sydney said.

"What if something escaped from a zoo or something?" Meya said.

"We'd get notified," Sydney replied. "Besides, there'd been no reports of wildlife escaping from any facilities." The ringing of his phone ended the conversation, much to Meya's relief. Giving up, she returned to her coffee. Sydney looked at the caller ID. It was dispatch. "Yeah?" he answered.

"Chief, I wanted to notify you we just got a call in regarding two missing persons. Names are Robert Nash and Susan Jean."

"Oh great," Sydney said. "Just what I need. Was there any mention of when and where they were last seen?"

"Both were reported to be heading to the lake last night…to meet with a Don Baker." Sydney processed the new information for a moment.

"Thank you, Dispatch," he said. "Keep me informed of any new reports." He hung up the phone and turned toward Meya.

"Everything alright?" she asked.

"There are people missing, who I think were involved with that accident," he began. "Where is Don Baker's room?"

"He's been moved," she said. "He had to be relocated to another hospital."

"Alright…which one?" Sydney said. Meya refilled her cup.

"I'm not at liberty to say," she said. "HIPAA laws prevent me from providing that information." Sydney became visibly irritated.

"You're not at liberty? There are two people missing and that guy knows what happened. I'm going to ask again…where is he?"

"Morgan!" she said, voiced raised. "I'm bound by LAW to not provide that info! You know…THE LAW…what you enforce. I can't give you such info without a warrant. Besides, the guy is sedated. He wouldn't be able to tell you anything."

"Then they can wake him up," he said.

"He's sedated because he's in severe pain," Meya said. Sydney waved his hand condescendingly and started toward the door.

"Don't give me a sob story about pain," he said, tapping his left leg. Meya angrily slammed her mug down, splashing coffee everywhere.

"Oh, right! I forgot, I'm talking with Mr. Sensitivity. I seem to remember him!" Sydney glared at her and thought of several things to say. He maintained just enough control to keep them to himself.

"Just finish your shift," he said and walked out into the hall. Meya heatedly followed him to the doorway.

"Listen, Hotshot! I don't work for you. I did this as a favor…after being up all damn night!" Sydney didn't listen and continued toward the lobby, where he'd find the building exit. Meya leaned against the wall, feeling the air flow from the vent. It helped to calm her down. She felt unappreciated, despite her best efforts. She cleaned up the mess from her coffee, and went to her office to sign a few papers. She rushed a few signatures and snatched up her keys. She went to her car to drive home. She was ready to sleep…for a month it seemed.

CHAPTER 14

"Here we go…" Dave Culverhouse gritted his teeth as he held his aching pole taut. The twelve-foot johnboat quivered in the water as he fought to bring in a northern pike, which tugged viciously at the spinner. It was strong and desperate, and not showing any signs of tiring out. He could feel the sweat rolling off his face, soaking his red beard. Though the cove was well shaded, the heat was still prominent, and it was worsened by the physical effort he exerted.

Anchored about five yards away, DeAnna Scott and Jeremy Rogers watched intently. The couple spouted a mix of cheers and guidance as Dave fought his perceived trophy, while also betting with each other on whether he'd bring it in. The line started to ease up, and Dave felt an opportunity arise. He pulled up on the line and began reeling in. At the exact moment he pulled upward, the fish suddenly made another strong dive. The pole arched to a near ninety-degree angle, and then suddenly shot back up to its normal form. The line went slack and weightless, and started to coil in small loops. The unseen fish swam off to freedom, taking the broken steel leader with it.

"Oh come on!" Dave yelled into the water. "That was not fair!" He sat down and started reeling in the excess fishing line while listening to the cackling laughter coming from the other boat.

"I saw it before it went down," Jeremy said. "It had to be thirty-six inches." Dave bit his lip and glanced over to his friends. Dressed in a red shirt and khaki shorts, Jeremy had his arm around his girlfriend DeAnna. A skinny individual of twenty-eight, Jeremy was enjoying his first real summer break in years, after spending the last five attending school year-round. DeAnna wore a blue shirt and shorts, and she was taking a cruel enjoyment out of witnessing Dave's defeat. They each had a fishing pole with crawler harnesses extending down into the lake bottom.

"Don't remind me," Dave said. The Marine veteran fumbled around his tackle box to grab a new lure to tie on. He moved aside a Smith & Wesson 686 revolver, something he kept with him at all times. This often earned made him the subject of jokes from his friends, but he didn't care. He kept an eye back to their cars, parked near the shore. They were locked and secured, but he was wary of the possibility of anyone coming by and noticing the shotgun in his back seat. He wasn't alone in having such habits. Many of the locals carried weapons in Rodney, especially the hunting crowds.

The cove was a fairly shallow area with several weed beds where bass liked to hide. With the trees providing ample shade, it was a prime area for fishing except for a fallen tree that had collapsed just off shore two years ago. The bulk of the trunk was just above the surface, with the mangled branches creating a blockage to the entrance of the cove. The branches were thick, nearly half the width of the trunk. Because it blocked off much of the cove, it was difficult to get the boats out further. They had to follow a specific path to travel over it. Even when going over this "gorge" in the tree, they could see the rotting wood beneath, inches beneath their boat.

Dave used his grey shirt sleeve to clean the sweat from his eyes, continuing to curse the fish that took his line.

"I'm surprised you're not swimming in after it," DeAnna said, giggling at him. Dave mocked her laughter with his tongue sticking out. He turned his attention back to his tackle box, deciding on a lure which resembled a bluegill.

"At least I had a bite," he said. He stuffed some chewing tobacco into his mouth and began tying on the lure. "Have you guys even had a bite? Nah. Probably just fishing each other's mouths." He looked over at them, wincing at the sight of the two lovers in the middle of a make-out session. "Oh God! Why'd I say anything?"

"Awww Dave…did your parents never give you the talk?" Jeremy joked.

"Better yet, I know to get a room," Dave said.

"Don't know why you'd need one; seeing as you've just been rejected," DeAnna punned, referencing the pike. Both she and Jeremy laughed hard at the joke. David made another mock laugh, while extending his middle finger. Suddenly, Jeremy's laughter came to a halt as he noticed the tightening of his fishing line.

"Oh! We got a call on line one!" he said, pushing DeAnna aside as he snatched the pole and slowly started reeling in. Dave gave a genuine laugh from his boat.

"Now who's been rejected?" he said. DeAnna stuck her tongue out at him. Jeremy cursed as he struggled to rotate the reel. After a couple turns, the line was locked tight. There was no struggle or force from the other end, and he could not get it to budge.

"Shit," he said. "I must be hung up on a rock or something," he said.

"That's what you get for laughing at me," Dave said. Jeremy tried pulling up on his pole, but to no avail. The line was snagged tightly. After struggling for another couple minutes, Jeremy realized he had two options; tug hard and hope the line either came loose or snapped close to the lure, saving him a few feet of line, or cut the line near the surface. With the water being at least thirty feet deep, he didn't want to lose that much line. The choice was simple. However, the hope remained that he could shake the hook loose of its snag. He got on his knees and reached down into the water, grabbing his line for better leverage. He tugged on it, jerking the line left and right to yank it loose. So far, he was only successful in splashing up water. A splash came up at DeAnna's face, drenching her hair.

"Thanks a lot," she said. Jeremy chuckled at her and continued pulling at the line. He leaned out farther. "Careful, babe," DeAnna said. He gave her a perplexed look.

"Careful? It's not like something's gonna come up out of the water and snatch me up." He returned his attention to the fishing line, splashing up more water as he attempted to free it.

****

The large fish traveled along the bottom of the lake, looking for prey while avoiding the bright sunlight that assaulted its fragile vision. Its eyes were still adjusting to the new environment, causing it to rely more on its lateral line and sense of smell. Over the past several hours, it was unsuccessful in finding prey at the bottom of the lake, which drove it to search elsewhere. It traveled along a large line of weed beds into shallower waters. Hunger caused it to fight against the pain in its eyes as it traveled the brighter areas.

A new series of vibrations triggered its senses. It detected something nearby, near the surface creating displacement in the water. Keeping as low as possible, the Carnobass swam in to investigate. The path it followed let it into a shallow cove, shaded by the tree line. With the direct sunlight being blocked off, the Carnobass was able to focus its sights. There were two floating objects up on the surface, with a small ragged movement coming from one of them. Moving in closer, it could see the red shirt on its prey. Unable to attack from directly beneath, the fish made a straight line at an upward angle toward the nearest target. With a strong flutter of its tail, it shot forward and opened its jaws.

****

A bizarre sensation in the water caused Jeremy to freeze. With his arm dipped in up to his elbow, he felt a bizarre fizzing sensation in the lake, as if some sort of force below was stirring it up. Inside of a moment, he saw the reflection of the two large eyes, and the white inside of the huge circular mouth. There was no time to react.

The water beneath him exploded upward as the fish breached. The boat lifted up over the water and rolled over in midair, flinging DeAnna into the lake. With the event being so sudden, she didn't have the opportunity to scream. Dave whipped himself around toward them, seeing the swell of water, the boat twirling in mid-air, and a gigantic largemouth bass arching its way back down, with Jeremy in its mouth. It crashed back down and tried to run deep with its prey, but its belly brushed viciously against the rough bottom. It flared its gills and opened its jaw to suck in its prey. Jeremy felt as if caught in a vacuum, as the sudden force yanked him back into a black abyss. The bass closed its mouth and swallowed.

Dave stood frozen on his boat, trying to wrap his mind around what he just witnessed. His friends' boat submerged beneath the sizzling water, with floating bait scattering in multiple directions. DeAnna emerged and drew in a deep breath. He saw her and snapped into action.

"Swim to me!" he called to her. She looked around, slightly disoriented until she located his boat. She kicked her legs and stroked her arms violently in the water. Dave quickly lifted up his anchor and prepared to start the motor on his boat to help her close the distance, but realized he'd likely overshoot his destination. Tucking his revolver under the belt in his cargo pants, he took a seat and grabbed the oars. He thrust them into the water and steered the boat toward DeAnna.

The fish felt the motion behind it. Lifting itself off the bottom, it turned around and saw the target swimming toward the other floating object. Driven by intense hunger, it pursued.

Dave heaved the boat backward, looking back to keep an eye on DeAnna. He was coming up close on her. He dropped the oars and leaned over to grab her. Still kicking hard, DeAnna accidentally bumped into the boat and dipped below. She came back up, spitting water as she reached for Dave's hand. Their fingers barely clasped as a huge swell lifted up behind her. The greenish bulk of the fish emerged, and the gills flapped open like huge flower petals. DeAnna gasped as an enormous suction yanked her from Dave's grasp. She disappeared into the mouth of the huge Carnobass. It turned sharply, hitting the boat with its tail. Dave fell to his hands and knees, nearly bumping his head on the seat. He stood up on his knees, putting on hand on the side of the boat for support. He drew his revolver and aimed it at the large swells caused by the fish.

Still unable to dive deep, the bass moved upward to the surface. Its large dorsal fin emerged. Dave focused the sights just ahead of the fin, and slightly beneath it, aiming to strike the creature in the neck. He cocked the hammer and squeezed off a shot. The bang caused his ears to ring. It was the first time he fired a weapon without ear protection since Iraq. The bullet crunched against the thick scales on its side, causing the bass to flinch violently. Dave fired the remaining five bullets, each one as futile as the other. The bass slashed from the water and turned his way, following the vibration caused by the gunshots and recoil.

"Shit!" he said. He dropped the gun and yanked the motor cord. Luckily, it started on the first attempt. He dipped the blades into the water, speeding the boat toward shore. With a burst of speed, the Carnobass pursued. He looked back, seeing the fish quickly catching up to him. He looked toward shore, suddenly remembering the downed tree…only about twenty-five feet ahead. "Oh crap!" he exclaimed. The passage was off to the right. He turned the motor, banking sharply as the boat quickly turned to the right. The boat barely cleared the tree, scraping up wood as it passed over the trunk.

The bass turned along with the boat, increasing its speed. It started to open its mouth to suck in its prey. Suddenly, its pursuit was stopped cold when it collided with a large wooden barrier in the water. The violent impact rocked the tree hard toward shore. Wood cracked as the Carnobass struggled within the thick branches in which it was wedged. Its tail swung wildly on the surface like a kite in a windstorm, spraying water with each motion.

Mud kicked up as Dave sped his boat onto shore. He looked back, seeing the enormous beast struggling in the shallows. He ran to his truck and grabbed his loaded Mossberg 500 pump-action shotgun from the back seat. He chambered a shell and stepped into the water, going up to his knees. He pressed the butt of the weapon to his right shoulder and squeezed the trigger. Dave ignored the plugging sensation in his ears from the intense blast, and continued firing.

The Carnobass didn't even feel the buckshot stopping against its rigid scales. Wedged between two thick branches of the tree, the fish twisted violently to free itself. It waved its tail from side to side, and lifted its head up above the water, then slammed itself downward. Dave could hear the sound of cracking wood as he shoved fresh shells into the shotgun's loading flap. He looked over at the fish as the branches gave way, breaking clear of the trunk. Huge pieces of wood flung upward with a spray of water and bark.

"Jesus!" he yelled. He held his position and raised his shotgun. The fish turned and started swimming out into the lake. Dave fired after it, unloading all six shells, unsure whether he inflicted any damage to the fish. With adrenaline coursing through his veins, he started fumbling with new shells from his pants pocket. He pulled out a handful and pressed the butt of the weapon against his thigh. "Damn it!" he cursed as he dropped a couple into the water. He began slipping the remaining shells into the gun until he noticed red flashing lights reflecting off of the water, followed by the sound of the quick on-and-off yelps of a siren. Holding the weapon by the barrel, he raised his other hand and looked back. "Oh shit."

With his hand placed on his holstered Beretta, Chief Sydney cautiously stepped down from his Jeep and approached. He saw the smoke wafting from the shotgun barrel and the alarm in Dave's eyes. More so, he saw the calming swells in the water where he was shooting at. Sydney wasn't sure what he saw in the water as he pulled up, but something had caused a massive stir.

"Let's start by putting that down," he said calmly.

CHAPTER 15

Dr. Wilkow sat in his office, keeping an eye on the office pod window just outside. He pretended to be working on grades on his computer while waiting for the last lab tech to leave. They usually passed by the faculty office pod on their way out, and his office was close enough to the small lobby where he could barely see out the window. He tapped a few things on his computer while waiting, studying the map and shape of Ridgeway Lake. He noted the locations of the reported incidents, which appeared to take place at the mid-point in the vertical portion of the lake.

He made a plan to go out the next day. Another tab on his computer had the Birchwood Lodge website on it. He searched through the site's shopping section, hoping they sold bathymetry charts.

"Bingo," he said to himself after determining they had one. He started to devise a plan, which would begin with purchasing the chart while renting a boat from the lodge. He'd check the deepest points near the recorded incidents, and use sonar to get a fresh new reading of the areas to determine if there had been any change. If Wilkow managed to locate any change in the lake bottom, he would use an underwater drone to investigate a possible crevice. He was convinced of his underground lake theory, and he was sure this was an opportunity to prove one existed beneath them.

The first step would be to check the Biology Department's storage area to sneak away supplies. To do this, he had to wait for the techs to leave, as no equipment was to leave the college without permission from the dean. And there was no doubt they would report him to Nevers.

Wilkow looked up from his computer, seeing someone in a green shirt walking by the window. He carefully stepped out of his office and slowly opened the pod door to peek out. The lab tech continued down the hallway to the stairwell doors. She stopped after putting her hand on the handle, and suddenly looked his way. She saw him peeking out at her. *Oh shit.*

"Oh sorry," he said quickly. "I thought you were the pizza guy. He always gets lost. You don't want any, do ya? Extra cheese."

"No thanks. I got food waiting at home," the tech said and left.

"Whew," he exhaled sharply. *That was close. Thank God she wasn't hungry. I need to come up with a better bluff.* He made his way into the lab and went straight to the storage room in the back.

Several different types of equipment were stored in the large room. He checked through field sampling supplies, diving gear, old chemistry sets, and anatomy charts. However, there was no sonar monitor, nor was there an underwater drone.

"Oh, come on," he groaned. He went through the room again, but with no success. The department did not possess the equipment he needed. Thus, the only way to obtain them was to get them himself. He locked up the room and returned to his office.

He got on the internet to look for places to purchase the items. He knew he could get the sonar at any fishing and hunting store, but the drone would be a different story. He checked websites of stores in the surrounding area which sold diving and electronic equipment. He grabbed his phone and dialed the phone number to one called *Aquatic Genesis*. He spoke with a customer service representative, who confirmed they didn't have the underwater drone. Of course, she mentioned she could special order it, and they would have it in a week. That wasn't good enough for Wilkow. He wanted to be on the lake ASAP.

Calls to other nearby stores went exactly the same way. It seemed the only way to obtain the drone would be to order online, which would require him to wait. Before he gave up, another store website caught his eye; a place called *Huron Valley*. It was a research drone from a brand called *Gladius*. Wilkow read about its features. It was able to dive down to six hundred feet. The unit had an attached camera which would send a feed to a monitor. Wilkow felt himself grow excited, until he noticed one little problem: The store was located in Alcona County…a three-hour drive. Unfortunately, it seemed to be the only option. He leaned back in his chair and thought about it.

I'd have to postpone until tomorrow, but if I leave now, I'll be back tonight. It became clear this was the best way to go. Before getting up, he noticed the price to the drone. $2,348.98. *Holy shit.* He didn't have that kind of money on him.

A thought came to mind. He knew there was a college credit card in Dr. Nevers' office, specifically for department spending. *This is technically a research project*, he rationalized in his mind. *What the hell.*

He went out into the hallway to Dr. Nevers' office. As expected, it was locked. He checked his pants pocket and dug out a paper clip. He straightened the metal to a long needlelike prong, while constantly glancing down the hallway to make sure he wouldn't be seen. He knelt down and picked the lock. After a few tries, he felt the latch pop open, and he twisted the handle. He observed Dr. Nevers' organized desk, and remembered where he once witnessed him store the card. It was in a desk drawer, which was also locked.

He kept a watchful eye on the office entrance as he picked the lock. Campus Security often passed through around this time, a fact he had just remembered. He hurriedly picked the lock with his paperclip. This one proved to be a more difficult endeavor.

"Come on, you little…stubborn…piece… of…sh—" the lock gave way and the drawer popped open. He sorted through some papers and a few of Dr. Nevers' personal belongings until he found the card. "Ta-da!" The sound of approaching footsteps cut his celebration short. He snatched up the papers inside the drawer, and pushed it mostly shut, just enough so it wouldn't latch. He then went to the office entrance, trying to appear not in any hurry.

Wilkow recognized the green polo shirt and black pants worn by the security guard as he approached the door. The guard stared at the professor in the doorway, and then glanced at the name on the sign, *Dr. Richard Nevers.*

"Did you guys change your uniforms?" Wilkow nonchalantly asked.

"A couple weeks ago," the guard replied. "May I ask what you're doing in here?"

"Oh!" Wilkow acted surprised. "The dean left his door unlocked. I was just dropping off some papers he wanted me to turn in." He pointed at the papers on the desk. The guard furrowed his eyebrows and glanced at them. "As you can see, I was just on my way out."

The guard eyeballed him suspiciously, then grinned. "Alright then," he said and started walking off. Wilkow quietly breathed a sigh of relief.

Twice now, I lucked out. He ducked back into the office to rearrange the contents of the drawer. This way, the dean wouldn't immediately notice the card was missing. He closed it completely shut and left the office. He looked at his watch, seeing it was nearly *5:00*. He only had so much daylight left in his long haul, and he would need to stop for gas. He left the building and hurried out to the lot. He programmed his GPS for *Huron Valley,* then started his car to leave. With his directions set, he left campus to begin his very long round trip.

CHAPTER 16

The beginnings of dusk cast a shadow over Chief Sydney while he leaned up against his Jeep and watched the County Sheriff deputies guiding a contractor's boat as it hauled the sunken rowboat from the cove. Although Sydney had arrived at the scene hours earlier after hearing the gunshots, late 911 calls had continued to come in. Sheriff Logan was notified and wasted no time coming out to Rodney yet again. He arrived and took charge of the scene, ignoring all of Sydney's advice and statements, including a warning about a fallen submerged tree. Consequently, the towing line and the boat itself got snagged on several occasions. Seeing the know-it-alls scramble to undo their mess brought minor amusement to the chief.

All of the RPD officers on scene stood by as Logan demonstrated his superiority. EMS also arrived, growing impatient as the sheriff's divers failed to retrieve any bodies. David Culverhouse gave a statement to the deputies, but was still taken into custody as a possible suspect in the disappearances of the occupants of the other boat. Once he described an enormous fish in the cove, it seemed he had lost all credibility with the police, who instantly believed he was mentally deranged. Sydney made some remarks in Dave's favor, informing the sheriff he thought he had seen something in the water, although he did not specify that it was a giant fish.

Sydney was still unsure himself of what it was he saw. His mind pondered which was real and which was his imagination. The splashing was definitely real, as was the terror in Dave's eyes. He thought he had briefly seen something beneath the sizzling water; something large of a greenish color. He wondered if that was his imagination. Whatever the case was, he knew deep down that Dave didn't murder anybody.

Standing by the parked ambulance was Joel, again on volunteer duty. He had arrived in his personal vehicle after receiving the call, meeting up with the ambulance. His old white van with emergency flashers on top was often the subject of jokes from his crew, and sometimes even from the chief. Right now, however, nobody was joking. Boredom had soured the moods of everyone on scene, as had the irritation caused by Logan's superiority complex. Joel walked over to Sydney, who continued to glare at the sheriff from his Jeep.

"What the heck has been going on here lately, Morgan?" Joel asked. "First that crash, then that thing with Mrs. Stanton, and now this… all in a couple days. Is there a full moon or something?"

"I wish I knew," Sydney said. At that moment, he cupped his hand over his mouth as he yawned. Being up most of the night and working all day had taken its toll on him. "God," he said. The drowsiness added to Sydney's frustration, which in itself amplified his leg pain. "There doesn't happen to be a coffee machine in that ambulance, is there?" It was a half-joke.

"Unfortunately, no," Joel said, cracking a small grin. "Great idea though."

"I used to be able to stay up all night and day, and barely be tired. One time, I did a forty-eight-hour stakeout. Now, only I've been dealing with stuff less than twenty-four hours, and I'm beat," he said. He took a long deep breath. "Maybe I'm just old. Perhaps…" he stopped and looked at Joel, sixteen years his senior. He suddenly felt a bit foolish. "Oops."

Joel laughed at him. "It's something you adapt to," he said. "Best thing to do is accept it." His eyes went to Sheriff Logan barking orders to his men. "And don't turn out like this idiot."

Logan started up the hill to Sydney. "My guys haven't found anyone in there," he said as he approached Sydney. "They found fishing poles, tackle boxes, and other stuff. But no bodies." He gestured toward Joel. "I guess you guys can take off." Joel snickered at him. *Like I take orders from you.*

"You cool with that, Chief?" he asked Sydney. It was only meant to piss off Logan. Although he didn't show it, Sydney could sense the effect. He resisted smiling.

"Yeah. Have a good night. Thanks for coming."

"Not a problem," Joel said. He got into his van and drove off, followed by the ambulance.

"I suppose you can have your guys clear out as well," Logan said. "We pretty much have everything under control." Sydney scoffed.

"Yeah, I can see that." He pointed to the boat. "And by the way, no, I'm keeping my guys around the lake. I'm issuing an order right now for the town that nobody is to be on the lake until we figure out what's going on."

"Close the lake?" Logan said, looking at Sydney like he was insane. "You're not telling me you buy that story about a big fish that ate people…"

"I'm not saying anything on that matter," Sydney said. "But I don't believe these waters to be safe. There's something weird going on, and until I figure out what, I'm not letting anyone else get killed."

"Chief, you can't just close the lake."

"Oh you bet your ass I can, and I will," Sydney said. "Listen, Logan, we…"

"Address me as *Sheriff Logan*," the sheriff said, attempting to demonstrate superiority. Their voices traveled, drawing the attention of all the officers on scene. Everyone slowly nudged closer to eavesdrop.

"Listen, *SHERIFF*, we've had three incidents within the last twenty-four hours, with now four people confirmed missing, at least one dead, plus possible others. Each incident occurred in the water. I'm declaring it unsafe until I can find out what's going on." Sydney started to walk away, but before doing so, he turned toward Logan one more time. "This is my jurisdiction, and you cannot supersede it."

"Oh you can bet that I can," Logan fired back.

"Not without clearing it with the mayor first," Sydney said. "Good luck getting in touch with him." Logan didn't respond. He knew Sydney was correct; Mayor Greene had not been pleased with the Sheriff's Department lately. But considering the current events, he figured he might make headway.

"Come on, guys," he growled at his deputies. They began boarding their vehicles and clearing out. As they did, Chief Sydney summoned his officers. They all approached and huddled in a semicircle to listen to his instructions.

"I don't give a crap what that moron says, we're closing the lake," Sydney said.

"Can you actually do that?" one of the officers said.

"We're GOING to," Sydney said. "I want officers patrolling the shore, and at least one unit on boat patrol. Keep a spotlight out." Rumbles of discontent spread through the small crowd. "What the hell's your guys' problem?"

"Well, uhh…" one of the officers stuttered. Sydney felt himself slowly losing his temper.

"Come on, spit it out!"

"Chief, it's a big lake, and there's a bunch of people here!" another officer spoke up, a tall, built man named Larabee. "It's the middle of July! People are here on vacation. Some are paying thousands of dollars to fish here. You seriously want us to tell them NOT to be on the lake?"

"Yes," Sydney said, bluntly. "I'll let the midnight shift know. Just get started. I'll speak with the owner of the lodge." He turned to get into his jeep.

"Uhh…Chief," another one of the officers said. Sydney looked back.

"Yes?"

"Beg your pardon, sir, but it's a big-ass lake to cover. That's gonna require a lot of manpower…and frankly…midnights has only three patrollers." At least it was an honest question and not a protest.

"I'll tell dispatch to see if anyone wants to come in. Otherwise, expect to stay over till *0300*. All of you." Immediately, the officers expressed their discontent in the form of irritated groans. Sydney climbed into his Jeep and inserted the key into the ignition.

"You've got to be kidding me, Chief," Larabee called out. "This lake is over three miles from one end to the other, and you seriously want us to tell everyone they can't be in the water. You realize we're gonna have a…"

Sydney's temper broke.

"Damn it, you guys! For Christ sake, give me a break here!" He started his engine. "Quit complaining and do your jobs. Work for your paycheck for once."

Sydney closed the door to his Jeep and took off. Even after he was out of sight, he could practically hear the angry rants from the shift. He was well aware they referred to him as an asshole, has-been, prick, jerk, and even cripple. While they followed his orders, there was no doubt there was a lack of respect for him, and that they questioned the validity of his orders. He didn't care.

The unexpected stress of the day was adding up, worsening the pain in his leg. As he drove, he kept one hand on the steering wheel, and another on his thigh. He found himself starting to pine for the *Meperidine,* despite the dreaded side effects. With one hand on the steering wheel, he grabbed the radio speaker.

"Unit 1 to Dispatch."

"*This is Dispatch. Go ahead, Chief.*"

"Prepare for a TX," he said. He put the speaker down and dug out his phone, quickly dialing the number. Dispatch answered after one ring. "Hey, it's Sydney. Do me a favor and start calling around to see if anyone wants to pick up a shift on midnights."

"*Will do, Chief. How many officers?*"

"As many as possible. I'll be in soon to prepare a bulletin. We're closing Ridgeway Lake."

CHAPTER 17

Tim Marlow stayed on the boat console, keeping his coffee mug steady as Officer Larabee stood on starboard deck, arguing with the vacationer in the rowboat. The boats flashing red and blue lights irritated his drowsy eyes, which wanted to clamp shut for sleep. Tim quickly regretted picking up the call for midnight shift, and he still had his regular day shift to go. With it only being *1:13* in the morning, he had a long ways to go.

"I'm sorry, sir, but nobody can be on the lake right now," Larabee said. It was the third time in a row he informed the angry vacationer of this. For Larabee, who was already irritated at being mandated to work overtime, his patience was wearing thin.

"This is bullshit!" the angler roared. "I spent over a grand for this trip, and I'm only here for four nights!"

"I apologize again, but this is an order straight from the chief; the lake has to be vacated," Larabee explained. "I promise we'll have the situation under control very soon, and you'll be able to come back out shortly." The fisherman cursed under his breath as he reeled in his line. He threw a few items into his tackle box and pulled up his anchor.

"Get that damn spotlight out of my face," he sneered as he started his motor. Larabee nudged the light to face away from him. The propeller blades swirled, pushing the small boat away.

"Thank you for your cooperation," Larabee said.

"Fuck yourself!" he heard the fisherman call out.

"Yeah, yeah," Larabee muttered, watching the boat speed from view. The propellers kicked up water as it went, as if the motor itself was angry too. Larabee sat in a seat on the deck, while Marlow accelerated the boat at a slow speed to continue patrolling. They had been wrangling tourists out of the water all evening and night so far. A few were understanding and reasonable, but many others did not take the news so well, much like the vacationer they just dealt with. The worst was right after Sydney gave his instruction, when several evening fishers had rented boats from the Lodge. Since then, they had been on patrol, keeping watch for any violators.

Marlow listened to the long eerie wailing call of a nearby common loon. It ended with a soft sound of splashing water, indicating that the bird had taken a dive. He looked back at his co-worker, who continued sulking while grabbing his coffee cup. Larabee took a sip, then quickly spat it out. "Bleh! Damn!"

"What's wrong?" Marlow asked.

"Damn bug got in my coffee," Larabee grumbled. He dumped it out over the side of the boat. He repeatedly glanced at his watch, impatient to go home. "Dude, I can't believe this shit, man. Twice in a row now. My wife is working tonight too. I had to call our babysitter to make sure she could stay late."

"Did it work out?" Marlow asked.

"Yeah, this time," Larabee said. "This is freaking ridiculous. We have this huge lake, and the chief wants nobody on it? For what? Does he think there's a shark in here or something? Dun-dun, dun-dun, dun-dun," he mimicked the famous *Jaws* theme.

"Yeah, but don't you think it's weird?" Marlow said. "I mean, we've had three unexplained incidents in the water now. I think the chief is just covering his bases."

"I think the chief misses being a hotshot for the state," Larabee said. He saw the disapproval in Marlow's face. "What? You don't think so? Oh right, aren't you two buddies, or something?"

"Hey, come on, man," Marlow said. "First of all, no. I never met him until I interviewed for this job. Second of all, I don't complain when I'm told to do something. We're lucky to be in a police department where staffing normally isn't an issue…and you're complaining about being frozen four hours over." Larabee waved him off, then took off his hat to swat off some insects buzzing around. After driving them off, he looked at his empty mug.

"Any more in that thermos?" Marlow checked it.

"Enough for about one more," he said. "You can have it."

"Thanks," Larabee said. He stood up and poured the remaining coffee into his mug, filling it just under the rim. "Sorry, I didn't mean to be a dick."

"Nah, don't worry about it," Marlow said. Larabee set the thermos down.

"You know, you're alright, kid. And I've got nothing personal against the chief. But I don't know if he's handling this the right way, especially with butting heads with the sheriff. Don't be shocked if we hear something from the mayor about closing this lake," he said. He lifted his coffee cup to his mouth to take a drink.

In the blink of an eye, water splashed up on the portside, joined with the sound of flapping wings. A black loon slammed into the fiberglass side of the boat, flapping its wings in a panic. It corrected itself and flew upward hastily, passing just inches over the officers as it elevated above the boat. Larabee and Marlow both jumped back, alarmed.

"JESUS!" Larabee yelled out. Hot coffee splashed out of the mug, splattering all over his uniform. The bird disappeared into the darkness of the night sky. Leaning back against the starboard railing, Marlow caught his breath.

"Well, that woke me up," he said.

"No shit!" Larabee exclaimed.

"I wonder what the hell pissed him off," Marlow said. "I've never seen a loon act so crazy." Larabee nodded in agreement. His brain registered the sensation of hot coffee on his shirt.

"Son of a bitch," he said, looking down at his stained uniform. "This…this is just lovely. This is the icing on the cake." He noticed Marlow covering his mouth with his hand, concealing a chuckle. "I hear that, you little dipshit," he said with a grin. It escalated into a full laugh. "Just take me back to the dock. I got a spare shirt in my car."

"Aye-aye," Marlow said. He returned to the console and started turning the patrol vessel around. "On the bright side, we can get some fresh coffee when we head in."

"And a travel mug with a lid," Larabee said.

****

The angry vacationer cursed and complained to himself as he sped his boat toward the Lodge. The sound of his voice was lost in the drone of the motor, which he had blasting unnecessarily at full speed. Keeping his eyes toward the dock lights, he took no notice of the mass that trailed about thirty feet behind, steadily closing in.

The beast had watched below, drawn by the vibrations from the two vessels above and the prey that they carried. Concealed by darkness, the creature was now hunting in conditions which better suited its senses. It had been stalking the smaller boat, but delayed its attack when the larger vessel moved in, sporting flashing red lights. It hesitated to strike, uncertain if the lights were indicative of a threat, as rival creatures in its previous world would sport lights either to attract prey, or to present a challenge to enemies. Before it could move in, the smaller target moved away. The enormous fish hesitated, undecided on whether to pursue the smaller target moving away or the larger one that remained. Instinct dictated that the smaller object contained easier prey, and the Carnobass began pursuit. It passed beneath a diving loon, which fled toward the surface.

The enormous fish stayed about twenty feet under as it closed the distance. However, its hesitation proved to be its misfortune as its target went into shallow waters. It moved upward toward the surface to continue its chase. With a flutter of its tail, it shot toward the small boat like a rocket.

It opened its jaws to enclose onto the metal stern. Sensory nerves unexpectedly fired through its body as propeller blades scraped against the inside of its jaw. As a reflex, the huge fish hooked around and dove, brushing against the lake bottom. It opened and shut its mouth, as if testing its jaw. No damage had been done aside from minor scraping and the loss of a few tiny teeth, all of which would grow back.

The brief grinding sound of the motor and the huge splash behind him caused the vacationer to look back.

"What the hell?" He didn't see anything besides stirring water behind his boat. *Maybe I ran over something that was floating,* he thought. He figured it was a rational possibility, as pieces of broken branches sometimes floated in the water after breaking off trees near shore. He slowed the boat down as he approached the beach. After bringing it in and tying it to the dock, he started collecting his items. He decided to look at the motor. He tilted it upwards, lifting the propeller blades out of the water. They were jagged and bent out of place.

"Oh great!" he said. "This'll probably come out of my wallet. Just what I need." He got out of the boat and collected his items.

The Carnobass swam back upward, only to find that its prey had already moved out of reach. Hungry and frustrated, the large fish swam back out into the open lake in search of food.

CHAPTER 18

Sydney resisted the urge to hit the snooze on his alarm clock. He had stayed out until after midnight to assist with keeping people off the lake. Speaking with Mr. Tindell, the owner of Birchwood Lodge, was the worst. Mr. Tindell did not take kindly to informing his customers that they couldn't go fishing or swimming. He came in to the station before going home, and dispatch was overwhelmed with calls regarding the order. People were aware of the police investigations, and a rumor of a possible lake-killer was starting to spread.

Sydney felt like a fragile old man as he got out of bed. As he sat up and stretched, his hip and shoulder simultaneously popped. At this age, his joints did this often, making him sound like a human walnut cracker each morning. To make matters worse, the little sleep he got wasn't quality sleep. His mind was fixated on the investigations, particularly the death of Amanda Stanton. There were no leads for him to go on, and he knew Sheriff Logan was going to continue hassling him on the situation.

Sydney stood up out of bed. As soon as his left leg felt the pressure of his body weight, the nerves within the muscles lit up like Vegas at night. He clutched his leg and nearly fell back into bed. Sydney squeezed the edge of the mattress, both out of pain and frustration. Each worsened the other.

He finally got up and limped his way over to the kitchen. He downed a protein shake and prepared some coffee. He grabbed the ibuprofen and gulped down a pill. Simply looking at the ibuprofen, knowing it wasn't going to numb the pain much, added to the stress and frustration. After looking at the clock, Sydney realized he needed to hurry up and get dressed. He knew he was in for a busy day, especially with angry tourists and residents wanting answers about the lake.

After he put on his uniform, he checked his phone. Surprisingly, he didn't have any messages, indicating that the night must have gone smoothly. He filled his travel mug with coffee and limped out the door, feeling the ache in his stomach from the ibuprofen.

****

As Sydney pulled into the station's driveway, he quickly saw the silver 2017 Chevy Silverado parked in the front row. He was well aware who it belonged to, and why he was here.

"Oh great," he said to himself. He knew he'd have to confront Mayor Shawn Greene about the situation, but he didn't plan on it being the very first thing. At the very least, he hoped to finish his coffee.

He parked his car and walked toward the front door, unable to conceal his painful limp. Mayor Greene was waiting in the lobby. At a towering height of six-foot-three, the skinny blond-haired man of forty leaned against the dispatch desk. He had been watching the hallway, where a couple of the officers had been waiting. His eyes turned toward Sydney as he walked through the entrance. In addition to his white dress shirt, grey slacks, and a blue tie, Greene wore a grimace which presented his irritation.

"Shawn!" Sydney tried to sound surprised. "Good morning. I'm glad you're here."

"Well, that makes one of us," Mayor Greene responded. "You've got a helluva lot of explaining to do, Chief." His voice carried, and Sydney knew he could be heard down the hallway where the officers were certainly listening.

"Well…let's go to my office," Sydney said, leading the mayor down the hallway.

"Was it too difficult to contact me?" Greene spoke in a booming voice. He wasn't bothering to wait until they were in the privacy of the office.

"Well, sir," Sydney said. "I had to act quickly to ensure—"

"My phone's been ringing off the hook all night and all morning. My personal phone has been blowing up all night. You closed the entire lake? What the hell are you thinking? Are you trying to kill this town?" They entered the office, and Sydney shut the door behind them. He offered a chair to the mayor, who declined simply by shaking his head. Sydney took a seat behind his desk. Looking up at the scowling mayor was no pleasant sight.

"Listen, Shawn," he began. "I'm not sure what's been going on around here, but I'm under the suspicion that the lake isn't safe to be on."

"Based on what?"

"Well, for starters, we've had three incidents in the last two days. All of which are still unexplained. We have several people unaccounted for, and at least one person dead."

"Oh yeah," Greene said. "About Amanda Stanton, was it correct when I was told you treated her husband Jimmie as a suspect? Are you aware that he's high up in a company that employs several people in this county?"

And has hosted several fundraisers for you, Sydney resisted saying out loud. He cleared his throat. "You do realize we have evidence that his wife had been fooling around? She was out with someone else, and brought him home. We found the door kicked in, with Jimmie's shoe print in the middle of it. Because of the conditions, I had to consider the possibility that he came home, found his wife and lover, and possibly murdered them. I checked with his employment and verified his alibi. We have to be thorough."

"What about this guy she was seeing?" Greene said. "Didn't you consider maybe he did this?"

"That'd be weird, considering he left his pants and shirt, along with his wallet and ID. Jack Penn. No trace of him so far either. And we have at least two other people reported missing, who were last known to be heading for the lake." Mayor Greene didn't seem to be fazed by this information. Rather, he appeared even more irritated.

"So, why close the lake?" he said. "It's broad daylight. We've got people who are here to enjoy the water. This is our prime season. I don't see why there's a need for the lake to be closed off."

"Because I don't believe it's safe," Sydney said firmly. He made a mental note to control his rising voice.

"Based on what?"

"Didn't I just expl—because we've had three incidents on the water; three that we know of."

"Sheriff Logan informs me that there's no danger in the lake," Greene said, crossing his arms again. Sydney glared at him and leaned back in his seat. He cracked a smile, but it wasn't a blissful one.

"Since when did you two become buddies?" he said. Greene ignored the remark.

"The point is, I already made a statement to the paper before coming here. The lake is open, and it's going to stay open. This is the lifeblood of this town, and I'm not gonna let you kill it."

"Oh yes…because that's totally why I took this job," Sydney remarked. "See, I was more concerned with someone or something that's actually killing people. Unlike your new pal, Logan. Why are you suddenly listening to him? I seem to remember why Rodney founded its own police department—"

"Morgan," Greene said. Being a formal person, he only used first names when really irritated, "don't push it. The lake is open. You can have one or two patrols on it, that's fine. But if you want to keep your job, quit this wild goose chase."

There was a moment of intense silence, which felt just as heated as their conversation. Sydney brooded in his seat, not pleased to hear his job threatened. Greene didn't feel there was anything more to say. Sydney stood up and opened the door for him, only as a show for the officers who he knew were listening outside.

"Have a good day, sir," he said. The mayor didn't say anything and simply walked to the front entrance to leave. With a frustrated groan,

Sydney went into the briefing room, where all of the midnight and day-time staff were waiting. As he walked in, the pain in his leg flared up. He stumbled, barely grabbing the podium before taking a fall. "God damn." He could hear some muffled chuckling from the back. That, combined with the pain and the frustration from Greene, nearly overloaded his temper. He straightened himself up. "Alright…as I'm aware you all know because you like to eavesdrop, the lake is open again. Apparently, the mayor and the sheriff believe there's no danger. However, I don't really care what they think. I want two patrols on the water, and other officers patrolling the shore." He looked to two of the officers sitting in the back, who he knew had laughed at his stumble. They were both midnight patrollers, who were about to go home. "You two," he said, pointing at them. They each perked their heads up, and all eyes turned toward them. "Grey and McMillan…congratulations, you're being frozen over. Eight hours." Clamors of protest echoed through the room, not just from the two unlucky midnight patrollers, but from several other officers as well.

"What the hell, Chief?!" one of them said.

"Chief, this is ridiculous!" another called out. Sydney didn't feel any guilt or intimidation, nor was he about to go back on his orders.

"Knock it off," he said, hammering a fist into the podium. The loud cracking sound of wood silenced the room. "You guys think this is a game? Clock in, clock out, maybe bust a drunk here and there? We've got something serious going on here. I don't know what, but I need you guys to help me keep it from getting any worse. Now, quit complaining and get to work." He limped away, ignoring the murmuring of discontent from the officers.

****

Joel placed the dead largemouth bass on the counter before him. With a swift motion, he slid the six-inch Rapala knife behind the gill slit, under the pectoral fins, along both sides of the spine, then deeper behind the rib cage. With a little bit of trimming, both fillets were clear of the fish meat in thirty seconds.

"Skin on or off?" he asked of the customer, a man and his wife. Each stared for a moment, impressed by the speed and efficiency of the fish cleaning. The husband appeared almost embarrassed, feeling less manly for not cleaning his own fish.

"Uhh…it can stay on," he said. Joel placed the fillets in a bag, along with the bluegill nuggets he cleaned for them as well.

"Here you go," he said, handing the bag to them. "Have a nice day."

"You too," the wife said. As they walked off, Joel could hear the husband mumble, "I could do that, you know. It's just that…we have a lot of other things to do and…"

"Uh-huh," he heard the wife say. Joel cracked a small grin and cleared away the fish guts. The morning had been busier than normal. Once the mayor released the announcement that the lake was open again, the vacationers at Birchwood Lodge all seemed to hit the water, as if in fear the chief would close it again.

The closing of the lake already was the talk of the town. Unhappy residents were questioning Morgan Sydney's suitability as chief of police. One of the loudest voices was Birchwood Lodge's owner, Mr. Tindell. As Joel arrived for work, he had to listen to his boss complain about how he had to instruct all of his tenants to stay off the lake. Several of them demanded refunds, and one customer even went as far as to write a negative review online, even though they knew it had been a police order and not the Lodge's choice.

Joel himself wasn't sure what to think of Sydney's decision to close the lake. On the one hand, it seemed like a drastic move based on a lot of uncertainty. On the other hand, however, he knew Sydney had a keen sense of a threat, and was not the type to make decisions he didn't fully believe in. In addition, in all of his years of hunting and being hunted, Joel developed something of a sixth sense when an unforeseeable danger lurked. He hadn't felt that feeling in years, up until recently, and it strengthened whenever he looked at that water.

He looked out the large window toward the large beach area. It was almost *10:00*, and already the sand was covered in tourists. Kids played volleyball and soccer games; women in bikinis were sunning themselves, while others were busy doing yoga. Naturally, the single men out there were eyeballing them, hoping to get the attention of an attractive female. Of course, the lake was filled with people enjoying the warm water. Joel glanced out the other window, which gave view to the dock. Most of the boats were already way out into the lake, and a few fishermen were loading into the boats that remained.

He recognized a certain duo that hobbled out to the dock. It was Jeff and Richie, the rude, overweight boozers that had checked in a couple nights prior. Joel quickly noticed the twelve pack carried by Richie, and one of the bottles was already open in Jeff's hand. They cackled obscene jokes to one another as they boarded the twelve-foot boat. Joel couldn't hear what they were saying, but seeing the offended expressions from some women nearby, he knew it wasn't of good taste.

Two other hefty individuals met up with Jeff and Richie, Brook and Diesel. Both were sporting full, untrimmed beards and ball caps. Diesel was much fatter than Brook, and the sight of his stomach nearly poking out from under his shirt was enough to rid Joel of any appetite he had. They started cracking jokes with Jeff and Richie while piling into the next boat. Joel winced as one of them bent down to lower a tackle box.

Those pants he wore barely held together as his waist stretched the fabric.

It'll be a miracle if that boat doesn't sink.

Tindell's voice carried from the front desk. The enthusiasm it contained likely meant he was renting out a boat. Because of the busy hours, almost all the boats had been rented out, leaving one remaining. Usually, two-thirds at most would be rented out at one time, meaning Tindell was making a pretty penny. With the sudden high demand, he had strongly considered upping the price to increase profits. However, Joel managed to talk him out of it. Tindell's voice drew nearer as he led the customer through the lodge. The customer carried with him two poles, a bucket, live-basket, and tackle box.

"Yes, sir," he said as he brought him through the fish cleaning station, "it's your lucky day. We have one last boat, at least until *1:00 p.m.* when some are scheduled to return. Typical twelve-footer with oars and anchor. Fifty dollars for four hours out, ninety for eight hours. We can also rent out a trawling motor for ten bucks." Joel saw the customer struggling to keep up with Tindell while trying to hang on to all of his items.

"Here, sir, I can help you carry those out," he said. The customer sighed with relief.

"Oh thanks, I appreciate it," he said.

"Not a problem," Joel said. He took the bucket and tackle box off his hands and got the door, shooting a disapproved look at his boss while getting the door. *Yeah, you preach customer service to* us, he thought. The three of them walked outside to the last boat.

"Alright," the customer said, "I think four hours is all I'll need for now. Can I pay in cash right here, or…?"

"That's just fine," Tindell said. The customer reached into his back jeans pocket for his wallet. He stopped and looked toward the front of the lodge, alerted by the sight of a man running toward them.

"Hey, hey, hey!" the man exclaimed. Dressed in a grey shirt and tan cargo pants, he hustled down the small hill, carrying two large boxes under his arms. "You got any more boats for rent! It's really important that I get—YAHH!!" He tripped over his own feet, flinging his boxes forward as he fell face first. "Shit!"

"You alright?" Joel questioned as he rushed toward him.

"I'm good!" the man said. He sprang to his feet and grabbed his boxes, stacking them on top of each other. He held out his hand to shake Joel's. "Hi! Dr. Mike Wilkow. Nice mustache! Are you the owner of this place?" Joel wasn't sure what to say, and he couldn't help staring at Wilkow as if he was a lunatic. He reluctantly shook Wilkow's hand.

"Over there," he pointed at Tindell. "That's the owner. I don't think we have any more bo—" Wilkow brushed passed him and walked over to Tindell.

"Hi!" he said. "I'm Doctor Wilkow. I know you're having some unexpected busy hours, but I was hoping you had any boats available for rent."

"Oh, I'm sorry sir," Tindell said. "I literally just rented out the last one to this gentleman here. However, we'll have a couple coming in at *1:00* this afternoon. Fifty bucks for four hours, ninety for eight."

"I happened to notice that this guy hadn't paid you yet," Wilkow said.

"Well, he's just about to. Like I said, there'll be another boat available at—"

"Tell you what…I'll pay you four hundred bucks for eight hours," Wilkow interrupted. Tindell stared flabbergasted.

Damn! He must really want to go fishing!

"Well, I…uh…" he looked to the other customer and back at Wilkow, as if unable to make up his mind. Joel could sense the gears turning in his head. The shit-eating grin was unmistakable, and Joel felt as if he could see dollar signs in boss's eyes.

"Hey, man, I was here first," the customer said, speaking to Wilkow.

"What's the big hurry?" Joel interrupted.

"Shut up, Joel!" Tindell barked. "Well, sir…perhaps we can work something out. If you could wait…"

"Let me cut in," Wilkow said. "Hey, bud, if you let me have the boat, I'll pay for yours." He whipped out his credit card; rather, the college's. The customer appeared angry, initially. As he rolled the thought around in his mind, he visibly became more at ease.

"Make it eight hours, and you have a deal," he said.

"Cha-Ching!" Wilkow said. He looked to Tindell, who barely contained his giddiness. A good business day had gotten even better. "Let's ring this in. By the way, do you have any bathymetry charts for this lake?"

"Yes, sir!" He pointed the way to the building for the professor. Tindell's voice trailed after his new favorite customer like a puppy dog after its owner. "Is there anything else I can get for you? Soda? Anything?"

Joel returned to the cleaning station and began to organize his counter. "I'll be darned if the guy doesn't try charging triple for the pop," he mumbled to himself.

CHAPTER 19

"Is there pressure up around the eyes?" Meya asked. Her patient, a twenty-five-year-old male with a red face and droopy eyes, nodded while sitting on the exam table. She jotted down notes on a sheet in her clipboard. "Mucinex isn't working at home?"

"Nothing's been helping with this," the patient said. His voice sounded as drained as he appeared. He turned and blew his nose into a tissue. Meya pulled out her prescription pad.

"Needless to say, you have a sinus infection," she said. "I'm gonna write you a prescription for Amoxicillin. Take one pill three times a day." She scribbled her signature and tore off the sheet. "You're all set to go."

"Thank you," the patient said. He took the prescription and left. Meya stayed behind and jotted a few more notes before calling for the next patient. Life seemed to have gone back to normal. Rather, her new normal: a near stress-free environment in which each case was a generic one. She grabbed the file for the next person, and picked up the phone to call the check-in desk. The nurse at the desk answered on the first ring.

"*Front desk. This is Angela speaking.*"

"Hey," Meya said. "You can send in the next one."

"*Oh, your eleven o'clock cancelled. So did your eleven-thirty. So far, nobody else has arrived.*"

"They cancelled to go to the lake," Meya said, more to herself than the nurse. "I guess they weren't really that sick. Okay, thanks." She hung up the phone, quickly realizing she had at least an hour to kill. She figured it was a good time to go to her office for some administrative duties.

The break lounge was on her way to her office. The smell of freshly brewed coffee filled her nostrils. It was hard to resist, being as she lived on nearly six cups a day for eighteen years. She entered the lobby and noticed two nurses seated at a break table. One was reading the local newspaper, chuckling at the front page.

"Wow," she began. "It says here he didn't even consult Mayor Greene." Meya glanced toward her table while filling her cup. She caught a glimpse of the newspaper, and the bold letters printed on top. She couldn't read the whole title, but the words *Police Chief* and *Lake* caught her eye, and it told her enough.

"I just can't believe he actually tried to close the whole lake," the other said. "What a shmuck. What do you think, Doc?" Meya realized she was now being spoken to.

"I'm sorry?"

"You hear about Ridgeway Lake, and our idiot police chief?"

"I don't know," she said. "I don't think he's an idiot. I think maybe...perhaps he's just..." her voice trailed off as she thought of Sydney. She felt a bit of regret for their sour interaction the previous day.

"He's just what?" the nurse asked.

"Just stressed," she answered. She left the lounge and went to her office, ignoring the nurses as they continued to verbally bash the chief. She shut the door behind her and sat down. She paused unintentionally before she could start her work. Her mind was fixated on Sydney, specifically the troubles he was going through. Her thoughts then went to some good times in their past, particularly by the lighthouse.

As if punishing herself for thinking of him, she lightly tapped herself on the cheek to focus back into reality. She logged onto her computer and began pulling up documents, forcefully keeping her ex-husband out of mind.

****

Wilkow dropped an anchor after reaching his next location. He tied the rope taut and looked at his bathymetry chart once more. It unrolled like a roadmap, showing the large shape of Ridgeway Lake. It was marked with green, blue, and red markings, almost appearing like the radar screen on the Weather Channel. The green blobs were indicative of areas deeper than two hundred feet. He was about a mile and a half south from the Lodge, and already checked three "deep zones" between there and his current location. So far, every sonar reading appeared to match the layout of what was on the chart.

He set up his sonar screen for the fourth time, and got the fish finder ready to send a ping toward the lake bottom. He paused for a minute after seeing a large speedboat starting to pass by, towing two cheering people on water skies. Swells of water rippled his way, bobbing his boat up and down several times until they settled down. The boat continued down the lake for an unknown distance, where it would eventually circle back.

"I haven't done that in a while," he said to himself. "I think I have a field trip in mind for class!" *Technically, I'd still be giving a lesson on water displacement and vibrations and stuff.* With that thought, he felt his skin beginning to burn. He'd been out on the water for nearly two hours, without any luck on finding any recent formation in the lake bottom. *Hopefully, I'll remember sunscreen next time.*

His fish finder fired a few pings, and the monitor lit up with green and blue colors. The screen was split into two images; the left showed an overhead map-like view of the area and marked depths. The right half of the screen showed a view of the basic shape of the lake floor. Everything seemed to match the information on his chart. Once again, no signs of crests or rifts along the bottom.

"Damn," he said. He looked at his chart for the next location. Everything around him seemed too shallow, with the nearest deep zone being across the lake in a southerly direction. He could only hope he could find some sort of anomaly, which would somewhat justify him stealing funds from the college. Either way, he knew he was in for an energetic conversation with Dr. Nevers.

He secured the monitor once again and started pulling up the anchor. He tugged upward, and the large, heavy cement block tumbled over the stern, dripping wet and covered in seaweed. Wilkow started the motor and steered the boat to the next testing area.

****

With the wind in his face, Aaron steered the speedboat. He kept his eye on a mirror, watching his two friends, Jordan and Rachel, as they each clung to their ski handles. Their cheers were as loud as the boat engine.

At least this is a kind of fun I don't have to accidentally walk in on, Aaron thought. He kept switching his view between the path ahead and the mirror, keeping track of his friends while monitoring his path. He sped by a fishing boat within which a man was flipping through multiple colored charts and fiddling with a fish finder. With all the boaters on the lake, maintaining a decent path was somewhat difficult. He would take the boat further along the side of the lake, and eventually turn around to do a pass in the opposite direction, then repeat until his friends decided they have had enough.

Knowing Rachel and Jordan, he'd likely be driving the speedboat all day.

****

Sydney pulled his Jeep up into one of the open parking spaces in the Lodge's driveway. He switched off the engine and appeared to stare at the large brown building. In actuality, he was staring off into space, deep in thought. For the past couple days, those thoughts were flooded with concerns regarding safety on the lake. The resistance he was receiving from the mayor, the sheriff, even his own officers, made things worse. It was as if the town believed they were in a safe bubble, and didn't want to believe a danger possibly lurked near.

But now, he thought of Meya: specifically, their last unpleasant encounter. He understood what it was; lack of sleep and overwork had gotten to them again. But he recalled his behavior, and felt a heavy sense of regret. He looked at his phone again, remembering her number even though it had been deleted long ago. He considered giving her a phone call. He knew what he wanted to tell her; he was sorry, not just for yesterday but for all the years they argued like that. Sydney wanted to tell her that and much more, but he ran into the same problem as ever: he didn't know how to say it. At least he thought he didn't know how.

Hell, she probably doesn't want to hear from me anyway, he thought. He put his phone away and stepped out of his Jeep. He walked over the grass and around the left of the building. The water came into view, as did the empty docks. All of the boats were gone, and further to the right was the beach. It was absolutely full, more than usual even for this time of year. There was so much splashing in the water, it almost looked like a human feeding frenzy. People drifted in inflatables, while others simply dove under and up. He looked further down the lake, seeing some of the cabins and lakefront houses further down shore. Their residents were also in the water, and his view of the lake was peppered with the sight of several boats of all kinds moving about. Jet skiers zoomed about, pontoon boats were full with loud music booming from them, and of course, several people were out fishing. It was as if the town and visitors were giving him the middle finger for trying to close the lake.

Joel did a quick fillet job on a customer's bullhead catfish they had caught on the dock. After bagging the fillets and sending the customer on his way, he naturally glanced out the window. He did a double take, seeing Chief Sydney standing outside with his arms crossed, watching the beach. He quickly washed his hands, then opened the door to peek his head out.

"Going for a swim there, Chief?" he called. Sydney looked over at him, sparking a small grin. At least there was one friendly face who didn't despise his existence.

"I do hear the water's warm," he joked. "Actually, I just wanted to keep an eye on things. I figured I better keep my distance though."

"With that in mind, you might want to wait here in the cleaning station. Tindell might not be too gracious if he sees you. Luckily, he only passes through here when he's selling something and...well, the whole town's out on the lake right now." Sydney nodded and went with Joel's proposal. After he came inside, Joel went to cleaning the fillet countertop.

"Has it been busy in here?" Sydney asked, simply making conversation.

"In the morning hours, maybe a couple people here and there, but normally quiet. This afternoon though, with everybody and their brother out fishing, I expect to be hustling. They normally come in around noon, but everyone has their knickers in a twist because they think you're gonna close the lake again. So they're staying out longer, it seems." Sydney understood the way Joel spoke as a polite way of trying to find out why he wants the lake closed.

"Well, I guess they have nothing to worry about," he said. "The mayor and apparently the sheriff have concluded that there is no danger in the lake. Despite the fact that we still have people missing and…ugh, I'm not going over the whole speech again." He looked over Joel's station, then at his hunting photos. He saw one of him and a large black bear, another with a lion. "Is that the one that nearly had you for dinner?" Joel turned and looked.

"Oh no," he said. "That one was much bigger." Sydney grinned and continued looking at the display. Naturally, he eyeballed the large Bandolero sword.

"I don't suppose you use that for filleting," he said.

"No, but I've had a few people ask me to," Joel said. "It was a gift from somebody in the service. We were into knives and guns and stuff. He had it custom made for me."

"Sounds like a nice guy," Sydney said. He grabbed the radio microphone. "Excuse me one sec," he said to Joel and then lifted it to his mouth. "Unit one to Unit Four?"

"*Unit Four. Go ahead.*" Sydney recognized Tim Marlow's voice.

"What's your status? Anything going on out there?"

****

Marlow slowly steered the boat south, keeping a distance from the shallow areas where most people were fishing.

"It's as quiet as a newborn baby out here," he spoke into the radio speaker. He waited for a response, but quickly realized Sydney likely didn't understand the remark. "As in, people are screaming all over. Speedboaters and jet skiers going nuts, fisherman yelling about something breaking their line, a couple people getting busy in a pontoon…"

"*Please tell me you asked them to take it somewhere else*?"

"Uhh, of course," Marlow said.

"*Alright. Keep your eyes peeled, and keep me informed,*" Sydney said.

"Will do," Marlow said.

"*Over and out.*"

Marlow set the speaker down. He kept the patrol boat going at a slower pace, actually having to keep an eye out in front of him as there was plenty of traffic on the lake for once. The music on the radio became mind-numbingly repetitive, which worsened his drowsiness. He switched it off, leaving the only thing to listen to was the pinball game that his partner was playing on his phone. The partner sat on deck, biding his time until shift change. Like most of the department, he thought the extensive lake patrols were a paranoid waste of time. This made Marlow feel a bit like an outcast, as he was the only one who trusted the chief's judgment. The mechanical sounds of the gameplay suddenly stopped, replaced by a downbeat musical score.

"Shit!" the officer said. Marlow looked back.

"Told you, you weren't gonna beat the high score."

****

Dr. Wilkow dropped his anchor at the next location. Once again, the previous two were a bust, and he was running out of deep zones in this section of the lake. He tied the anchor down and set up his equipment for what seemed like the hundredth time.

Next time, I'm bringing a pole and bait with me.

His phone vibrated. He glanced at the caller ID. It was the general phone number for the University. It went to voicemail. Although he didn't want to, he listened to it. As he anticipated, it was Dr. Nevers' voice.

"*I swear to God, Dr. Wilkow, you better have an explanation for this. I got an alert regarding thousands of dollars in charges placed on the college credit card, which interestingly is missing from my desk drawer. I only know one person who would purchase a Gladius 4K underwater drone and a bathymetry chart! And where the hell are you? Get your ass back here STAT, you hear me?*"

"Wouldn't you want to ask that at the beginning of a message?" Wilkow said, expressing his sarcastic wit even with nobody to witness it. He tucked his phone away and returned to his sonar monitor. The fish finder sent a ping to the bottom of the lake, and immediately the colorful images began to arise on the screen. Wilkow looked at his chart to compare the images. Glancing back and forth between the chart and the monitor, his eyes widened and his jaw dropped. His heart thumped with intense excitement. The layout of the lakebed showed what appeared to be a deep fissure in the bedrock.

"YEEAAAHHH BABY!" he cheered. The approximate depth of this area was two-hundred-ninety feet. He scooted to the other side of his seat and tore open his other box. He lifted the large, yellow Gladius drone out along with its one-hundred-meter tether. The drone was flat, with a solid exterior for resisting water pressures and twin propellers at the rear. At its maximum depth of three-hundred-thirty feet, it was capable of going at a horizontal distance of five hundred feet.

Wilkow synced the drone's video feed to his laptop computer. The video came through nice and clear. He held up the drone and turned the camera toward his face. He admired his own image on the monitor screen before activating the recording device.

"Hi! I'm Dr. Mike Wilkow! Today, we're going to take a peek into the deep dark crack of Ridgeway Lake. What we'll see, well…we're just gonna have to…ehh fuck it." He dropped the drone over the side and snatched up the control device as he sat back down. Hunched over, he looked like a young video game player, staring intently at the feed on his computer screen while operating the controller. The image on the screen displayed a pleasant clear blue milieu, with streaks of golden sunlight reaching downward. As the drone dove deeper, those golden streaks turned brownish and eventually disappeared into a murky green locale. The tether unreeled with a whirring noise, and Wilkow used the amount of cable left to help determine his depth.

Finally, he got a visual of the lakebed. Seaweed gently waved in the water like leaves on a tree from a light breeze. The plant life wasn't well grown due to the lack of exposure to sunlight. Other than that, there wasn't any life at this depth, except for the odd catfish here and there. Wilkow looked at the sonar images to see how far off he was from the rift. He steered the drone northeast, watching the video feed carefully. He began to notice a disparity in the lake floor. It suddenly became more rocky, very uneven. The drone came upon an upward hill. Wilkow steered the drone up above the peak, and cracked a wide smile as he dipped the camera downward.

It was like a miniature Grand Canyon underwater. There, two-hundred and ninety feet down was an opening like that of the mouth of a cave. Wilkow backed the drone up to get a better view, and switched on the lights. The drone's headlight cast a white illumination on the dark chasm. He snapped several still pictures, which instantly saved onto the computer's hard drive. Wilkow studied the gap, estimating it to be roughly thirty to forty feet wide, and perhaps fifty feet long. He noticed signs of instability around it as well, such as cracks in the surrounding earth. This area seemed to be made of a rocky structure, which was weakened by the constant exposure to water. Wilkow hypothesized that this area had weakened, and that the tremors from the blasting in the Corey Mine caused it to give way.

Wilkow moved the drone closer. He checked the tether, and determined he had roughly forty feet before maxing out. Wilkow put the drone directly over the opening and pointed it straight down. Its light traveled deep into the dark, profound tunnel. Gently moving his thumb on the control pad, he moved the drone inward. The drone descended slowly, snapping photos every couple feet. New details came to view on the monitor. Wilkow could identify layers of sediments and areas of compaction. Looking down into the distance, Wilkow thought he could see something attached to the "wall" of the cave. As he moved the drone closer, the tether tightened. It had maxed out.

"Crap!" He angled the drone as best he could to cast the best light on the object. He nearly put his eye right against the monitor screen to see as best he could. "I'll be damned." The object resembled a form of plant species. It was charcoal in color, shaped like a bulb with three large arrow-shaped leaves extending out. *How can that be growing underground, with no exposure to sunlight?* Assuming it was a plant, of course. If it was, it would require photons from light to survive. *Unless it wasn't getting them from the sun, but from something else.* He thought of the possibilities. Likely, there were species of fish using lights to lure prey or attract mates, just as fish do in the deep Mariana Trench. There were likely species of fungus that gave off light. Even rocks or other minerals could do so as well. Wilkow grew excited as he thought of all the possibilities for discovery. He snapped a few photos of the plant and slowly backed the drone out of the cave.

"Okay, Dr. Nevers," he said, "I think I have my explanation."

Only about ten yards to Wilkow's starboard side were two twelve-foot boats, steadily trawling with fishing lines trailing. Jeff and Richie were on the front boat, each with a beer in hand while cracking jokes to the other duo, Diesel and Brook, who were roughly twenty feet behind them. They had hardly any luck catching any fish, and their excessive intake of alcohol was certainly to blame.

"I should've kept that turtle!" Diesel called out. "I've never tried the soup!"

"You wouldn't be impressed," Brook said. On the other boat, Richie stood up. He tilted his head back and downed the remainder of his beer. He swallowed, waited for his stomach to stop gurgling, then let out a loud burp which sounded like a frog croak. "You expect congratulations from us?" Brook said. Richie mimicked a stage bow. Jeff belched out a booming laugh. His friends weren't sure whether he was laughing at the joke, or the burp, or nothing at all. In fact, Jeff himself didn't even know. At this point, he was a walking beer keg.

"No more for him," Diesel said. "He can't hold it like I can!"

"Well, no shit, Diesel," Brook said. "You've got three times as much room to store it." He pointed to his friend's protruding gut.

"Go f…" his curse word came out as a heavy belch, "yourself!" The four vacationing slobs erupted in laughter. Richie doubled over as he cackled. While bent down, he found himself looking directly at his fishing pole. The line was tight, and the pole itself was starting to bend.

"Oh shit!" he yelled. He fell to his knees and grabbed the handle. "I got a bite!" He yanked back on the pole and started reeling in. Immediately, he felt something heavy on the other end, although it didn't seem to be fighting back. "What the hell?"

Wilkow stared confused at the tether as he reeled it in. It stretched a bit outward, as if something was trying to pull it away from the boat. The winch continued reeling it in. After several seconds, Wilkow noticed a red lure coming up with the tether, along with several feet of fishing line. He looked at the man on the boat struggling with his pole, and quickly realized that he had snagged his tether line.

"Whoa! Hold up there, bud," he called out. "You're hooked to my line here."

Richie didn't listen and continued yanking back on his pole, seemingly unaware as to why it couldn't reel in any further. Wilkow stopped the winch from bringing it in any further. He reached for the fishing line to untangle it. He felt the line to find the tangle, just as Richie pulled back again. The hooks swiftly jolted to the side, nearly piercing his hand. Wilkow reared backward, falling back into his seat.

"Holy…" He looked over at Richie and stood back up. He cupped his hands around his mouth, although they weren't too far away. "Hey!" Richie looked toward him.

"Little busy!" he called back. "I've hooked the big one, and boy, he's not giving me a break! I think I'm about to break some sort of record!" He returned his attention to the water and tugged with his pole. Wilkow gave him a blank stare, losing his faith in humanity as Richie continued his attempt to reel in his boat.

"Hey, genius!" He pulled up on Richie's line and held it up as best he could. Richie finally looked toward him again and saw the line in his hand. "Unless the record is how much booze you can have in an hour, I think the only thing you're gonna break is your lure." Richie wasn't amused. He yanked back on the pole even harder, as if in a blind rage.

"You douche! Give me back my line!" He spoke as if Wilkow deliberately snagged it. Wilkow dropped the line before it could cut into his skin. He quickly realized he was dealing with an intoxicated lunatic who quickly resorted to anger.

"If you just hang on, I can undo this," he called out. Richie didn't listen and continued to tug mindlessly. To make matters worse, his drunken friends started shouting obscenities at Wilkow. He determined the quickest way to get out of this situation was to untangle the snag, particularly without breaking the line. If that happened, the drunkards would certainly blame it on him and take offense, which would worsen the situation for him. He manually unwound the tether a bit, but couldn't get his hands on the fishing line as it repeatedly jolted outward with each tug.

The Carnobass felt an internal pain throbbing within itself due to a lack of sufficient nutrition. Its attempts to hunt at the bottom of the lake proved yet again to be fruitless. As it patrolled the dark depths of the lake, its eyes caught sight of something in the distance.

The drone hovered several feet over the lakebed, its light still shining. It swayed back and forth, and tilted to and fro like a wounded animal struggling to swim. Curious, the Carnobass moved in closer to inspect. The drone changed direction with each sway, and every few seconds, it would bounce upward. Instinct drove the fish into action. It lunged forward and engulfed the drone in its jaws, then quickly turned to run with its prey.

Wilkow fell backward as the tether yanked downward, dragging the boat downward. The portside tilted upward, and water started seeping over the submerging edge of the starboard side. With a metallic popping sound, the winch popped off. The boat fell back into place and leveled out as the tether and winch disappeared from view. Richie watched his pole bend at a near ninety-degree angle, before his line snapped.

"What the…?" he yelled. He looked at his broken fishing line and threw his pole down in a drunken rage. "You fuck! Look what you did?"

Wilkow's mind didn't register Richie's rant. He was still trying to grasp what just happened. He revisited what he witnessed in his mind, thinking strongly about how the tether seemed to pull straight down. For him, there was only one logical answer: the fish was beneath them. He quickly stood up and started pulling up on his anchor.

"Guys! Hurry and get out of here!" he called out to the fishermen. Unfortunately, their intoxicated brains misunderstood his meaning, and instead took it as Wilkow simply ordering them what to do.

"What's that, you say?" Jeff shouted.

"You think you own this lake, you little punk?" Diesel called from his boat. He started to stand up to present a threatening presence, only to drunkenly stumble. His hefty figure and bodyweight caused his boat to rock strongly back and forth, nearly dipping Brook over the side.

"Jesus, dude!" Brook said. "I swear, you're getting a Stairmaster when we get back!"

The inorganic material of the drone did not sit well inside the fish's gullet. It arched its body from side to side, opening and closing its mouth rapidly. With a massive flare of its gills, it regurgitated the drone, which sank to the bottom. The fish swam upward as it pumped water through its gills to recover from the effort. Its energy quickly returned, and immediately its senses picked up on intense vibrations from up above. It angled itself upward to see the boats floating on the surface. The sunlight still pained its eyes, but to a lesser extent as they had begun to adapt.

The natural need to feed intensified, and the beast didn't waste time to examine the prey. It flapped its tail hard and shot upward like a cruise missile, aiming directly at the quivering boat.

"Shut up, Brook," Diesel said. He continued to rock the boat while trying to stand upright. "You can kiss my chubby white ass." He then pointed to Wilkow. "And you, you're up for an ass kick—"

The lake beneath the boat exploded upward, sending it twirling upward. Directly underneath it was the fish. Every muscle in Wilkow's body tensed as he witnessed the twenty-five-foot bass breach the water. Its scales, like green armor plating, reflected the glow of the sun. Diesel and Brook were both flung from the boat. The bass hit the water, followed immediately by the boat and its former inhabitants.

Diesel sank several feet beneath the surface, completely disoriented. Unable to determine which direction was up, he flung his arms out wildly and kicked his legs. His eyes were clamped shut for several seconds, unconditioned to being underwater. He finally opened them, just in time to see the enormous shape speeding toward him, jaws extended. A burst of air bubbles vacated his lungs as he let out a stifled underwater scream. The Carnobass flared its gills and sucked him in, then clamped its jaws down over him. As a last-ditch attempt for escape, Diesel threw his arms out. The jaws shut over one of them, snapping the bone and tearing some of the muscle tissue. Held together mostly by the skin, the arm dangled outside of the Carnobass's mouth. It sped along the surface as it turned to locate its next victim.

As the fish's head briefly emerged, Wilkow saw the arm dangling out of the corner of its mouth. He saw the fish beginning to circle back. Just then, Brook broke the surface nearly thirty feet away from him. He drew a breath and began to swim toward Jeff and Richie's boat. Unbeknownst to him, they were watching the fish speeding his way.

"Pull me up!" he cried as he neared their boat. Richie and Jeff didn't respond. Jeff stumbled toward the anchor with a switchblade and sawed away at the rope while Richie lowered the outboard motor and pulled the cord. The propellers sprayed Brook in the face as it started pushing their boat away. "Hey!" the abandoned drunkard yelled. The boat only moved slowly at first while it gained momentum, but soon started making some distance from him.

"Swim to me!" Wilkow called to Brook. The man turned and paddled his way. Wilkow leaned over the side with his hand extended outward. He looked toward the fish's direction, realizing it had disappeared. "Oh shit." Just as he spoke, he witnessed Brook lift from the surface in a watery blast, carried into the air by the breaching Carnobass. Wilkow shrieked and ducked down into the boat. Water trickled down on him as the fish passed overhead, followed by heavy splashes after it crashed down along the other side of his boat. In one flare of the fish's gills, Brook was reunited with Diesel.

Wilkow started the ripcord to his motor. The boat moved slowly for about five seconds. "Come on, come on," he urged it. It finally picked up speed and swiftly moved forward. As it did, the water sprayed where the boat had been two seconds prior, and the fish thrashed about. After missing its target, the fish dove down about ten feet. It sensed the vibrations of two different targets. Each contained prey, and were moving in different directions. It sensed the motion of one target being more jagged. Its brain interpreted this as an "injury" in its prey, meaning it would be easier to attack, and the Carnobass quickly began its pursuit.

The johnboat's bow angled upward as the 20hp motor pushed it forward at full speed. Both Jeff and Richie cursed as Jeff steered around a couple jet skiers that zoomed in their path. The boat barely missed the last one, tilting hard to the right as it turned sharply. Jeff kept his hand on the throttle grip and steadied the boat, while Richie watched behind them as the Carnobass leapt over Wilkow's boat. Jeff noticed Richie's facial expression grow more terrified.

"What is it?" he asked. Richie babbled, unable to form a coherent sentence. He pointed his finger back behind them, trembling both from fright and intoxication. Jeff looked behind him. "HOLY SHIT!" Like a black spiny razor blade, the large dorsal fin sliced through the water directly toward them. The boat was moving at top speed, yet the fish was gaining on them.

Jeff looked back to stern, just in time to see the pontoon boat directly ahead. It carried six people; three men, three women all college-aged. They all shrieked as they saw the crazed fishermen speeding their way. Jeff pressed the handle to his left, swiftly turning the propellers to portside. Richie slid off his seat and the boat hooked to starboard. The vacationers screamed and rushed to the other side. The boat barely missed them, spraying a stream of water onto the pontoon deck.

The Carnobass fluttered its tail to ram its prey. It shot forward, just as the target turned suddenly to the right. It sped past the turning johnboat, heading directly toward the pontoon boat.

The fish hit the boat with the force of a semi-trailer. Bits of metal and fiberglass spiraled in several directions. The boat vehemently flipped over, flinging all of its occupants off its deck. The boat settled upside down in the water, with its propeller still spiraling above the surface. They all hit the water, scattered, confused, and dazed. Some suffered broken ribs from the crash. Eighteen feet from the stern of the boat, one of the females broke the surface. Immediately, a panic attack set in. She screamed for help, while feeling down her left leg with her hand. She felt down by her knee; it was bent…in the wrong direction. Intense pain flooded her nervous system, and throbbed even harder as she instinctively tried to kick to remain afloat. Another person, her boyfriend, swam up to the surface after sinking several feet. Seeing his girlfriend in agony, he quickly started swimming toward her.

The fish picked up on the muscular vibrations of the six organic creatures. Swaying its fins, it hovered several feet beneath the surface, looking upward to identify its prey. The nearest one was directly ahead, staying afloat with lopsided movements…a classic sign of wounded prey. The Carnobass opened its mouth and moved in for the kill.

The girlfriend desperately reached out for her man as he neared. He reached his arm out to her. As their fingers touched, the boyfriend's eyes suddenly opened wide open, and his jaw dropped. He retracted his arm out of instinct and let out a horrified scream as he saw the swell rising up just behind his girlfriend. The white inside of the fish's mouth could just be seen under the water, where his girlfriend was sucked downward.

It seized its prey and quickly dove downward, hooking its body as it turned. Its black caudal fin swept the surface from below like a broom. The boyfriend saw the webbed tailfin sweeping upward…directly toward him. It struck him in an upward motion, hard enough to launch him several feet into the air. Several bones snapped and all of the air was blown out of him. He fell back down, landing right on the boat's propeller. The swirling blades repeatedly sliced through his flesh, spraying blood upward like a gruesome fountain. The remaining occupants screamed in horror as they watched their friend be torn apart like paper in a shredder.

Jeff and Richie both looked at the devastation behind them as they sped away. They felt a flood of relief overtake them when they realized the fish was no longer after them, but attacking the pontoon boat instead. They looked at each other and shared the moment with booming laughter. They cackled and pointed at the capsized pontoon boat, growing further away with each moment.

A deep loud droning noise cut their laughter short. They looked to each other, confused. The loud noise blared a second time, from up ahead. They turned around to face the bow, seeing the large speedboat cruising directly toward them at full speed.

Aaron clenched his teeth when he looked up from the rearview mirror and saw the fishing boat in his path. His muscles tensed and his heartbeat became rapid.

He sounded the horn a third time. In only a few short moments, the boats would close the distance. He grabbed the helm to steer.

"Oh shit!" Jeff shouted. He grabbed the motor handle and cut the boat hard to the right, precisely as the speedboat driver turned left to avoid collision. Both fishermen screamed as the larger boat slammed into their portside. Their boat bent inward and flipped. Jeff landed in the water only inches ahead of the ongoing speedboat. He barely felt the sensation of the water before the hull crushed his skull.

Richie hit the water a few feet past Jeff, and sank a bit deeper. The boat passed above him, grazing him with its underside. He rolled a few times under the water until the boat and its water skiers cleared. He stroked upward toward the sunlight, drawing a gasping breath after emerging. He looked back at the speedboat, which was slowing down and circling back. The sound of a second motor drew his attention. He looked back at his submerging johnboat; a piece of metal pressed against the motor lever, causing the propellers to spin at maximum velocity. The motor shook uncontrollably against the transom. Finally, it broke free, bouncing off the stern like a ricochet bullet…straight toward Richie's face. The powerhead slammed into his forehead, caving in his face. The slowing propellers pushed his lifeless body downward into the depths.

****

"JESUS CHRIST!" Tim Marlow yelled out after witnessing the crash through his binoculars. McMillan leaned over the deck, watching the event unfold in the distance. Marlow grabbed the microphone extender and lifted it to his mouth, simultaneously turning on the emergency flashers. "Chief! Chief, it's Marlow! Are you there?" He pushed the throttle forward, speeding the boat toward the scene.

"Uhh…Marlow?" McMillan said.

"What?"

"Hand me the binoculars." Marlow tossed them to him, and he looked in the distance past the speedboat, seeing the capsized pontoon boat. He passed the binoculars back to Marlow. He looked to where McMillan was pointing.

"*This is Sydney. What's going on?*"

****

"*Chief, we've got two separate accidents over here out by Rig's Place, almost right in the center of the lake. A speedboat just collided with a johnboat going way faster than what it should, and we have a pontoon boat completely overturned!*"

Sydney and Joel looked at each other in disarray. Sydney quickly started moving out the door.

"Dispatch, you copy this?" he questioned into his radio.

"*Affirmative, we copy,*" Dispatch responded.

"Alert EMS and Fire Rescue. Unit Four, I'm going to the dock right now. Once I get a boat, I'll meet you out there. In the meantime, do what you can and keep us informed."

"*Ten-four.*"

A second voiced boomed over the radio. "*This is Unit Five. We also copy and are en route.*"

Sydney climbed into his Jeep and immediately switched on the siren and flashers. He backed out of his space and sped out of the parking lot. Cars pulled to the side at the sight of the red flashers. Once on the road, he floored the gas pedal.

****

The sound of crashing metal and horrified screams permeated the air, drawing the attention of several boaters, lake-home owners, and anglers. After confirming that the fish was not pursuing him, Wilkow slowed his boat to a stop. He stood up and looked toward the source of the screams.

His heart felt as if it jumped into his throat upon seeing the devastation. The same speedboat he had seen earlier was circling around, while the skiers trailing behind, screaming in panic from what they had just witnessed. The shock worsened with the sight of the pontoon boat, and the struggling people in the water trying to climb onto it for support. Further in the distance was a police vessel, cruising towards the scene with siren lights blazing.

Wilkow's first instinct was to continue fleeing to shore. He grabbed the motor lever, only to stop and look back once again. He knew the fish was picking off the swimmers and would likely attack the other boats.

"Oh…hell!" he groaned. He knew they needed to be warned. He started the motor once again and curved his path to take him to the incident.

****

The stern of the johnboat slowly disappeared under the water as it sank to the depths. As Marlow approached, the speedboat had come to a complete stop. The water skiers were in the water, kept afloat by life vests. The boat driver kept moving from side to side, looking into the water for the anglers he had, crying, "Oh my God" repeatedly. Marlow brought his boat alongside his.

"You guys all right?" The boater looked up, appearing even more upset when he saw the police.

"I don't know what happened!" Aaron said. "I was just towing my friends, and then these guys suddenly darted in our path. We tried to get out of the way, but I guess they did too…and then…"

A scream from one of the young skiers cut him off. He rushed over to the side to look out to her. She was backstroking in a panic, away from Jeff's floating body. He was facing upward, and his head was completely disfigured. The boater felt the blood rush from his face and he quickly turned away. The realization that he killed that man hit hard and quickly overwhelmed his senses.

Other screams drew the attention of the two officers. The people on the pontoon boat were piling up on the underside, waving frantically.

"Help us!" they cried. "Please help!" Marlow realized they were gathering near the bow, staying away from the stern.

"What the hell?" he mumbled to himself. He raised the microphone to his mouth. "Stay calm, we're gonna come to you!" He then turned his attention to Aaron. "Listen to me!" The boater kept his back turned, taking shallow, shaky breaths. "SIR! HEY! Listen!" Aaron finally looked at him, looking very pale. "We have more units coming. Just stay put, and get your people out of the water!" The boater looked to his friends. The female skier, Rachel, was frozen in a panic after seeing Jeff's mangled face. The other skier, Jordan, swam to her. He grabbed her by the shoulders and attempted to calm her down. The boater looked back to Marlow.

"Okay," he said.

Marlow throttled the boat toward the pontoon. The screams grew louder as he got closer. Two of the occupants stood up on the underside, while the other two clutched the side of the boat, still in the water from the waist down.

"Is everyone okay?" he yelled out to them.

"There's something in the water!" one of the people cried out.

"Nathan…he…he's dead!" another one screamed. The hairs on the back of Marlow's neck stood up. He brought his boat near them.

"Okay, we're going to help…oh my God!" He saw Nathan's bloody mangled corpse on the propeller blades. The small crowd continued shouting at once.

"Something's in this lake!"

"Vanessa's gone!"

"Get us the hell out of here!"

"Hurry! Get us out!"

The distant echo of somebody else calling out got Marlow's attention.

"Now what?" Looking past the pontoon, he saw a johnboat speeding their way. With one hand on the motor handle, the man onboard waved at the officers. The sound of the motor muffled his voice, making it difficult for them to understand what he was saying.

"What?" McMillan called out to him. "We can't understand you."

Dr. Wilkow switched off the engine as he drew near. Its droning sound settled down, and he cuffed both hands around his mouth.

"GET EVERYBODY OUT OF THE WATER!"

"We got EMS en route, and we're going to get these people…"

"No, you don't understand!" Wilkow shouted. "There's a giant frickin' prehistoric fish in this lake!" He instantly regretted using the word prehistoric, especially seeing the surprise in the officers' faces. "I'm not joking around! It's in new territory, and I think it's staking its claim! It'll see every boat around here as a natural competitor!"

If the situation at hand wasn't so dire, Marlow would probably be rolling on the deck laughing. Wilkow certainly looked and sounded like a madman, but yet Marlow was finding himself convinced of a threat in the water.

****

Gravel kicked up as Sydney arrived at the police dock. The docks consisted of three square wooden platforms by which both police vessels would moor. Both the police cruisers were already out on the water, leaving the police jet ski. Sydney had barely shifted the Jeep to *park* when he yanked his keys from the ignition and dash down the small hill as fast as he could.

Almost midway there, the pain in his leg fired up. As if he had suffered an electric shock, Sydney's leg seized up. He shrieked and fell to his hands and knees. He gritted his teeth while quickly pulling himself back up.

He dragged his foot while scuffling down to the deck. He snatched a blue life jacket and put it on. With all of his weight on his good leg, he jumped onto the small watercraft like a cowboy onto his horse, landing perfectly in the seat. He engaged the throttle and slowly moved the jet ski out. He flipped a switch to activate the small emergency flashers on the sides. A small radio was installed just below the steering control. Sydney snatched up the speaker.

"This is the chief; I'm on my way," he said. He replaced the speaker and accelerated the throttle. The motors moaned like a racecar engine as the jet ski quickly gained speed, leaving a swishing trail in the water behind it that soon settled back to normal.

****

Circling back from its dive, the Carnobass moved upward into its kill zone. The shapes above, like silhouettes, contrasted sharply against the bright background. The images registered much clearer to its brain. The sunlight, which had brought so much pain to the creature, was no longer straining to its eyes. The creature was finally adapted to its new environment.

The police vessel moved into its feeding ground up above. Seeing the boat's considerable size, the fish believed it to be a challenger, just like many it had encountered its underground world. The Carnobass aligned itself at a forty-five-degree angle with its head facing the boat. It flapped its tail hard, creating a jet propulsion that sent it speeding toward its target. Each flap generated force for a ramming attack used to shatter bones and exoskeletons of other giant species with ease.

****

Marlow was in mid-sentence, directing the victims on the pontoon boat, when suddenly his vessel shook violently following the sound of crunching metal. Both he and McMillan fell to the deck and rolled toward the stern, as the bow tilted upward. The boat tilted up for one long moment before gravity pulled it back down, generating a huge splash.

"What in the name of—?" Marlow yelled out. The cruiser rocked heavily as it leveled out while large swells of water rolled outward. The pontoon boat bobbed in the waves. Water crashed along its side and over the exposed underside. The two people standing on top fell to their stomachs, while one male swimmer clinging to the side lost his grip. The pontoon boat moved with the swells and a distance of a few meters formed between it and the swimmer.

The swimmer quickly started paddling back. He stopped when he believed he saw another swell coming up. It was when he looked to his right that he realized it wasn't just an upsurge of water, but the huge green bulk of the bass. He screamed and paddled harder, only to be sucked backward into the creature's mouth.

Marlow's jaw dropped open, simultaneously as the Carnobass's mouth shut. He couldn't believe his eyes. He realized the nut on the johnboat wasn't as crazy as he sounded. McMillan instinctively drew his Glock and pointed it toward the large fish. He placed his finger on the trigger, but did not yet shoot. Marlow grabbed the radio speaker.

"Chief! Where are you? There's a giant…FISH, in the water!" He eased his thumb off the transmitter.

"*What the hell are you talking about?*" Sydney's voice clearly expressed his bewilderment.

"I'm not making this up," Marlow said. "This thing is bigger than our fucking boat! It's swimming over to…oh SHIT!" The bass circled back along the surface, and made another attack run toward the cruiser. McMillan yelled as he fired off several rounds from his Glock. The bullets shattered against the solid armored scales. The fish didn't even flinch. It rammed the port quarter, sending the cruiser into a brutal tailspin. The railing shattered into bits of metal, while the side of the boat caved inward. The deck splintered near the point of impact, and water slowly began to seep in at the breach. McMillan fell to the deck, accidentally firing off his last round. The bullet whizzed right by Marlow's ear. Instinctively, he ducked, and then checked himself for any injuries.

"Shit, man!" he yelled.

Several yards back, the speedboat driver went from his catatonic state to sudden alert. With a racing pulse, he yelled out to the skiers to hurry in. Though still in shock, they could sense the alarm in his voice. Still crying, the female skier finally began to paddle, followed by the man.

"Hurry! Hurry!" the driver yelled at them.

Marlow could hear the boat's engine still running, and could only hope the twin propellers weren't too badly damaged. He engaged the throttle, and to his slight surprise, the boat moved forward.

"What are you doing?" McMillan shouted as he shoved a fresh magazine into his Glock.

"Drawing it away!" Marlow answered. "Don't worry about what I'm doing and keep your eye on the damn thing! Where is it?" McMillan didn't answer, but rather made a rush for the armory compartment. He pulled a loaded Remington Autoloader and chambered a round. Marlow looked back over his shoulder towards the stern. Suddenly, he had his answer. Less than thirty feet behind them was the creature. In the brief moment he looked at it, it had already shortened that distance by half. His muscles tensed as he braced for impact.

The bass crashed into the stern. The bow lifted slightly, and the twin propellers detached, crushed from the impact. Marlow fell against the console as the bow came back down. Dead in the water, the boat bobbed and slowly turned in a clockwise motion. Marlow grabbed the second shotgun and ran to the starboard side, while McMillan took the portside. He looked over the railing to assess the damage.

"Oh shit, Tim! We're taking on water!"

"Watch for the damn fish!" Marlow yelled.

With the creature sidetracked, Wilkow sped his boat over to the pontoon. The three survivors gathered on the side closest to him.

"Get in here!" he called to them. They started moving before he even spoke. The man jumped clear from the pontoon right into the johnboat, which rocked hard when he landed. The girls slipped into the water and pulled themselves over the side.

"Come on, man, get us out of here!" one of them shouted.

"Oh really? I figured, now that you guys were in my boat, we'd hang and cast a line!" Wilkow sarcastically remarked.

"There!" Marlow yelled and pointed to the large fin circling around his side. He raised his shotgun and quickly fired off several deafening blasts. The water kicked up around the fish near the fish as the pellets tore through. Each one was stopped cold against the fish's solid scales. McMillan joined Marlow and started firing. The fish turned toward them, appearing to be readying for another run. The head emerged. The enormous eyes seemed to stare right at them. Both Marlow and McMillan felt chills, and realized this next attack would certainly sink their boat, ultimately leaving them helpless. Marlow quickly started inserting more shells into his shotgun.

The bass started moving forward, only to stop suddenly from the tiny stings of projectiles striking its face at the speed of sound. Marlow looked and saw Chief Sydney speeding in from the south. He kept on hand on the controls while he aimed his Beretta with the other. He lined up with the fish and squeezed off several more rounds. One struck the fish just below the eye. Although the bullet was crushed by the armor scales, the impact triggered a stinging nerve pain that drove the fish down. Sydney pulled up beside the boat.

"Are you guys alright?"

"We're fine, but the boat's busted," Marlow said. "The propellers are gone and we're taking on water." The distant sound of sirens echoed through the air. McMillan suddenly rushed to the front of the boat, pushing past Marlow.

"That's Unit Five," he said, pointing to the police vessel approaching from the northeast.

"They're coming fast enough!" Marlow said. He chambered a shell in his freshly reloaded shotgun. "Chief! Don't stay put! This thing is fucking fast, and STRONG!"

"What the hell is it?!" Sydney said.

"Some sort of big ass fish!" Marlow said.

A thunderous smashing sound filled the air, and the boat suddenly rolled to starboard. After ramming its enemy, the Carnobass dipped under the water, ready to pick off the two bite-sized prey that fell into the water.

The breach widened into a massive gorge in the portside. Water rushed inside, causing the boat to quickly sink. Within seconds, water was up to the officer's waists. Marlow ditched the shotgun as he felt the deck disappear beneath his feet. Sydney pulled up to him and reached out. Taking the chief's hand, Marlow pulled up onto the jet ski and sat right behind Sidney. Despite the intense situation, both men couldn't help but notice the awkward position.

"We will never talk about this," Sydney said to him. McMillan started swimming their way, and Sydney steered the jet ski closer to him. His eyes went further past him to the disturbance in the water. The fish was swiftly approaching. He quickly shoved a fresh magazine into his Beretta and started firing. He hit the approaching fish along its back, but to no effect. "FUCK!"

The skiers boarded the speedboat. Shaking from adrenaline, the driver Aaron throttled the speedboat forward, intent on returning to the lodge. The motor moaned and the boat quickly sped up along a path that would pass by the police officers. Aaron suddenly recognized that the cruiser had sunk and one of the officers was in the water.

His eyes then went to the bass's dorsal fin…directly ahead. He shrieked as the boat passed over it. The hull grazed the fish just behind the head, driving it downward. The panicked driver didn't look back, and continued pushing the throttle to its top speed.

The fish felt the displacement from the fleeing vessel. Believing the impact to be a sign of aggression, the Carnobass lost interest in the prey in the water and turned to pursue.

Wilkow steered his johnboat over to McMillan. The surviving vacationers, while still shouting and crying, reached over and helped him up. In this same moment, the other vessel arrived. The officers on board stared with baffled expressions, unsure of what had just occurred.

"Alright, you're getting on board with them," Sydney said to Marlow. He lined up the jet ski with the cruiser.

"Sir, what's happening?" one of the officers said.

"There's a large animal in the water!" Sydney said. "It's a big fish of sorts."

"It sunk our boat!" Marlow said as he climbed up the ladder to the cruiser. He looked at the distancing speedboat, and could just barely see the fin trailing behind it. "Oh hell, boss! It's following the boat!"

"Fuck! The idiots are leading it right to the damn lodge!" He then saw Wilkow, recognizing him as the doctor from the university. "You? What are…?" he stopped, as there was no time to waste. "Get out of the water now!" He then pointed at the officers on the cruiser. "Come on! We gotta get to the lodge!"

Sydney sped his jet ski forward, spraying up water in his path. He pulled his phone from his pocket and attempted to dial the lodge telephone number. In the upper corner of the screen read *No signal.*

"Son of a bitch!"

****

Aaron could see the busy shore by the lodge. Fright and adrenaline fried any rationale in his brain. He had no plan other than to blare the boat horn and speed on through.

"Oh my God!" Jordan called out. Aaron glanced back at him briefly. He was looking back over the transom, watching the fish close in on them. Aaron turned his eyes back toward shore.

"Come on… almost there…ALMOST THERE!" The beach area was getting closer and closer. He could see the rubber rafts floating about and people splashing as far as three hundred feet from shore.

The Carnobass angled downward and thrust its black tail to generate extra speed. After diving several dozen feet, it hooked back upward. It then tilted back upward to line up for another ramming strike. With another strong thrust of its tail, the Carnobass rocketed upward right in the path of the speedboat. The strike made its mark directly in the middle of the hull with pulverizing force.

All three boaters suddenly felt weightless as their boat went airborne. Lifted from the tremendous impact, the sixteen-foot boat twisted in mid-air in a corkscrew motion. Jordan and Rachel screamed for dear life as they were thrown from the deck. Aaron hugged the helm and held his breath while every muscle tensed. He heard the splashes as his friends hit the water. Gravity pulled the boat down, with the bow tilted at a downward angle. Aaron attempted to scream. With his muscles tensed, all he could get out was a low-pitched squeak.

Twisting like a screw on a power drill, the boat hit the water upside down.

Water splashed all around, and lifeless human figures bobbed all around the boat. The six-year-old boy on the beach yelled "Boom" to mimic an explosion as he crashed his toy navy boat into a group of action figures. Playing in a foot of water, he grabbed a second toy boat to pretend to fire make-believe bullets at his G.I. Joes.

"Ahhh!" he mimicked screams of the "bad guys." His make-believe yells were joined by the real-life screams all around him. Confused, he looked up around him as several adults stood up on the beach and looked far out into the lake. Screams echoed through the huge crowd as people witnessed the speedboat crash into the water and repeatedly flip forward in a summersault roll. The boat broke into pieces of wood, metal, and glass, most of which sank beneath the waves.

Aaron drew a breath after his life vest pulled him up into the middle of remaining floating debris. Amazed to be alive, he patted himself for any obvious injuries. Nothing. Miraculously, he hardly suffered a scratch.

His amazement and relief was so immense that he was shortly relieved of the terror that had stricken him. It was short lived. The greenish shape emerged from the side, and the jaws opened up to a dark throat. Aaron tensed and gave another squeaky scream before being sucked into the huge jaws.

Widespread panic hit the beach. People shrieked at the sight of the giant bass as it devoured the man. The boy's father rushed out into the water and picked him up, while much of the crowd started moving in from the lake in terror. Nearby fishermen dropped their poles and sped their boats to the dock.

From the cleaning station window, Joel watched the large crowd running inland from the water. Standing beside him was Mr. Tindell, who watched the same event unfolding.

"What the hell is this? The Normandy Invasion?" he said. Joel walked outside for a better view. He stood baffled when his eyes locked on the Carnobass swimming into the shallower waters. The green color of the fish contrasted strongly with the clear beach waters. Though several people had already come ashore, there were many stragglers far out in the water.

Joel's instinct for taking action took immediate effect. He ran to the dock where several anglers rode their boats ashore. He picked the first vacant johnboat and tossed out the gear left behind. He moved to the bow and pushed the boat back out into the water. Once knee-deep, he heaved himself over the side and started the motor.

The bass could feel the multiple vibrations flowing through the water. Prey was in abundance in this area. Although its hunger had been temporarily satisfied, the fish did not want to pass up this opportunity for further sustenance. With so many targets to choose from, it jetted for the nearest one.

Laying face down on his blue inflatable air sofa, the twenty-year-old vacationer paddled his hands in the water like oars. His girlfriend had previously accompanied him, but she departed in favor of the speedier escape of swimming to shore. He favored the watercraft. "Good luck," he snorted as she dove off.

He paddled as hard as he could. He thought to be home free, until he noticed a large shadow overtake him. He looked up, and there it was.

The bass had jumped clear out of the water, momentarily blocking the sun. It angled down directly on him, jaws hyperextended. The sheer force of the creature coming down on him brought instant death, sparing him of the horrific experience of being swallowed alive. The inflatable air sofa made a popping sound like a giant birthday balloon as it escaped the Carnobass's jaws.

Immediately, the bass identified another target; a yellow rubber raft with three people on it. There was no rationale in its choosing. It just acted as a mindless killing machine. It launched itself, ignoring the swimmers between itself and the raft. Like a semi-truck speeding through a crowded area, its bulk pummeled many people in its path. Several of them were hit squarely by its head and knocked to the side, resulting in multiple fractures. One swimmer, a man in his thirties, ended up rolling over the top of the bass. Initially, he thought he'd roll along like a log. But then he came over the fins, just as they flared. A spine entered his abdomen, exiting his back. He hung along the top like a medieval trophy until the force of the waves shook him loose.

The people on the raft stroked the water to steer inland, but hardly gained any distance. They noticed the fish coming right for them. Two of them quickly bailed and dove, while the third one suffered the deer-in-headlights effect. The bass lifted its head, and without slowing down, engulfed him in its mouth.

Sydney cursed the fish as he watched it come down onto the vacationer. He raced into the beach area, followed by the patrol cruiser carrying Marlow and two other officers. All three of them had shotguns handy, although Marlow and Sydney were aware of how ineffective they were. For the first time in years, Sydney felt a deep fear strike him. He hated putting his officers at risk, especially after the creature had already ravaged one patrol vessel. The worst part was, there was no clear plan of action. Only an objective; drive the fish away from the populated area.

"*Holy crap, Chief, it's going crazy! What are we going to do?*" Marlow said. Before Sydney could answer, another officer yelled into the radio.

"*WHAT IS THAT!*"

"Listen!" Sydney said. "Whatever you do, don't stop! This thing will smash that boat to bits like it did the other one. Empty your shotguns into it, but check for friendlies. Right now, we just want to draw it away!"

The Carnobass banked left to go after a paddleboat. The married couple on board pedaled hard for shore, completely unaware they had been targeted by the rampaging fish. It hit the small boat from behind like a battering ram. The hit sent the paddleboat rolling over like a soccer ball. Both occupants found themselves under the water and separated by several yards.

The Carnobass detected the rapid movements of the two struggling lifeforms. It caught sight of the nearest one, the husband, and moved in along the surface to scoop him up in its mouth. Sydney watched the dorsal fin curve as the fish adjusted its position. With his Beretta in hand, he rested his arm over the center of the controls to steady his sights. He aimed several feet ahead of the fin in hopes of hitting the creature's head. He squeezed.

Several rounds mushroomed against the thick scales near the gill slit. No damage was inflicted and the creature felt no pain, but it was startled. It attempted a deep dive, only to smash along the shallow lakebed. It flapped its body in a fury, kicking up an immense cloud of muck.

"It's down there!" Sydney pointed to the brownish haze under the water. The cruiser aligned towards the designated zone like a battleship with its starboard side facing the underwater cloud. Marlow, still dripping wet, stood at the stern with a shotgun handy. The driver left the controls and snatched up his shotgun to join his partner at the railing. Sydney took quick notice and snatched radio speaker.

"No! Get back on the console! You need to be ready to make a run…" The fish jumped clear up out of the water. Its body arched to the side and back in midair. It came down fiercely on the cruiser's bow. The whole front of the boat dipped hard, causing the rear to lift up like a see-saw. Marlow was flung from the stern as if from a catapult, and landed several feet away in the water. The other officers fell to the deck and grabbed anything they could for dear life. Water flooded over the crushed bow railing and quickly spilled into the lower compartments.

Sydney quickly hooked around the damaged boat to rescue Marlow. The rookie quickly emerged while fighting with his heavy gear to stay afloat. Sydney throttled up while keeping an eye out for the bass. The fish had swum under again, concealed by the now thrashing surface.

"Hang on, kid! I'm coming!" He slowed as he neared him.

"I hear ya, Chief!" Marlow called back, spitting water with each word. Sydney was mere feet away, and reached out. Marlow reached back. As he was about to grab Sydney's wrist, another watery surge erupted around him.

"NO!" Sydney yelled as he witnessed the young officer sucked down, out of his grasp, into the mouth of the Carnobass. Marlow, still reaching out to him, disappeared as the jaws clamped shut. The Carnobass quickly began to swim off. Its gigantic bulk passed closely by Sydney. The chief felt a unison of guilt, sorrow, and intense rage. This combination led to a raging madness. He gritted his teeth and fired off the remaining rounds in his magazine. Empty cartridges hit the water off to his right until the slid locked back.

"You...motherfucking...bastard...devil!" He continued squeezing the trigger, drawing nothing but dull clicks. He ejected the empty mag while throttling the jet ski to pursue the beast. He let it drop into the water and fumbled for a fresh one.

The cruiser regained its buoyancy and evened out. The tip of the bow was smashed in and the decking suffered major damage. The officers stood up in shock, having witnessed Marlow's horrible demise. One of them finally moved to the controls. Surprisingly, the engine was still functional. However, the damage was critical, and there was obvious hull damage. They moved the boat closer to shore, picking up stragglers in the water along the way.

Sydney grew frustrated after losing sight of the creature. It had dove again while swimming out into the outer reaches of the lake. He patrolled in circles around the immediate area, hoping for another chance to shoot it. Overcome with rage, his irrational mind believed the minute possibility of getting a lucky shot, perhaps in the softer tissue of its eye or mouth. He still struggled to get the magazine in his pistol while operating the jet ski. Finally, he stopped and looked down to his weapon. He properly inserted the magazine and chambered the first round.

He looked back up, just as the creature emerged dead ahead. It was speeding right toward him.

"Shit!" he yelled in alarm. He turned left and throttled. The huge open mouth passed by, and the body scales scraped against the hull. Sydney lifted his gun to fire point blank. Just as he begun to squeeze the trigger, the Carnobass whipped its tail and struck the hull. The jet ski hurled to the side and quickly sank beneath the waves. The force of the blow caused Sydney to roll over several times underwater. As he attempted to straighten his position, the jet ski rolled overtop of him. His head banged against the rigid hull. The next thing he was a red cloud of his own blood forming in the water around him. Finally, his life vest pulled him to the surface. Though disoriented, he managed to draw a breath. Through his foggy vision, he could see the black spiny fin cutting along the surface in his direction. The natural instinct to survive kicked in. Sydney thrust his arms along the water and kicked his legs.

The nerves in his injured leg fired up, causing Sydney to yell with each kick. The pain quickly increased his fatigue, and finally he gave up and watched the bass steadily approach. It was a bit slower, having fed on more than sufficient food, but that did not stop its intent on killing its next target.

"Chief!"

The familiar voice drew Sydney's attention to his left. A fourteen-foot johnboat raced toward him, with Joel at the motor. Seated in it were four people he rescued from the water. Joel steered the boat in front of Sydney and reached far over the side. He grabbed the chief by the shirt and throttled up again, dragging him alongside just as the bass opened its mouth. They cleared the fish's path by inches and quickly turned toward shore. Joel held on to Sydney, and looked to the people huddled in the boat.

"Would you guys mind…?" They realized what he meant and rushed to help pull the chief in. Sydney lay on his back, slowly slipping into unconsciousness. "Hang on!" Joel yelled as he shifted the motor into the highest gear. The bow lifted nearly two feet and the boat bounced in the swells as it raced forward. He slowed as they reached the shallow docking area, eventually coming up alongside an empty dock.

With the area now void of prey, and its hunger satisfied for a short period, the Carnobass swam out to the depths of the lake.

CHAPTER 20

Activity at Readfield Hospital went from quiet to near chaotic. After the attack in Ridgeway Lake, many people rushed to the ER. Every available paramedic unit was dispatched to the resort area, while outside departments were notified for assistance. In addition to the ambulances on route to the hospital, several people transported themselves to the ER seeking treatment for injuries. The tourists had become their own worst enemy in fleeing the beaches. During the mass panic, people trampled over each other, fought over floatation devices, looted belongings, and worse.

Nurses were overburdened with the rapid influx of patients. To make matters worse, people arrived with minor injuries such as small cuts or bumps and bruises. But each person had to be evaluated, and it made it harder for the staff to make way for the more critical patients. There were two ER doctors on duty, and they too were quickly overwhelmed. And the most critical patients hadn't even arrived yet.

At the check-in counter, Meya argued with the oncology doctor on the house phone.

"*But ma'am, my patient's condition is severe. She may need—*"

"Is she dying?" Meya asked. Withholding the anger in her voice was growing increasingly difficult.

"*She very well might be,*" the oncologist said.

"In the next hour?"

"*Well, no...*"

"Then tell her you'll meet with her again shortly. We have a dire situation here, Doctor, and we don't have enough staff. Get to the ER now!" She slammed the phone down and went back to the ER lobby. Almost every seat was full with patients waiting their turn to be seen. Meya scanned the room in search for the RN supervisor on duty. She had just emerged from an exam room, escorting a patient out.

"Lisa!" Meya called out. The supervisor heard her name called and stopped. "What's the word? How many answered?"

"I called every nurse," Lisa said. "Only five answered, but they're coming now."

"Call the others again. Tell them they HAVE to come in," Meya said. Lisa sighed. Those would not be pleasant phone calls, mainly because it was never stated in the contracts that nurses were obligated to mandated overtime. But it was an extraordinary situation, and she knew Meya wouldn't take no for an answer.

"Yes, ma'am," she simply said. Meya walked away and took the next patient. It was a man who claimed his wrist was broken. She took him into an exam room.

"Hold your hand flat," she instructed him. He did so. "Now make a fist." He squeezed his fingers into his palm. It was weak, but he had range of motion. "It's not broken," she said.

"Are you sure?" the patient began to argue.

"It's sprained," she told him. She opened a drawer and grabbed a wrist bandage. She wrapped it over the wrist and palm and taped it up. She snatched up a prescription pad and jotted a few notes and her signature. "This is for 800 mg ibuprofen. Come back if it gets worse." She quickly left the room and went to the counter with the next patient. She picked up a clipboard at the counter to call the next patient.

"Oh God, look at that," somebody called out. Several people looked at the forty-inch lobby television. The news was covering the incident, and the footage showed the twenty-foot police cruiser resting on the sandbank. The hull was dented in, and the whole top of the bow had been crushed inward several inches. The next shot of footage showed people scrambling on the beach.

The next shot made Meya gasp. People were lifting an unconscious law enforcement officer out of a fourteen-foot johnboat. The voiceover broadcast narrated that the police chief had been injured during the incident. Meya turned and found Lisa again.

"Lisa! I need two nurses. I'm going to Birchwood Lodge right now."

"You're leaving?" Lisa nearly yelled. "Why? We're short staffed and we need every able-bodied person." Meya realized she needed a rational answer.

"I...we're going to set up a medical tent there. That way we'll condense the inflow of patients to the ER. Now get me a couple nurses. Have them meet me at the loading dock." Without waiting for an answer, Meya hurried to the rear of the hospital. There, she quickly started loading gear into a transport unit.

****

Paramedics and police officers covered Birchwood Beach like ants. Rescue officials continued pulling stragglers out of the shallow waters, while police attempted to seal off the area. A sheriff's deputy used a bullhorn to announce "place vacate the beach," but not everyone complied. Loved ones reunited with each other after being separated in the confusion. Other people called out for missing friends and family that never returned from the lake.

Morgan Sydney had slipped in and out of consciousness since Joel hauled him out of the boat. He was now fully conscious, but still in a daze. Paramedics sat him up near an ambulance and looked at the gash on his head.

"You're still bleeding, Chief," one of the paramedics said. "I'm gonna wrap a bandage on it, but you're going to need to see a doctor." Sydney didn't listen. He stared out into the water without blinking. It wasn't a blank stare, however. It was more like a vengeful trance. He looked at the glassy blue surface, knowing that something horrible lurked under it. The sight of Tim Marlow trapped in the creature's jaws, while reaching out to him, replayed in his mind like a sadistic torture. The one officer on the force that gave total dedication to the job, and absolute respect to Sydney, had paid the ultimate price. Sydney knew, had he been just two or three seconds faster, Marlow would have been saved. The only part worse than that, was that Sydney wasn't sure his death was at least instant.

"Sir" The medic tried to get the chief's attention. "Sir, can you hear me?" After receiving no response, he looked at Joel, who stood nearby, and shrugged his shoulders. "How hard did you say he hit his head?"

"I didn't see it," Joel said. "Maybe I should be the one to take him to the hospital."

"No," Sydney spoke out.

"But Chief," the medic said. "You're definitely gonna need stitches, and I believe you have a concussion."

"I have work to do," Sydney said. His voice was iceberg cold. As the medic began to plead further, Joel put his hands on his shoulder to stop him.

"Just wait," he whispered. He knew Sydney was fixated on Marlow's death. The news of the fallen officer had spread across town as quickly as that of the fish. Tim Marlow had become the first police officer to fall in the line of duty in the Rodney Police Department.

"I'll see him," a female voice called out. Sydney recognized the voice. He turned and saw Meya walking toward him. A large white medical tent had just been set up behind her, with aides setting up tables and equipment. Sydney's natural instinct to protest kicked in.

"I don't need—"

"You don't get a say, Morgan," Meya interrupted him. Sydney's initial response was to stand up and walk away. However, when he tried to stand up, he realized how dazed he really was. The pain in his head throbbed as if all his blood had been pumped there, and the beach seemed to spin. He nearly fell back down in his seat, caught in time by Joel who rushed in to grab him.

"I concur," Joel said. Sydney conceded only with a slight nod. A very slight one. Having dealt with patients equally as stubborn, Joel recognized it. He tucked his arm around Sydney's back and helped him to the tent. Once there, Sydney sat in a chair, which looked more like a simple folding chair than anything from a hospital. He didn't care. Joel left the tent to grant him privacy. Sydney hardly noticed. He simply stared out into the lake through the tent opening, fighting the fresh horrible memory that plagued his brain.

"*I hear ya, Chief*," Marlow yelled, demonstrating his wit even in the worst of circumstances. Sydney had reached, and nearly had hold. Then those jaws emerged, white on the inside, with lines of small teeth within. Physical pain broke his memory, a sharp prick piercing his forehead.

"Ow, goddamnit," he cursed and jolted. Meya stood, with the suture needle now covered in his blood. She grabbed him by the top of the head and forcibly straightened him out.

"Seriously, Morgan, hold still," she said. He grimaced and stared ahead at the water while she applied the stitching. "Oh, quit the tough guy act," she said. Sydney gave no reaction. Meya took a moment to consider he had been through a lot today, in addition to being injured. Then the thought hit her; once again, he had nearly lost his life. That feeling of worry crept into her mindset for the first time in years. She completed her stitching and started to apply the bandage. "I guess it's been a while since I've had to tend to you," she said.

"You always hated it," he answered.

"I always knew it was a matter of time before I would have to do it again," she said. She looked him in the eye. "How's the pain? How are you feeling?" Sydney exhaled strongly.

"What do you care?"

"I was married to you for nine years," Meya said. "I'm allowed to still be concerned." She finished taping up the bandage. "I heard about the young man." Sydney looked up at her and back at the lake.

"His name was Tim," he said. He leaned back, feeling the world starting to spin again. The pain throbbed hard enough to make him groan.

"You're gonna need to sit out the rest of the day," Meya instructed. "You might miss the busy life of a state cop, but today, you're confined to rest. Doctor's orders."

"I *thought* I missed the busy life of a state cop," he said. "But I don't have it in me anymore. I don't know if I'm too old, or too beat up, but I just don't have the energy."

"You are too old, and definitely too beat up," Meya said. "And you're not a state cop anymore. You're chief, here, in Rodney." He didn't speak. "It's not a bad thing."

"What do you expect me to do?" Sydney said. "Sit around in a patrol car and eat donuts?" He thought about his own question for a moment. "I guess it's best. Better than getting one of my men killed."

"Oh knock it off!" Meya said. "Listen, Morgan…you were right about the lake not being safe. Your judgment is as good as ever." Sydney looked away. Her words were gentle, but they didn't help mask the anguish of Marlow's death.

Crowds of concerned residents and crazed media personnel rushed to the parking lot as the Chevy Silverado came to a stop. Mayor Greene had barely stepped out of his vehicle as a wave of reporters quickly began shoving microphones in his face. An onslaught of questions invaded his ears at once. He couldn't manage to make one out over another.

Finally, several officers cleared a path for him in the crowd. People continued shouting questions as he made his way to the beach, but they became more discernible.

"Mr. Mayor, you issued an order to reopen the lake. Do you assume any responsibility for this incident?" One said.

"Mayor Greene," another one shouted, "how long has your office known of a giant fish in Ridgeway Lake?" Microphones protruded through the wall of deputies, prodding the mayor in the chest and sides. He ducked down as he walked, as if seeking cover from enemy fire.

"Listen," he said. His voice was quickly lost in the barrage of questions. "LISTEN!" he spoke with volume and authority. The chatter downed a bit. "Now look, the situation is unprecedented. I assure you, however, that this is the very first we've known of this animal."

"Then why was the lake closed?"

"There had been various incidents concerning the lake these past few days, but there was no evidence that led us to believe something like this creature existed."

"What's going to be done about it?"

"I'm on my way, right this moment, to consult with our law enforcement officials. We will determine the best and speediest way of exterminating the threat. Until further notice, the entire lake is closed. Thank you." Greene turned around as the crowd yet again erupted. He slipped under the yellow caution tape that cordoned the beach. He walked to the medical tent and peeked inside. Sitting in the front was Morgan Sydney, with a white bandage taped to his forehead. When Greene glanced in, Sydney appeared to be staring downward. But those eyes soon rose, up at him.

Greene quickly continued walking. Being confronted by Sydney was something he wasn't enthusiastic about. Greene knew he would hear about how the beach should have remained closed, and now people are dead. Greene briefly questioned in his mind whether he was truly to blame or not. He did open the lake, and as a result, many people were killed, and many others injured. But how could he have known? After all, who was to know there was a man-eating fish in the lake. Or anywhere, as a matter of fact?

Greene saw a nurse approaching the tent with supplies in hand. He waved his hand to get her attention.

"Excuse me," he said. She stopped. "How's he doing…the chief?" He kept his voice low.

"He got banged up pretty good," the nurse said back to him. She spoke loudly. Greene cringed slightly, fearing Sydney would overhear. That fear was vindicated less than a moment later.

"You son of a bitch!" Sydney called out. Greene looked back to him. The chief clung to the tent support as he stepped out. Meya stood behind him, already exhausted in her attempts to protest his actions.

"Listen, Chief," Greene said. He wasn't sure what to say, so he said the first thing that came to his mind. "Okay, I get it. You were right. The lake is closed now."

"Oh you can't do that," Sydney said. "That'd kill the town, remember? The tourists, the lodge, your voters!" After steadying himself, he marched toward the mayor. Greene backed away, in fear of being struck.

"Chief…Chief…" Sydney didn't stop. His right hand clenched into a fist. Greene's eye went big when he saw this. "MORGAN!" Several eyes turned toward them, and many officers quickly rushed in to separate them, including Sheriff Logan.

"Morgan, don't!" Meya called out. Sydney immediately stopped and looked back at her. After a moment, he relaxed his posture and looked back to Greene. He didn't offer any apology, but Greene didn't need one. Not being punched by someone he severely pissed off was enough. The deputies and RPD officers gathered around.

"Listen, Chief," Greene said. He hated that everyone was gathered to hear his apology. "I'm sorry. I'm truly sorry, not just for failing to hear your advice, but for the loss of your man. Officer…uh…" an assistant leaned in close and whispered into his ear. "Officer Tim Marlow."

"I'm sure you are," Sydney said. "Listen, my boats are banged up. If you're truly sorry, let me go out there and kill this thing. I'll need new boats, but more specifically I'll need…"

"I'm sorry, Morgan," Greene said, "but what you really need is a leave of absence. Not a penalty, but because you're injured and under grievance."

"You've got to be fucking kidding me," Sydney said. He nearly stumbled, but steadied himself. His lack of balance was noticeable, however.

"I'm not kidding," Greene said. "I'm leaving it to Sheriff Logan to create a plan of action." Now Sydney stumbled.

"Why don't you just put my balls in a vice?" he shouted. Logan stepped in-between them.

"Listen, Chief," he said. "It's not a time to be dick measuring."

"Says you, the guy who's been trying to manage each of my cases the past few days. Listen, *SHERIFF,* you don't know what you're up against. I guarantee, all you're gonna achieve is getting your men killed." Logan opened his mouth to retaliate with a snide remark, *like you did,* but held back. Not out of courtesy, but knowing how he'd sound to everyone gathering around. With the mayor giving Logan support, Sydney knew he'd lost this dispute. He backed away, but stayed close enough to overhear. Logan watched him, resisting the urge to continue the argument. He heard the mayor clear his throat in an obvious attempt to get his attention.

"Sheriff, we need to do something soon. Very soon. People are vacating. The year is dead as we know it. If we don't deal with this, people will never come here again. The news is already going nuts with this. We're already being dubbed Carnage Lake."

"I'm getting every available man ready," Logan said. He spoke loudly, as many of his deputies were hearing his plan for the first time as well. "We have patrol boats being transported here. Lots of them. We're going out there TONIGHT. We're going to bait the son of a bitch, and unload everything we have into it. Plain and simple." There was a mixed reaction from the surrounding deputies. Some of them were iffy about going into the water, especially after seeing the ravaged RPD cruiser, but others were feeling gung-ho. Knowing they'd have the opportunity to unload some firepower was gratifying. Sydney shook his head at the ground.

"Do you wake up in the morning, and ask yourself in the mirror, how stupid can I be today?" he spat. Logan's expression grew heated.

"If you don't like the plan, tough," he said. "As the mayor said, I'll handle the situation. Go home."

"That thing will capsize every one of your patrol boats," Sydney persisted. "It moves too fast, and even if you do hit it, I don't think your bullets can penetrate it."

"You know he has a point," a voice called out beyond the crowd. All eyes went toward the man approaching. Sydney pushed his way through the crowd once he recognized Dr. Wilkow.

After overhearing the chatter regarding Logan's plan, Wilkow couldn't help but put his two cents in. He approached the crowd, but was unable to see either the chief or sheriff. Then suddenly, like stage curtains opening up for a show, two people were simultaneously pushed in opposite directions. From the opening emerged the chief, approaching him like an enraged maniac.

"YOU!" he growled. Wilkow stopped in his tracks. He had heard through the grapevine of the officer that died. He suddenly questioned whether he should have arrived.

"Oh, whoops," he said, and started to turn away. "I thought you were discussing having overhead covers installed. Just be careful with those sharp turns…"

"Did you know that thing was out there?" Sydney questioned angrily. Meya caught up with him. She placed a hand on his shoulder. Surprisingly, it seemed to have a calming effect. Wilkow looked at both him and her, and finally answered.

"When you brought in the scale, I had a suspicion," he said. "I've had this theory for forever. Everyone thought I was a nutjob, but today I proved them wrong!" He cackled an exaggerated laugh. He noticed that neither the chief nor any of the other officials were amused. In fact, they looked at him as if he actually was a nutjob. He cleared his throat. "I discovered it before it attacked. I also discovered where it came from." The crowd gathered, as if listening to the reading of a story. Mayor Greene stepped to the front of the crowd.

"You know what that thing is?"

"I call it a Carnobass," Wilkow said. "Basically your typical largemouth…only bigger, obviously. It came up through a tunnel at the bottom of the lake. Now that it's here, it'll feed on whatever it can find."

"Wait, wait…a tunnel?" Greene said, holding both hands up.

"To where?" Meya asked. Wilkow suddenly felt as if he was teaching a class.

"That's the cool part," he said. "Ladies and gentlemen, there is a huge underground lake underneath us. There's an entire ecosystem down there. Possibly ancient species that roamed this earth long before we shat all over it."

"What the hell is this guy talking about?" Logan cut in. "Who the hell are you?"

"He works at the university," Sydney said. "He knows about that thing out there."

"Let's back up there, Chiefy," Wilkow said. "Most of what I know is mainly theory. This is the first proof I have that these things exist. But I can say one thing, I agree with the chief about the use of weapons. I've analyzed the scale, and it's composed of concentrated ketamine and layers of…" He saw the confused faces of everyone in front of him. "It's really tough. You won't penetrate it with bullets."

"Listen, Doc," Logan said. "We have armor-piercing rounds that'll cut through anything. I appreciate your help, but we won't need you." Wilkow raised his hands in defeat.

"I'm just saying, this guy will be hungry again tonight! His metabolism works fast up here. He's used to eating stuff like oversized crayfish and other creatures with shelled plating. Trust me, the people he ate today look like Swiss cheese by now." He instantly regretted saying that after remembering one of those victims was a police officer. Sydney didn't appear angered, but sickened. Wilkow's voice grew softer. "The point is, the bass will be ready to feed by the time you head out there. I would suggest..."

"No...*I suggest*, that you turn around and leave. You see those barriers there," Logan said, pointing at the yellow caution tape. "You shouldn't be past those. Out you go. Bye." Wilkow gave an exaggerated frown and left.

Your funeral.

"Alright, I need everyone to clear out," Logan said. He scanned the area for the Fire/Rescue captain and spotted him. "Will you have your crew and EMS on standby, in case we do have things go sour?"

"Of course," the captain said. "We've got volunteers called in as well. Everyone's on duty tonight."

"Good," Logan said. He looked at his deputies. "Alright guys, let's get to work."

Meya heard her name called. It was the nurse, calling from the tent. There were patients needing to be seen. She waved and nodded to indicate she'd be right there. She looked back to say something to Sydney, but he was gone. She saw him disappear into the lot, where one of his officers would give him a ride to his Jeep. For a man with a limp and a nasty bump on the head, he moved fast. She sighed and returned to the tent, knowing that he needed more medical attention than he had gotten. "Stubborn bastard," she mumbled.

Joel had stood aside the whole time while listening to the conversation. He had already been paged about being on volunteer EMS duty tonight to assist the sheriff. "The wife's gonna be ticked," he said to himself.

CHAPTER 21

Sydney slammed the door behind him and went straight into the bedroom. His uniform felt as if it was peeling off his body as he stripped. After throwing on some jeans and a black T-shirt, he limped to the refrigerator. He snatched a beer, intended to be the first of many, and tore the tab off. Bottoms up.

He had spent the past two hours with Mr. and Mrs. Marlow in their residence. He gave the typical speech of how their son served with distinction, and how he'd be missed. Informing a mother of her son's death was almost as bad as seeing Marlow killed. What made it worse was when they asked if they could see him. Sydney choked on his own words as he figured out the most respectable way to explain their son was eaten alive. Sydney stayed with them to offer comfort. Other loved ones were notified, and people started arriving at their house. Sydney found himself answering the same questions over and over. Each time, he had to relive the horrific experience. Some people were sympathetic to him, having been so close to rescuing Marlow. Others looked at him with contempt, as if he was to blame. Sydney wondered which view was correct.

Hardly a moment passed and the bottle was half-empty. He raised it again to finish it off. A knock on the door halted his progress. The chief glared at the shut door, and decided to ignore it. He went to drink again, but another knock pounded the door. It was just a little harder this time, but it demonstrated just the right level of persistence. Sydney went to the door. He opened it, ready to curse out whoever was on the other side.

The open doorway revealed Meya. She was dressed in blue scrubs after working all day. She still wore her stethoscope around her neck.

"Hi," she said. There was a long silent pause between them. Sydney stared at her as if looking at a ghost. Meya quickly noticed the beer in his hand. *Either he's really surprised to see me, or he's already had too many.*

"Hi," he said. "How'd you know where I live?" She grinned nervously. It wasn't the most welcoming response she hoped for, but she did just drop in unannounced to her ex-husband's doorstep.

"Someone mentioned you were in this neighborhood," she said. "You're pretty well known around here. I just looked for the house with the Jeep Rubicon." It was a reasonable enough explanation for Sydney to accept. He watched her eyes stare down to his beer bottle. He looked at it, and lifted it up.

"What?" he said. "You gonna give me a lecture about this?" Meya shook her head.

"No. Actually…I, uh…" she paused for a moment. "I haven't tried any of the local bars yet. I figured…" she tapped her foot on the pavement, "perhaps…we both had a rough day. Might as well get shit-faced." It was not the answer Sydney expected, and it was visible in his reaction. Both his eyebrows had raised, and his jaw dropped an inch. His not-yet-intoxicated mind weighed the options. He could tell her "hell no" and send her on her way. That action would fit the mood he was in.

Then he realized misery loved company. Sydney could tell from Meya's appearance that she had a rough day as well. If he was going to get drunk at home, he'd be doing it with cheap beer. That would take a while.

"What the hell? As you heard the mayor say, I'm officially off duty tonight," he remarked. He limped to the bedroom to dig his wallet out of his discarded work pants. Meya took the liberty to step inside. Naturally, she viewed the interior of his home. Surprisingly, it was neat and well cleaned. Sydney emerged from the bedroom. "There's a place called Gamby's," he said. "Luckily for us, I doubt it'll be crowded with vacationers."

"One thing before we go," Meya said. She approached him and put her hand on his head. Sydney felt a rapid increase in his pulse.

"What are you…?"

"I need to change your bandage first," she said. She unwrapped the bandage and peeled away the gauze. There was still a bit of dried blood around the wound. Sydney never found time to clean up during the day. She produced a small vial of sterile saline from her pocket and soaked a small square of gauze with it, then used it as a rag to wipe away at the crusted blood. Afterwards, she checked the stitches to make sure they were holding properly, then dressed the wound with fresh gauze. "There," she said. "All set. Now, do we want to drive together, or separate, or…?"

"Can't imagine a third way," Sydney said. He tucked his wallet into his jeans. "I'll drive." He shut the lights off and led her out the door.

****

The sun sank into a low point in the horizon. Its golden rays of light stretched at a near perfect horizontal angle. At that angle, it was blinding to look toward the west. Luckily, the lake was in the opposite direction, so Joel took a seat on the dock and watched his shadow gradually grow longer into the calm surface. He and the fire chief stood on standby, per orders from Sheriff Logan. Throughout the lake were other emergency responders, prepped to provide assistance in case the police ran into trouble.

They listened to the police chatter over a radio on their docked boat. Logan had announced the order to begin the operation moments earlier. The plan was for patrol units to travel in groups of two cruisers. One would troll ahead of the other, while chumming bits of fish guts as if trying to bait a shark. The second boat would have officers ready with Bushmaster M4 rifles to shoot the creature when it surfaced.

When Joel heard the plan, it took everything in him not to shoot his mouth off. He knew it would be of no use, however. Logan was not the type to take advice from anyone but himself. Joel kept thinking of the RPD police boats and how easily they had been wrecked. But there was nothing he could do about it now but wait and hope for the best. Without saying a word, he stared out into the deceivingly calm lake. Without any wind or major boating activity, the water was like a sheet of glass. A mild fog was beginning to form over it, and Joel knew it would thicken further into the night.

The unit teams were spread across the lake to maximize efforts in locating the bass. One unit headed south from Birchwood. Two officers were manned on the chumming boat, while three were on the escort. It patrolled several meters behind them, off to the portside. Two of its officers stood at its starboard rail, with rifles barrels pointed toward the water.

Nick stood at the stern of the chumming boat. A slightly stout officer with a height of five-foot-seven, he was only referred by his middle name. Squinting from the blinding sunlight, Nick begrudgingly dipped the scoop into the large white tub of fish guts. When he heard he was going to be chasing after a large fish, he initially was overjoyed. Then he found out he was assigned to chumming, and his enthusiasm went away. He wanted to be the one to shoot the thing.

He tossed another scoop of guts out into the water. The scoop bumped on the transom, sending several drops of blood spilling everywhere. Some of it landed on Nick's uniform shirt.

"Son of a bitch!" he yelled out. The other officer looked back from the console. Officer Brannan was initially concerned, then he saw the guts on Nick's uniform and laughed.

"Does your wife like chum?" he snickered. Nick glared at him.

"Keep that up, and you'll get some too," he said and pointed the scoop at his partner. Brannan just continued laughing. He snatched up the radio speaker and pressed the transmitter.

"Unit 4 to other units, I'd like to report I have a walking piece of fish chum named Nick. He figured he'd get bait all over himself and go out for a swim." He lifted his thumb from the transmitter, and quickly the radio blew up with responses from the other officers.

"You're hilarious," Nick said to Brannan. He grabbed a cloth and scrubbed at the guts on his uniform. He could hear the laughter coming from their partnering cruiser. As he did, Sheriff Logan's voice broke out over the radio.

"*Alright, guys, knock it off,*" he said. "*Focus on your task. If we nail this bad boy, then drinks are on me...once the shift is over of course.*" Responses rapidly come in.

"*Hell yeah, Sheriff!*"

"*Roger that, sir.*"

"*Nick might want to change his shirt first.*"

Nick gave mock laughter and scrubbed away at his shirt. The guts were gone, but the stain remained and quickly dried.

"That's just lovely," he said. Before returning to the bucket, Nick glanced at the fish-finder monitor near the controls. The screen showed little dots, representing fish beneath them. Those dots seemed to quiver in place, and lines of static buzzed in several places on the screen. Brannan paid no attention to it, as he was more interested in his Dr. Pepper. Nick went up to the screen and slapped the frame with his hand. The frozen image remained.

"Dang it, Brannan. Don't you pay attention?" he grumbled.

"Me? Pay attention?" Brannan scoffed. "Coming from the guy who can't seem to aim his chum?" Nick switched off the unit and restarted it. After a moment, the image came back on, this time refreshed.

"Damn thing froze up," Nick said. "We don't want that. It's supposed to help us detect the thing if it comes up from underneath us."

"I know how a fish-finder works," Brannan said. "I'll keep an eye on it."

"That's all I ask," Nick said. He picked up the scoop and continued chumming.

****

Business was slow in Gamby's Bar. Most of the tables were vacant, with the exceptions of a few lone patrons. The incident at Ridgeway Lake drove much of the business away, leaving mainly the average neighborhood drunks and people drinking away their sorrows resulting from the day's tragedy. The servers spent much of their time wiping down tables repeatedly, even the ones that were already clean. The bartender did much of the same. Only two people sat at the counter, with a fifth of Jim Beam and two shot glasses between them.

Sydney threw back another shot. He winced as he swallowed, feeling the burn of the whiskey as it made its way down. Meya threw her head back and laughed at his expression as he washed it down with a glass of water. This action had been repeated several times with no sign of stopping.

"I'm disappointed in you," she said to him. "How is it I can handle this stuff better than you?" Sydney allowed the water to cool his throat.

"I'm out of practice," he said. He tilted back on the stool while the intoxicating buzz set in stronger. "I'm a police chief, remember? I'm technically always on call."

"Nice excuse," Meya said.

"Thanks."

Meya threw back a shot. The only expression to follow was a satisfying smile. The whiskey washed away the stress of the day. Sydney recognized the effect, and it made him wonder how overwhelmed the hospital really was.

"How bad was it in the ER?" he asked. Meya moaned miserably and refilled her glass.

"We didn't have enough people to handle the overflow," she said. "Most of the critical had to be transported to other hospitals." She threw back the shot and immediately refilled the glass. "To make matters worse, our chopper pilot wouldn't come in because he has that flu. So I had to spend the majority of the afternoon choppering people out myself, while giving instructions to my staff by phone." Sydney refilled his glass while munching on a basket of pretzels.

"Sounds almost as bad as pulling people out of the…" he stopped suddenly and looked at her, puzzled. "Wait…*you* flew them?"

"Uh-huh?" Meya said while pouring down her glass.

"When did you become a pilot?" Meya chuckled. Sydney wasn't sure if the answer was funny, or it if was his expression, or just the booze taking effect.

"A little over a year ago," she said. "I was dating this helicopter pilot guy, who was an instructor. I figured, why not?" She started to chuckle, but stopped when she noticed Sydney. He was staring down at his glass, slowly twirling it in his fingers. He appeared forlorn, and didn't say anything. Meya's awareness peeked through the fog of the buzz, and she realized what she had said. Instantly conflicting feelings crowded over each other. Part of her felt guilty admitting she had been dating, while the other part wanted to justify it. After all, they were divorced; free to move on with their lives. "Haven't you been seeing anyone?"

"I got stood up once," Sydney said. Meya burst out with laughter. The booze had reclaimed its hold on her inhibition. Sydney stared at her with contempt, but after a moment joined in. "I think she saw me and left."

"What makes you think that?" Meya asked through her laughter, while refilling her glass.

"I had the cane with me," he said. "I don't think anyone wants to go out with a grouchy cripple." Meya laughed harder, feeling herself turn red. Even as she laughed, she hated herself for finding such drunken amusement in her ex-husband's misery.

"Sorry," she said. She exhaled sharply as she tried to regain control.

"Nah, it's alright," Sydney said. He continued staring down at his glass, which was still full to the rim. He threw it back, and winced once again from the burn. Meya watched, and felt herself slipping into another fit of laughter.

"Good lord, Morgan," she cackled. "How long has it been, seriously?"

"It's been a while," he said. "I guess too long." Meya could judge from his tone that he was avoiding the answer.

"Oh, come on," she said. "It's obvious you haven't had a serious drink in forever. When was the last time?"

"Since I was served those papers," Sydney blurted. His eyes went big at the realization of his own admission. *Great, now the booze is doing it to me.* Meya's smile disappeared, replaced with a saddened gaze. He hated that look as much as the thought of her seeing other people. "Oh, I know that look," he said. "It's not like I became a raging alcoholic. Actually, I avoided this stuff since then, because I could tell that's where I was headed." He immediately regretted saying that as well. "Damn," he said to himself. Meya looked back at him.

"You know I hated everything that happened between us," she said.

"Me too," Sydney said. "But don't be too hard on yourself. It wasn't your fault. I'm the jerk who got paranoid and nearly started a fight with your co-worker, remember?"

"I do remember that," she said. "But I'm to blame too." Sydney snickered.

"I suppose we both had our faults, but come on," he said. "I'm the one who pressed you when you were going through a hard time. I get it. It's tough when you have a young kid die on your operating table." Meya stared into her glass, as if judging her distorted reflection.

"I never told you the whole story," she said. Sydney perked his head up. She hated this sudden need to be honest, but she hated the secrecy even more. Even after these past two years apart, she never felt like she had true closure. And she was now devoted to telling the truth, as she could see Sydney's expression in the corner of her eye. It was clear he was feeling antsy. It was time to reveal something she never told him, to revisit her worst memory.

Yes?" he said. His voice was quiet and shaky, as if he wasn't sure if he wanted to know the answer.

"I was depressed and withdrawn during that time because…well, I lied about the child. There was no kid that died on the table." She paused, and Sydney remained quiet. She took a quivering breath. "I never told you this, because…I guess there was too much tension already. I was pregnant." Sydney leaned back slightly, and put his glass down. It was certainly not what he expected to hear.

"What?"

"I was ten weeks along," she said. "I wanted to tell you, but we were too busy with our jobs. I thought a baby would bring us closer together. But I miscarried." She wiped away a tear that ran down her cheek. "I didn't know how to tell you, so I didn't say anything. Of course, I couldn't stop thinking about it. That's why I was the way I was. When you thought I was screwing around, I knew I had to say something, but I was afraid telling you would create more problems. So I made up the story about the kid." She poured half a shot and drank it. "So, I'm sorry I…" her voice trailed off. It was hard to say anything more.

Meya couldn't bring herself to look at Sydney. What could he think of her now, after never being informed of such a thing? Meya fought back the welling in her eyes, not wanting to make a fool of herself in a public place even though there was hardly anyone there.

She felt his hand placed on her shoulder. Finally, she brought herself to look at him. There was no anger in Sydney's eyes. It was nothing but compassion, which was also displayed in his touch. She rubbed his hand with hers. The first true affection in years. After several moments, Sydney refilled both their glasses. He lifted his high, as to make a toast.

"Well, here's to Tim…and Baby Boy Sydney," he said. Meya smiled and lifted her glass in unison. They both drank. Naturally, Sydney coughed again. He noticed Meya grinning at him.

"What makes you so sure it was a boy?" she said.

"I…" Sydney tried to think of a clever line, "I'm just good at guessing these things." *That sucked.* "You know, I'm chief. I know everything. I even know—" His words were halted by her lips on his. *I didn't know that.*

As they kissed, the rest of the world seemed to fade away. For the first time in years, the pain in Sydney's leg lifted.

CHAPTER 22

The air cooled as night set in over the town. Sheriff Logan gripped the rail as he stared out into the water. His patrol unit patrolled the east side of the lake, escorting another vessel that chummed several yards ahead of them. The fog had thickened, which created limited visibility. Their boats switched on their spotlights, but they did not improve range of sight.

Along with the night came the bugs. Mosquitoes and flies started buzzing about. Every few seconds, Logan slapped something that landed on his neck. He removed his cap and thrashed it in the air around his head. For a moment, it seemed like the bugs had vacated, but they quickly returned.

For the past two hours, hardly anybody had spoken. There was no sound other than the thrum of the many boats' motors, and the nightly sounds of nature. Logan listened to the frogs croaking and the random splashing of fish and birds in the water as they snatched up hovering bugs. The other deputy stood at the cockpit, growing impatient with the search while he kept the boat slowly cruising forward.

"How much longer are we gonna continue this?" he said to the sheriff. Logan didn't skip a beat with his answer.

"Until we find and kill the son of a bitch," he answered strongly. He could hear the frustrated sigh from his deputy, but didn't care. Nothing would keep him from being the hero tonight.

****

Nick felt the warm, sticky sensation of the chum as he accidentally dipped the scoop in too far into the tub. He cursed quietly and sent the scoopful of guts over the transom. He set the scoop down and walked to the cockpit. He was in need of two things; to clean his hand off from fish guts, and to get some coffee. He found a towel and scrubbed his hand. After rubbing in some sanitizer, he grabbed the coffee thermos and filled a cup. He tasted it, and spit it out. The coffee was cold.

"That's just what I need," he said to Brannan. He figured his partner would offer some sarcastic response, but surprisingly there was nothing. Nick looked at Brannan, and noticed how he was leaning on the helm. Nick walked up to him and tilted to see his face. Brannan had dozed off.

"Hey!" he called out. Brannon awoke as if struck by a bolt of lightning. He jumped in place and shuttered.

"Sorry…uh…I was just shutting my eyes for a sec," he stuttered.

"Yeah, sure," Nick said. "Need me to drive?" Brannan shook his head.

"What? No! No, I'm good," he said. Nick shook his head as he started to turn away. He could tell Brannan simply didn't want to take over the task of chumming.

Great. We're traveling in fog, and now the boat driver is dozing off.

He stopped midway to the stern. He heard something; like water bubbling up. The sound was off to the portside. Nick grabbed a spotlight and shined down. Though the fog made it hard to see, he was able to spot the ripples just before they settled. They were several meters away, and quickly dissipated into the flat surface. After a moment of silence, he figured it was nothing. He started to take a step back, when suddenly more bubbles boiled on the surface. The disturbance in the water was a few feet wide. He felt a chill run down his spine. His eyes then went to the fish-finder monitor. Static lines covered the screen. The thing had frozen again. Nick's eyes darted back to the ripples.

He decided not to waste any more time. He snatched his radio, which he had placed near the console, and depressed the transmitter.

"Sheriff?" he questioned as he tried and failed to withhold the nervousness in his voice. Several moments of silence passed before Logan answered.

"*Logan here. Go ahead.*"

"Sheriff, this is Nick. I think we have something here. The fish finder is acting up, but I think I saw something. We're near, uhh…" Nick shined the spotlight inland. It was hard to see through the fog, but he could barely manage to see the corner of a man-made drop-off. He recognized the location. "We're by the Hampton Ledge."

"*We're right across the lake from there. Just hand on. We're on our way.*"

Nick put the radio down. He could hear the commotion from the other boat. The officers on board had withdrawn from their ready stances earlier and took seating, enjoying some coffee in the meantime. But after hearing the radio traffic, they had snatched up their rifles and returned to the starboard rail.

Nick put his radio down and went to the monitor. He tapped the monitor, but his attempt to get it to work was fruitless.

More bubbling caught his attention. This time, it was closer. He stood up straight and drew his Glock. He slowly leaned over the rail, holding his pistol close. Brannan watched silently from the helm. He wasn't sure what Nick had seen, but he was more than ready to put the boat into full throttle. Nick watched the ripples settle.

"Hey guys," he called out to the other boat. "I think it's here!"

"You sure?" one of the officers called back. Nick nearly jumped at another disturbance on the surface.

"Yeah, I'm sure," he said. "Get ready." He took several deep breaths and watched the dark water beneath him. Suddenly, the water erupted into a frenzy. A pair of loons burst from the mayhem they had created, and hurriedly flew upward past Nick.

"Shit!" he called out in alarm and fell backward, bumping the spotlight in the process. His finger leaned on the trigger, but he retained just enough control to avoid discharging. The birds flew off, echoing some panicked calls. Several moments passed, and Nick felt the rush in his veins slowly wind down. The air then filled with the sounds of laughter, from both Brannan and the officers on the escort vessel.

"Watch out for those terrifying monsters there!" he heard one call out.

"Yeah, they might carry you away!" another cackled. Nick bit his lip and stood up. He holstered his Glock and then extended his middle finger toward the boat, right into the path of the spotlight they shined upon him. The laughter grew more intense.

The laughter suddenly turned into yells of "Oh shit" and "Jesus Christ" as a mass exodus of small lake birds suddenly took flight. Even in the dense fog, the flock seemed to form a white sheet over the boats as the birds took off in unison. Nick was no bird expert, but he recognized the alarm in the chirps and rapid flight. The birds ascended and disappeared into the night sky above the fog.

Nick relaxed, despite the foreboding feeling that overtook him. He saw the crooked position of the spotlight. He grabbed it and straightened it out. That's when he saw it.

Something submerging. Something large. An immense bulk with a black, spiny sail-like appendage on top. Nick swallowed hard.

"Oh, no."

****

Logan stood at the port rail, looking ahead for any spotlights from the other patrol boats. The fog that coated the lake impeded his vision. Judging by the speed of the patrol boat and the amount of time past, he knew they were nearing the other side of the lake. He snatched up the radio speaker.

"Nick, this is Logan," he said. "Any update?" He eased off the transmitter and waited for the response. There was none. Logan and his deputy looked to each other, each sharing the same puzzled expression. Logan picked up the speaker again.

A loud booming echoed from up ahead that resembled the crushing, crunching sound of a car crash, followed by the sound of splashing water.

"Nick, come in!" Logan spoke into the speaker. No response came through the radio. Then through the fog was a new sound. The hairs on the back of Logan's neck stood on end. He could hear screams. "Nick? Ramirez?" The bang from several gunshots cracked through the air. Logan recognized the specific sound from the Bushmaster rifles. "What's going on out there?"

Another large crashing noise reverberated, followed immediately by thrashing water and more screams. The screaming and shouting came to a sudden stop. Logan looked at his deputy at the helm.

"Can we go any faster?"

"We are, sir," he said. "We're just about there." Logan snatched up a rifle and aimed it outward, pointed slightly up to avoid pointing it at any of his deputies that might have been in the water. He held on to the weapon by the handle with one hand, using the other to adjust the spotlight. The fog began to thin up ahead, and he tilted the light that direction. First he saw rippling water reflecting his light. Then within those ripples he saw something else. Bits of decking floated about, along with small fiberglass fragments and other material. Empty life vests floated in the water. Beside one of them was something small and plastic. The sheriff focused the light on it. It was the scoop for the chum.

"Oh, damn," Logan mumbled. He looked back as two other patrol boats arrived from the north, with a third approaching from behind. The two other boats grouped at the wreckage site, with only a space of a couple dozen feet between them. He snatched up his radio. "Spread out! That thing is out here somewhere!" He then snatched up his bullhorn and called out into the darkness, "Is there anyone alive out there?" Unfortunately, he knew it was a wasted effort, but he was going to give the benefit of the doubt.

"Hey, what the—?" one of the officers on the other boats called out. Logan looked their way, just in time to see the enormous swell of water rising up. The spotlight reflection sparkled on the thick scales as the huge fish burst from that swell. It collided with the portside hull, indenting the whole section of the boat. The boat rolled over to the right, flipping over completely. The officers on board dove as their vessel flipped over overtop of them. All three quickly emerged several feet apart as the boat quickly took on water and submerged.

"Get them out!" Logan yelled. It was mainly directed at his deputy at the helm, who quickly turned the wheel. Their boat turned toward the men overboard.

All three started paddling towards the sheriff, forming a triangular formation. After a few quick paddles, the middle deputy froze in fear. It was as if a sixth sense had struck, and he felt a foreboding presence in the water beneath him. That sense proved correct as he noticed the white inside of the creature's mouth directly beneath him. The deputy reached out with both arms as he was sucked downward, and the water that filled his throat immediately muffled his screams. The Carnobass shut its mouth on its prey and dove.

Both deputies shrieked at the sight of their partner devoured. Both turned in opposite directions, kicking against the water in their attempt to escape. Logan's vessel quickly closed in on the nearest deputy, while the other swam toward the other vessel.

The patrol boat and its three deputies moved alongside the swimming officer. Two of the deputies quickly reached their hands down under the port rail for him. The swimming deputy reached up, his hand beginning to secure a hold on one of the arms.

In the blink of an eye, the water beneath him expelled upward, and the deputy found himself moving up with it. While lifted up, he also felt himself simultaneously slipping down, right into the beast's open mouth. The officers shrieked and jumped backward. The fish clamped its jaws down in midair as it fully breached the water. Gravity pulled it down from its massive jump, right down on the middle of the police boat. The two deputies on deck dashed for the stern, but the third one stood at the helm, paralyzed at the sight of the monster. It crashed down across the boat, crushing the helm and the officer who operated it.

Logan pulled his deputy onto his boat when he saw the creature jump and land on the other vessel. He shoved the driver out of the way and quickly throttled the boat in their direction.

The structure of the patrol boat crumbled under the creature's weight. Cracks and indentations formed in the side of the hull, and the engine groaned, as if giving a last breath before death. The Carnobass rested momentarily, flapping its gills. As they peeled open, the muffled screams of the officer inside reverberated, followed by a crushing groan and the sound of bones mashing. The remaining officers snatched up their Bushmaster rifles, shouldered them, and emptied their magazines into the creature's hide. Scales splintered and cracked, but the armored exterior stopped each bullet from entering the flesh.

Standing on the left, one of the deputies dropped his rifle after its mag ran dry. He quickly drew his Glock and squeezed the trigger. The first two bullets were crushed against the scales. The creature wiggled to drag itself back into the water. The third bullet hit its scales, now tilted at a slanted angle. The bullet ricocheted off the armored plating, and hit the other deputy in the thigh. His leg gave out, and the officer quickly collapsed. Confusion mixed with adrenaline, and as water flooded the deck as it sank below the waterline, terror had set in.

With a single flap of its gills, the Carnobass pumped in several gallons of water, and its lamellae took in the dissolved oxygen. With a burst of energy, it whipped its body in a counterclockwise motion. As it turned, its tailed thrashed the standing officer. Nearly every bone in his body broke as the strike launched him into the stern railings. The fish, and the boat, submerged just as Logan's vessel arrived. The two deputies with him quickly hauled out the injured officer from the water and began wrapping his bullet wound. Logan throttled the boat at full speed toward shore, while picking up the radio transmitter.

"Sheriff Logan to all units…return to shore now! Wherever you are, just go for the nearest land. Everyone, get out of the water now!"

CHAPTER 23

Sydney awoke in bed to the sight of sunlight streaming through the open bedroom window. For the first time in what seemed like forever, he had slept through the entire night without getting up due to his leg pain. Feeling pleasantly rested, he laid on his back and enjoyed the morning breeze coming in.

He felt Meya's hand planted on his chest. He looked over at her. She lay bare under the covers beside him and returned his gaze, having just woken up as well. It was a pleasant moment of relaxation and satisfaction that neither had felt in many years.

"You snore," Sydney said.

"You talk in your sleep," Meya replied. They both smiled and continued resting for a bit longer. Finally, Sydney looked at the clock near his bed. It was *10:12* a.m.

Damn! He could not remember the last time he slept in so late. He and Meya did not stay out very late either. He didn't care, however. In fact, he felt happier than in a long time. His leg throbbed a bit, but not nearly as bad as it normally did. Meya felt her spirits lifted as well. She was back in a place that she had longed for, even during the proceedings years back. She never thought she'd be granted a second chance. The only regret she had was not trying harder to fix it back then. She wondered what would have happened had she been up front.

"I'm sorry I never told you the truth about what happened," she said.

"Shhh," Sydney said. "It's okay. It's behind us." Meya smiled and rested her head on his chest.

"Oh, let's just stay like this forever," she said. Sydney smiled and stroked her hair romantically. Unfortunately, their cuddle was short lived when his body sent him signals of a full bladder.

"Unfortunately," he gently pushed her off and stood up, "under the circumstance, that might not be such a good idea." He threw on some sweatpants and went to the bathroom. He relieved himself and flushed. He took the opportunity to wash his hands and brush his teeth. Not since their first few months together had he been so conscious of his hygiene around another specific person. He returned to the bedroom to Meya getting dressed.

"Want to catch a brunch?" she asked.

"Not a bad idea," Sydney said. After all, he was off duty. He dug through some fresh clothes and dressed himself in some jeans and a grey T-shirt.

"Any ideas where we should go?" Meya asked. Sydney thought for a moment.

"I guess, since you're still new to town, you haven't tried *Kosakowski's.* It's a nice breakfast joint."

"No, I haven't," Meya said. "But it sounds like a good plan." She looked down at her scrubs, the only clothes she had with her. "I suppose you wouldn't mind if we stopped off at my place first so I could change?"

"Of course," Sydney said. He slipped on his boots and tucked his shirt in. He looked up from his tidying after hearing the sound of a car door slamming just outside his house. More door slams followed, clearly coming from his driveway. He barely took two steps into his living room when someone started knocking at his door.

Sydney opened it, revealing a small group of people. Mayor Greene stood at the front, with Logan standing off to the side behind him. Behind them were a couple of RPD officers, one of them being Larabee. Behind them were two of Greene's assistants, and at the back stood Joel, clearly struggling to keep his eyes open. Like everyone else, he had been up most of the night performing rescue operations. Logan looked more than tired; he looked defeated. His very body language lacked the authoritative, confident figure he always exuded. The sheriff looked more at the ground than he did at Sydney.

"You guys look like you could use some coffee," Sydney said.

"Honestly, I wouldn't say no if you offered," Greene said. Sydney looked past the group at the vehicles. There was the sheriff's vehicle, a RPD patrol car, and Joel's raggedy van. There was no sign of Greene's truck, or any other vehicles for his assistants.

"What's with this?" Sydney pointed at the vehicles. Greene exhaled heavily.

"Joel was kind enough to transport us," he said. "We had a press conference today. It didn't go well. We had an angry crowd, and people started throwing things. One of those things was a beer bottle that went through my windshield." Sydney winced, feeling the mayor's mental anguish. That truck was new.

"Oh," he said. "For a sec, I thought Joel was just here for the coffee."

"I am," Joel said, and started walking toward the door. Sydney gestured for them to come inside. Sydney started a fresh pot of coffee for everyone, and pointed out where the mugs were. Joel helped himself into the kitchen, and stopped suddenly when he saw Meya. Through his drowsiness, he did manage to notice a certain spark within the chief, and now he knew why. It was a pleasant surprise.

She was surprised too, but not for the same reason. She looked into the living room to see everyone piling in.

"What's going on?" she asked.

"That's what I'm trying to figure out," Sydney said. He looked to the mayor. "You mentioned there was a press conference that didn't go well. May I presume you're guy's operation didn't work out to kill the fish?" Everyone looked at him with stunned silence. The only one who did not stare at him was Joel, whose eyes were fixated on the brewing coffee.

"Did you not hear?" Greene asked.

"No," Sydney replied. "What happened?" Greene took a breath, and Logan turned away, as if humiliated about what was about to be disclosed.

"Several deputies were killed last night," Greene said. After a pause, he added, "By that thing out there." There were several seconds of solemn silence, except for the brewing from the coffeepot.

"Nine," Logan said.

"Nine?" Sydney digested the news. Meya put her hand over her mouth. Mayor Greene put his hands on his hips and looked down. He finally looked Sydney in the eye.

"That thing out there is out of control, Morgan. We HAVE to destroy it," he said.

"I thought that's what you had Mr. Know-it-all over there for," Sydney retorted and pointed to Sheriff Logan. Greene took a step forward and held up his hand.

"Good lord, Morgan, give him a break," he said. His expression was strict, but quickly eased up when Sydney retaliated.

"A break?" Sydney nearly snapped. "I warned him. I warned *YOU*; don't go out on that water! I warned you guys of what that thing could do, and you idiots wouldn't listen. Now look what happened; nine police officers, all dead." Neither Logan nor Greene did not argue. Finally, Logan looked Sydney in the eye.

"Yes, you're right," he said. "In fact, the whole damn town pointed that out. Hence the near riot we had at the press conference. I, uh, told Mayor Greene that we need your expertise to kill this thing." Sydney stared at him, then at the mayor.

"Morgan, we need your help," Greene said. Sydney paced around. He was enraged at them for proceeding with the operation, despite his warnings. The consequences he warned about were even worse than he feared.

Both his officers stepped forward. Larabee raised his hand, as if requesting permission to speak.

"If I may, sir," he said. "Everyone in the department wants to get this thing. For Tim." Sydney looked at him and listened. "But we don't know how. We need your help." It was something Sydney never expected; true respect from his officers.

"Obviously, I'll help you guys," Sydney said. Greene blew a sigh of relief. He noticed Joel pouring a cup of coffee, and moved to the pot to help himself to a mug.

"Do you have any ideas on what we should do?" he asked Sydney.

"First things first," Sydney said. "I want to speak to that nut job professor guy: Professor…uhh…" He struggled to remember the name.

"Wilkow," Meya reminded him.

"Him!" Sydney said. "We need to find him. He's the only one who had any knowledge of this fish."

"Where would he be?" Logan asked.

"We could check the university," Meya said.

"Well, let's not waste time," Sydney said. He moved toward the door. "Let's get moving." He realized nobody was following him out the door. He looked back, and saw everyone lined up at the coffeepot. "Oh, for Christ sake…"

CHAPTER 24

The radio roared classic country music while Dr. Wilkow cast his line into the pond. The song on air was referring to it being a great day to be alive; a sentiment Wilkow was feeling. Dr. Nevers was not at the University today, so Wilkow was spared the likely endless verbal assault regarding stealing college finances and equipment. The dean's absence allowed Wilkow to review the footage recorded on his laptop, and update his thesis.

With the news of a giant new species of fish being in the lake, scientists from all over were undoubtedly on their way to Rodney. Some had already arrived in town, but with the lake off limits, they were unable to conduct any research. This meant Wilkow was the only one with any data collected. That, plus the new evidence supporting his theory, meant that he was going to be in high demand for any research facility intent on studying the creature.

"Yeah, baby!" he yelled excitedly as he hooked a fish.

****

Meya rode shotgun in Sydney's Jeep, admiring the summer breeze that came through the passenger window. As they drove to the University, she watched Logan's car and Joel's van through the rearview mirror. Her thoughts were on Sydney, and her hopes that he would not place himself in harm's way when hunting the creature. The fact that one creature had killed so many people gave her a nervous ache in her stomach, and the thought of Sydney going out there to kill it only made it worse. She glanced several times at him, but forced herself to look away to not draw his attention. She figured he was deep in thought regarding the situation. However, her eyes were drawn to him like a magnet. In the corner of his eye, Sydney could see her looking at him. He grinned.

"Don't worry. We'll have that brunch another time," he said.

"I wasn't concerned about it," Meya said. They pulled into the university lot. Sydney looked at the buildings and tried to remember the correct one.

"How are we gonna find this guy? You think he'll be in the same place we saw him the other day?"

"I hope so. Otherwise, I don't know how we'll find him," Meya said. Just as she finished speaking, a loud call rang through the air.

"HEEELLLL TO THE YEEEAAHHH!"

They both looked across the lot. There he stood at the pond with a fishing pole in hand and a cigar in mouth. Just as when they first saw him, he was busy reeling in a largemouth from the pond. Sydney and Meya looked at each other, equally amused and relieved.

"Well, that was surprisingly easy," Sydney said. He turned his Jeep and drove along the service drive up to the pond, followed by the other vehicles.

Wilkow held the bass by the lower jaw as he watched the vehicles come to a stop by the curve. Sydney and Meya were the first to step out. Wilkow quickly recalled Sydney's aggressive advance toward him during the previous day at the beach. He naturally took a step back.

"Oh hell," Wilkow said. He held up the bass. "Not the same chap you're looking for, just in case you're wondering!"

"Relax," Sydney said. "You're not in trouble." Wilkow eased his tension.

"I appreciate that," he said. "What do I owe this lovely visit?"

"I was hoping you'd be interested in helping us catch a different fish," Sydney said.

Wilkow's eyes went to Joel's van. The sight of the old white van with cherry lights on it was amusing enough, but it was seeing the mayor stepping out of it that nearly dropped Wilkow to the ground in laughter. "What's the matter, Mr. Mayor? Doesn't the town pay enough for decent transport?"

"It's a long story..." Mayor Greene started to say.

"Nah, don't worry. I watched the whole conference on TV," Wilkow said. "That was a heck of a start to my day." The assistants stepped out of the van, pushing aside the assorted tools and junk that was piled in there. He snickered once again and looked at Logan. The sheriff's defeated demeanor hadn't left him, and Wilkow knew the reason. "This guy warned you," he pointed at Sydney. "He warned you, and I warned you."

"I'm well aware," Logan said. *Everyone* was aware. Even the families of some of his fallen deputies were aware. His humiliation had been well broadcast.

"Listen, you're the only one who seems to know anything about this thing," Sydney said. "We just need you to help us kill the bastard." Wilkow unhooked his bass and tossed it back into the lake. He picked up his fishing rod to secure the hook.

"You know, this would probably be a good time to offer me a bribe," he joked. He started collecting his fishing gear. "A new sports car, set of golf clubs, season tickets to the Detroit Pistons..."

"We can make that work," Greene said. Wilkow stopped what he was doing. Another grin creased his face. He debated in his mind whether to accept the mayor's offer, or admit he was just kidding.

"What are your ideas, Chiefy?" he said to Sydney.

"First thing; no boats in the water unless absolutely necessary," Sydney answered. "We all know what that thing can do."

"That's a good start," Wilkow said. "I'm also assuming you've realized firearms are useless against it. Unless you have a bazooka." He leaned down to pick up his tackle box, then stopped to look at Sydney and Logan. "Do you guys have bazookas?"

"No," they both said.

"Damn," Wilkow said. "The movies are always wrong." Meya glanced up at the *Liberal Arts Building*, remembering that they had all sorts of lab and chemistry equipment.

"Could we try poisoning it?" she asked.

"Poison could kill it," Wilkow said. "The problem would be getting the solution into its system. You can't really inject it through its exterior. Same problem as the bullets; the scales are too tough. And good luck getting some in its mouth."

"What about coating a lake with some sort of poison mixture?" Logan asked.

"Yeah, and kill the entire lake in the process?" Wilkow remarked. "Aren't you trying to make it a place people can go fishing again? Oh, and swimming?"

"He's right," Greene said. "We can't do that. Forget the vacationers. The EPA would string us all on a cross and leave us to bake in the sun."

"Wouldn't do well for my Nobel Prize candidacy," Wilkow said. He closed his tackle box and picked up his pole. From the van, Joel stared at the reel, and then eyeballed the hook.

"Why don't we just suffocate it?" he said. All eyes turned toward him.

"The plumber has an interesting idea," Wilkow said. "Of course, you'd need a way to get the Carnobass out of the water, and keep it out long enough to die of oxygen deprivation." Joel looked at himself, in his EMT uniform, and then shot Wilkow a scolding look.

Do I look like a plumber?

"Hang on a sec," Sydney said. "That gives me an idea."

"What? The plumber?" Wilkow said. "You want to drain the lake?" Everyone stared dumbly at Wilkow.

We're asking advice from this guy? Mayor Greene thought to himself. Joel thought something quite similar.

"No," Sydney said after a pause, "I was thinking we'd do what you were just doing." He pointed at the fishing pole. "We could commandeer one of the cranes from the Corey Mine. We could set up a makeshift net, or a hook, or something to hold the fish and hoist it out of the water. If it works, we can keep it lifted long enough for it to suffocate."

"That..." Wilkow was about to bash the idea, but thought about it further, "...might actually work."

"Can we hire someone to operate the crane?" Meya asked.

"I can do it," Joel said, raising his hand. Sydney looked back at him.

"You can drive a crane?" he asked. Joel nodded. "Damn, Joel. You're just a jack of all trades."

"I'm no expert on cranes, though," Wilkow said. "That fish weighs a couple tons at least. Can those cranes lift that much?"

"And then some," Joel said.

"Okay. And I think we can get supplies from that mine to make a net strong enough to trap the Carnobass in," Wilkow said. "But that leaves us with one more issue." Sydney waited for him to give an answer.

"And that is...?" Wilkow plucked a worm from a tub and tossed it into the pond. After only a few seconds, the squirming pink figure was snatched up by a shape under the water, which quickly swam away with it.

"We'll need bait," he said. "We're gonna need something, or someone, to guide the fish into the trap. Is it safe to assume none of you want to be the worm in this case?" Sydney stared at the pond as he thought.

"You're right; we will need something to lure this bastard in," he said. "I DO NOT want any boats out there. The people who've managed to outrun this thing were just plain lucky. No boat can go faster than it, it seems."

"Well, more to the point is that these bass make quick bursts of speed," Wilkow explained. "It doesn't actually move continuously for too long. Bass are lazy. They take time to observe something, then if they're interested, they make a move toward it. Granted, this isn't any ordinary bass, but it seems the principles of hunting are generally the same. Except it's much more aggressive. The point is, we need something that'll attract its attention, but can move out of the way if it makes its run."

Sydney continued staring into the pond.

He could see the little fish swimming about in the shallow areas. They nipped at petals and bugs that landed on the surface. Finally, a dragonfly buzzed nearby. It circled and chased another, possibly a mating ritual. Unlucky, the dragonfly landed on the water, seemingly *standing* on the surface. After several seconds, the shape of one of the fish emerged from beneath it. Just as the fish moved in, the dragonfly took off again into the air, narrowly avoiding the jaws of its predator.

"I got it," Sydney said. He turned to Logan. "Does your department have a chopper unit?"

"We do," Logan answered.

"Good, I know what we'll do," Sydney said. "We'll have a pilot fly over the water. We'll dangle some bait down with a cord, and use radar to keep track of the fish's position if it comes up. The pilot then can lure the fish toward the crane."

"Once it gets close enough, the crane operator can dip the hook into the water. It'll be loaded with bait, of course. It'll attract the Carnobass, and it'll move in right for the trap. Snag, lift, struggle, dead."

"Alright, we have a plan," Sydney said. Mayor Greene stood silent for a moment as he visualized the whole concept. A lure, bobbing in and out of the water, drawing the creature in. It bites on a hook, connected to a line that will hoist it from the water.

"So…we're literally going fishing for this thing," he pointed out.

"Damn," Wilkow said. "Too bad Birchwood isn't hosting a Rapala Fishing Tournament! Can you imagine the looks on everyone's faces when we weigh that sucker in?" Sydney looked down and shook his head.

"Well, let's not waste any more time," he said. "Let's go to the Corey Mine and see if we can get ourselves a crane." Everyone started back to their vehicles. Wilkow loaded his gear into the car and prepared to follow everyone to the site. Meya started climbing into Sydney's passenger seat.

"Are we sure they'll even give us one?" she asked. Sydney stepped up into the driver's seat.

"Oh, I'm sure they'll be very cooperative," he said.

****

"Absolutely not!" The mine foreman nearly shouted at Sydney. He lifted his arm over his face as a gust of wind kicked up a cloud of loose gravel. Even at the front gate, there was much residue from the digging and blasting that made its way up.

"Look, man, I don't think you realize how important this is," Sydney said.

"No, I do!" The foreman shouted. "This equipment is worth more than what all of you combined make in a year." He pointed his finger at Sydney, and everyone who stood behind him. That included Mayor Greene, his assistants, Dr. Wilkow, Joel, Sheriff Logan, and Meya. Greene stepped up.

"Sir, I can assure you that the equipment won't be damaged in any way," he said.

"You can't assure that," the foreman said. "You want to use our crane to catch that big ass fish in your lake. How many boats did that thing sink?" Nobody offered an answer.

"The crane won't be in the water," Sydney said.

"Yeah, but what if it gets pulled in?" The foreman argued. "No. Just…no! I'm not letting you take any of our equipment. Get your own."

"That'll take too long," Greene said.

"Too bad. That's your problem," the foreman said. He turned to begin walking away. Sydney walked a fast pace, stepping in front of him. His determination blocked out the pain in his leg and prevented it from slowing him down. The foreman stopped. His facial muscles tightened with anger, but quickly eased up. He saw the look in Sydney's eyes, and knew better not to mess with him.

"It's your problem," Sydney said. "If that thing kills anyone else, it'll be on you if you don't let us use your equipment. And if you don't, believe me, I will do anything and everything I can to make your life a living hell. Trust me, on any normal day, I have plenty of free time." The foreman looked back at the mayor, as if to ask, *you're gonna let him do this?* Greene shrugged his shoulders at him.

"Hey, you heard him," Greene said. The foreman took a long, deep breath. He took a quick moment to consider all of the people the creature had reportedly killed.

"You just need the crane? None of my guys have to drive it?"

"Just the crane," Sydney said.

"Alright. Come with me," the foreman said. He led the group down a long dirt path, passing trucks and several workers along the way. The walk took over fifteen minutes to get to the first drop-off. A crane rested on the edge of a pit, and its cable lowered down to a crew on the next level down to deliver supplies. The cable was reeling up as they approached it. The foreman lifted his two-way radio to his mouth. "Hey, Harold," he said. He saw the operator inside look at him through the window.

"*Yeah?*"

"Back that thing up for me, will ya?" He could see the confused expression from the operator. The back-up alarm echoed, and the crane slowly moved in reverse. Harold stepped out.

"What's going on?"

"We're giving this crane to the chief here," the foreman said. He looked back at the group. "Is this good enough for your liking?"

"I think so," Sydney said. Joel walked over to the crane and stepped in to inspect the controls. He rose the arm, and slowly moved it from left to right. It was more a refresher for him than anything else. "Looks like he's got the hang of it," Sydney said. "You have any lifting hooks?"

"Yeah, we have a bunch of them," the foreman said. Joel stuck his head out of the crane door.

"Particularly a Founton Eye Hook," he said. He noticed Sydney looking confused. "The throat gap on many of the other kinds will be too narrow for what we're trying to do. If we get the Eye Hook, I can sharpen it with a welding torch, and also weld a piece of metal onto it to use as a barb." The foreman nodded, still slightly reluctant to give up his equipment.

"Yeah, we have one of those," he said. He started to lift his radio to have someone deliver it up.

"Hey!" Wilkow called out. "Think of it this way. If this stuff gets smashed up, just think of it as a tax write-off." The foreman stared at him blankly for a moment.

"Who's the funny guy?" he inquired. Sydney cupped his hand over his face.

"Never mind him, he's just a…nevermind," he mumbled, resisting the urge to roll his eyes.

"Hey Chief," Wilkow said. "We might want to find any scrap metal while we're here. For the lure."

"Right," Sydney said. He turned to face the foreman once again. "Listen, I hate to ask for more, but like the knucklehead said, do you have any scrap metal you're willing to get rid of?"

"Gosh, why don't you ask for one of my kidneys while you're at it?" the foreman remarked. "Yeah, we have some." He walked away to speak on the radio. As he did, Sydney and the group stepped together, as if in a football huddle.

"I'll take a look at the metal," Wilkow said. "We'll need a flat piece, as well as a few smaller pieces to attach to it to create as much water displacement as possible. Basically, an oversized spinner."

"We can do that," Sydney said.

"Also, we'll need to visit a meat shop," Wilkow added. "We'll need a big, fresh, slab of beef to put on that hook. A yummy last meal for the Carnobass."

"I'll put someone on it," Greene said. "When can we expect to be underway?"

"I want us to have some daylight," Sydney said. "Can we have everything ready to go by seven?"

"Yes, sir," Joel said.

"I'll have my deputies ready," Sheriff Logan added. "I would like to suggest we set up at Hampton's Ledge. Good place for the crane, and that's where we ran into it last night."

"Alright," Sydney said. "Everyone know the game plan?" Everyone nodded, ready and even eager to get to work. Sydney clapped his hands together. "Okay then. Let's go fishing."

"Oh, yeah! LET'S KICK SOME BASS!" Wilkow shouted, with his fist raised in the air.

CHAPTER 25

Located in the southwest edge of Rodney, a small bar called *Ringside* was seeing normal business. It was known as a cheap bar, as that was what was mostly served. While high-class whiskey was on the menu, it was hardly ever in stock. The only thing keeping the place afloat was the usual crowd, who saw the bar as a good hangout more than anything else.

It served mainly a redneck crowd, as that was the type to reside there. The usual patrons were mostly hunters, dockworkers, bikers, and some freeloaders who relied on their buddies. Inside were twenty circular tables, eighteen of which were occupied by mainly bearded patrons, and a cheap wooden bar counter. The owner, who was also working as the bartender, wiped down glasses and silverware in a nearby sink. It allowed him to act as if he was busy. In reality, there weren't many dishes to clean. Most of his customers drank from the bottle.

Dave Culverhouse sat at the bar counter. He rested his elbow on the scratched countertop, while drinking a beer and watching the television. Like everything else in the bar, the T.V. was cheap, an old box television. On screen was a replay of the live news coverage from that morning's press conference.

He shook his head disapprovingly as Mayor Greene stood at a wood podium during the outside conference. He spoke vaguely of the Sheriff's Department attempt at catching the creature, and explained that it failed. A large group of people with cameras and microphones stood only about twenty feet from the podium. Microphones extended in Greene's direction, following a jumble of assorted questions, not just from the reporters, but also the residents of Rodney that gathered behind them.

"*Please, please,*" Greene spoke inside the monitor. Dave could easily tell he was unequipped for the onslaught of questions and criticism. Greene's face and shifting body language clearly demonstrated his discomfiture. "*One question at a time, please.*"

"*What about the lake?*" one reporter shouted out.

"*Until further notice, the lake will remain closed. Anyone caught going into the water will be arrested by police,*" Greene answered. The crowd erupted with disorderly dialogue. Cameras flashed, not just toward Greene, but at the angry residents. Greene started visibly sweating.

"*We are currently working on getting rid of the creature as quickly and efficiently as possible. As soon as Ridgeway Lake is deemed safe, we will notify everyone.*"

"*What is the plan?*" someone else shouted.

"*I've lost customers because of this!*" Another individual shouted. Greene didn't answer, and simply started turning away to step from the podium.

"*We'll keep you posted,*" he said. The crowd erupted again with chaotic shouting. Deputies approached the people to maintain order, while Greene walked with Sheriff Logan to his truck. As the mayor placed his hand on the door handle, a brown twirling object comes into frame. A timely narration from the news anchor explained that it was a beer bottle. It smashed through the windshield, sending bits of glass and beer everywhere, including Mayor Greene's shirt. Dave couldn't help but laugh at Greene's flabbergasted expression, holding his hands up as suds dripped from his sleeves. The footage then showed Sheriff Logan moving into the crowd with his deputies. The suspect made a brief attempt to flee, but was brought down with a taser, and then put into handcuffs. Logan personally escorted the suspect to one of the patrol cars.

Another individual sat next to Dave. Dave glanced to his right, recognizing his buddy Luke, and slid his beer away so Luke wouldn't steal it. There had been numerous occasions in which Dave would mysteriously find his beverages drained prematurely. Luke usually wore a guilty grin on his face.

"Was that the guy who had you arrested?" Luke asked and pointed at the T.V. image of Sheriff Logan.

"Yep, that's the asshole," Dave answered.

"Has there been any word on what they're doing?" Luke asked.

"The mayor's leaving it to the sheriff," Dave said. "That guy has no idea."

"Hell no, he doesn't," the bartender said from behind the counter. "That guy's an idiot. Probably can't even jerk himself off properly."

"Thanks for that image," Dave said, wincing.

"I still can't believe those morons thought you killed those friends of yours," the bartender said. "Bunch of loonies, if you ask me. Every one of them."

"No, the chief's alright," Dave said. "That sheriff, however…well, you get the idea."

"Hey, bud," a voice called from one of the tables. Dave looked back. A patron with a white beard and black biker vest pointed a finger toward him. "Are you the fella that encountered the big fish the other day?"

"That's me," Dave said.

"Wait," somebody from another table said. "You saw it? Did it try to eat you?"

"Emphasis on *try*," Dave said. "Instead, I gave it a serving of lead." Luke burst out in laughter, leaning his head on the countertop. He looked back up at his friend.

"Are you sure it didn't just take one look at you and lose its appetite?" He laughed at his own joke. The rest of the crowd quickly joined in.

"Oh, ha-ha-ha," Dave mocked them. He held up both middle fingers, and then reached back for his beer. He took a slug, only to realize it was empty. "What the…Luke, you douche." Luke turned away, playing innocent. "Son-of-a-bitch. I don't know who I'd like to kill more; you or the fish." Luke laughed again, in a high-pitched laugh that made him sound like the Riddler.

"You want to kill that thing?"

"Yeah, it killed Jeremy and DeAnna. Yeah, I want to kill the thing."

"I don't know," someone called out from one of the tables. "I hear it can't be killed."

"Yeah," Luke said. He agreed mainly to get on Dave's nerves. "You'd be just a can of spam to that thing." Dave nearly choked on his fresh beer.

"Spam? You've reduced me to canned process meat?" The other rednecks started laughing again. "Funny!" He took another drink. "Besides, it's just an oversized fish." Chatter started to build up inside the bar, with the patrons debating amongst themselves about the Carnobass.

"I concur!" a voice called out over the others. All eyes turned to the back corner of the room, where a husky individual sat at a table by himself.

It was Jimmie Stanton's first time at this bar. Normally, he'd go to higher class bars on the northern part of town. Since the death of his wife, friends and family constantly stopped by to visit. While he appreciated the support, he found himself just wanting to be alone. Sadly, when he'd go to any of his normal hangouts, there'd be at least one person there that knew him, and naturally wanted to cheer him up somehow. *Ringside*, however, was one they wouldn't think to look.

Unfortunately, no amount of alcohol would rid his mind of the horrific image of his wife's ravaged corpse. The appearance of terror and pain embedded on her lifeless face made the haunting memory increasingly worse.

Then there was the fact that his wife was cheating on him. Stanton felt a strange combination of intense anger and guilt. His head felt as if it was in an endless tailspin from the thousand unanswered questions. How long has the affair been going on? How many men had she been seeing? Why did she do it? He wondered his busy schedule was what drove them apart, or if his increasing weight was a factor. That's where the guilt came in. He started placing the blame on himself, believing if somehow he didn't drive Amanda away, she wouldn't have cheated; and therefore wouldn't have been killed.

Listening to the rednecks talk of killing the bass sparked a unique ambition. Like many others, he had lost faith in the law enforcement officials' ability to exterminate the creature that undoubtedly killed his wife. He believed that if, somehow, he carried out the deed himself, the retribution would redeem his failures in marriage. Perhaps it would make the guilt disappear, to do one last thing for Amanda. Stanton understood the type of people amongst him in the bar. They were most likely gun owners, and by the looks of them, wouldn't mind making some serious money. And to kill the beast, he would need assistance.

"It is just a fish," Stanton said as he stood up from his chair. He casually walked to the center of the bar. His clothes were wrinkled, having been slept in, and his mustache and hair were a mess. Despite this, he had a commanding presence amongst the drinkers. "You're right about something else; the police don't know what they're doing." He lifted his beer to his lips, swallowed several gulps, and swiftly lowered it down to his waist, spilling some from his mouth in the process. He looked around the room. "Now I don't know any of you, but if I may—you guys strike me as a bunch of gun-toting fellas. Am I correct?"

All at once, the patrons revealed assorted handguns from their vests, pockets, and belts, and held them proudly in the air. At the counter, Dave held up his Smith & Wesson revolver, which had recently been returned to him from the county. The bartender pointed his finger at the room, and his face shriveled up with frustration.

"Hey! How many times have I told you fucks not to bring those in here?"

"Relax," Stanton said to him. He leaned against the counter and looked to the crowd, appearing like a politician running for office. "Now, I want this bastard fish dead. I don't care how, or who does it. I just want it done. So hear me out…" he paused to make sure he had their attention. "…Thirty grand…CASH…to whoever kills the bastard." If he didn't have their attention before, he certainly did now. All eyes went wide with interest, including Dave's and Luke's. The room went entirely silent for a moment, while everyone let the offer sink in.

"You're serious?" Luke asked.

"I'm DAMN fucking serious," Stanton said.

"Wait, wait, wait…hold on just a sec," Dave said. He had seen several scammers before, and wasn't ready to commit trust to this individual. "How do we know you're on the level?" Stanton walked up to him, standing close enough to look him square in the eye.

"Because that thing out there killed my wife," Stanton said. Conviction set in. Those eyes that Dave looked into did not lie. This man wanted the creature destroyed, and was willing to do whatever it took. "Thirty grand," he said, still looking directly at Dave. He then turned to the crowd. "Thirty-thousand dollars…to the one that kills the fish!" Dave was the first to stand up.

"Well, HELL! What am I waiting for?" he said. His motive had changed. Yeah, there was a satisfaction to avenging his friends, but thirty-thousand dollars was more money than he ever had. He tossed some cash onto the bar counter to pay for his drinks, and then marched straight for the door. Luke followed suit.

At that same moment, everyone stood up and started rushing for the door. Like a stampeding herd, each of them was eager to cash in on Stanton's offer. The bartender pulled out his double-barreled shotgun from under the counter, and switched off the lights. He placed a sign on the inside window. *Closed.*

Stanton stepped outside along with him, and watched his posse load into their trucks and motorcycles. Although the painful guilt still resided, he could feel the burden begin to lift.

"This is for you, babe."

CHAPTER 26

The large crawler crane, yellow in color, rested just a few feet from the manufactured drop-off at Hampton's Ledge. Joel sat inside the platform and tested the controls. The booms slowly extended outward, to a maximum length of one-hundred-fifty feet. The newly carved hook hung from a cable just over a foot from the tip of the upper sheave. He slowly rotated the winding drum, swinging the boom to the left and right. The motion was slow, but it functioned properly.

Some construction crews were hired to dig a small trench for the crane to position within. They packed loads of gravel in front of the tracks in order to help prevent the crane from being pulled into the water. Joel's worry was that, should he successfully hook the fish, that it would undoubtedly make a run. It would likely swim outward toward the open lake. He didn't want to risk its sheer force possibly tilting the heavy crane into the water.

Sydney approached the crane and gazed at the sharpened hook. A pointy piece of metal protruded outward near the tip of the hook, acting as a barb that Joel had welded. Sydney stood, dwarfed by the huge machine. Joel had properly gone over the specifications. The counterweight sat at fifty-three tons on the upper, and ten tons on the lower. Its lifting capacity was well more than necessary to lift the fish from the water. The sound of approaching footsteps crunching gravel drew his attention. He looked over his left shoulder as Meya stepped alongside him.

"You think this'll work?" she queried.

"I do," he said without skipping a beat. Joel stepped out of the platform.

"Joel, you forgot your hard hat," Meya called out to him. Joel chuckled.

"I'll need one when I get home," he said. "I'm in the dog house again."

"Uh-oh," Sydney said. "Your wife?"

"Yeah," Joel said, long and drawn out. "I told her I was working with you all again tonight. I've been busy twenty-four hours a day since this excitement started, so she's ready to have me home."

"Well, that's sweet," Meya said. "At least she likes spending time with you."

"I like to think that," Joel said, smiling. "But I know the real reason: she wants to hand me the honey-do-list."

A brown pickup truck rolled into the nearby parking lot. It slowly pulled up past the gravelly spaces and stopped a few feet from Sydney. Wilkow stepped out of the truck, covered in fish guts and bait. Dressed in khakis, a flannel shirt, and a round fishing hat, he looked as if he was ready to go out on a boat with a pole.

"Sorry 'bout the smell," he said. "I had to get our beef. Fresh off the steer!"

He opened the bed of the truck, and Sydney looked inside. It was a freshly sawn hide, with the ribs and fat still intact. The muscle tissue was bright red, and some remaining fragments of brown skin dangled from the meat.

"What's that?" Sydney pointed to a large blue tub, full of red, mostly liquid, ingredients.

"Oh, my very own recipe," Wilkow said. "Blood. Fat. Intestines. More fat. A bit of coagulant thrown in." He climbed onto the bed of the truck, and opened the tub. "Wanna see?" The smell hit them both like a freight train of stench. Meya and Sydney both covered their noses. The smell was wretched. Meya, despite her experiences with gory sights and smells, could hardly stand it. Standing several feet away, Joel had to clench his nose shut as well. He casually walked back to the crane, leaving Sydney and Meya to suffer Wilkow's company.

"Good lord," she said. "Put that back on!"

"Why do you even have that?" Sydney said. Wilkow replaced the lid and stepped down off the truck.

"Because I'm gonna coat the lure with it," he said. "That stuff should stick fairly well to our makeshift lure. You think that stuff smells, 'blech!'" He waved his arms out and stuck out his tongue in an exaggerated disgusted expression. "But that fish out there, when he gets a whiff of this, he'll be thinking, 'Mmmmmmm.'" He rubbed his stomach to express his point further.

"Well, he can have it," Meya said and walked away. Sydney started to join her.

"Hey!" Wilkow called after them. "Where's the lure?"

"The other side of the crane," Sydney answered as he continued walking, not even looking back.

Wilkow shrugged to himself and climbed back into the bed of the truck. He slid the tub toward the edge, then stepped down again to lift it. He groaned as he picked it up by the side handles, and slowly hobbled his way toward the crane. Joel watched the embarrassing sight from the platform.

Oh God. He's coming towards ME with that.

Wilkow moved around the crane, eventually reaching the lure to the right of it. He lowered the tub, nearly dropping it as his body gave in to its heavy weight. After leaning back to crack his back, he looked down at the makeshift lure. It was a large, oval-shaped sheet of metal, curved slightly inward in the middle. Along the edges were several holes with wires tied around to attach smaller pieces of metal. It was just like a spoon for catching pike, except this one was six feet long.

Wilkow took a brush from his vest pocket. He dipped the bristles into the mixture, and coated the lure with it. Joel watched from the window as Wilkow applied the guts as if painting the lure. The smell worked its way up the platform, and into Joel's nasal cavities.

"You sure the water won't wash that off?" he called out.

"Not right away," Wilkow said. "Once I have this thing covered, we'll let it sit for a little bit. The substance should stick to lure. We may have to recoat it after." He applied a few more coats of the mixture, then looked at the brush. "Oh yeah!" He held it up toward Joel. "I hope you don't mind. I borrowed this from your van. I'll give it back when I'm done." Joel stared down at him for several long and quiet moments, fantasizing about putting Wilkow on the hook instead of the beef.

"Keep it," Joel said.

Sydney and Meya walked toward the lot. The air freshened and cleansed their nostrils of the foul stench. Meya glanced down at Sydney's injured leg. He wasn't limping as bad, but it was still apparent.

"Maybe when this is all over, we'll get you a new appointment," she said. Sydney put his hand over the area of the injury. He wanted to shrug it off, and claim the pain didn't bother him, but knew she would see through the lie.

"To do what?" he said. "Put the muscle back in?" He made a small chuckle.

"No," Meya said. "However, there are other techniques we can do, and better medication. And one other thing."

"What's that?"

"This time, I'll be around to help you through it," she answered. They shared a brief glance at each other. Though unspoken, Meya could read through Sydney's eyes that he would gladly accept her offer.

Their moment was cut short when they heard the sounds of yelling from the vehicles. Their attention turned to the source, and they continued walking. The yelling did not sound to be caused by panic or shock, but anger. They recognized the two voices; clearly Mayor Greene's and Sheriff Logan's. Sydney and Meya stepped around the front of Joel's van, and saw the two bickering by the sheriff's vehicle.

"I don't care," Greene said. His white shirt showed many signs of wear from the day. Dirt stains were plastered all over it, and the top two buttons had popped off. The tie had been removed, only to be lost in the day's confusion, and his trousers looked equally as bad. Worse was his temper. "Get somebody to do it!"

"Damn it, Mayor, I don't HAVE anyone else available," Logan said. Sydney and Meya quickly approached.

"Hey, hey, hey!" Sydney called their attention, as if breaking up a brawl. "What's going on? What's the problem?" Logan took a breath and tried to regain his composure.

"Our fucking pilot backed out," he said.

"Huh?" Sydney said, flabbergasted.

"Yeah," Logan said. "He strictly refuses to do this. Apparently, he thinks the fish will grab the lure and pull the chopper down with it." He turned around and angrily kicked his vehicle tire.

"Well, it is a genuine concern," Meya said.

"More to the point is that he doesn't trust the sheriff's judgement after last night," Greene said. He noticed the sheriff shoot him a glare. "It's not a personal jab, Sheriff, it's just the truth of the matter."

"Yeah, and you're blaming me for it," Logan snapped. "What do you want me to do about it?"

"Get us another pilot," Greene said. Feeling his muscles tense with anger, Logan turned to walk away, only to turn back once more. His face had nearly turned beat red, through his dark complexion.

"We don't have one!" His voice came out as a hiss, resulting from his struggle to keep from shouting once more.

"You don't have any other certified pilots?" Sydney asked.

"No," Logan said. His defeated expression returned, after having lifted during the day's work to set up the operation. "This guy was our last. We had another, but he…" Logan's voice trailed off into a long, drawn-out sigh, "…he was one of our men who was killed last night."

"So now what?" Greene asked. The question was clearly directed at Chief Sydney. "Could we just use the bait on the crane's hook and see if the bass will still come?"

"We could try," Sydney said, "but it's a big lake, and if that fish isn't in the immediate area, it won't pick up the scent. That's why we need the chopper unit to lure the fish in."

"Except now we don't have a freaking pilot," Greene said. He clapped both hands and held them out, palms facing up. "Well, I'm out of ideas."

"Like you had any to begin with," Logan mumbled, just loud enough to barely be heard. Greene's eyes turned to the sheriff and stayed locked on him as Greene mentally eased his temper.

"We have a pilot," Meya said. All eyes went to her.

"Huh? We do?" Greene said. Sydney's eyes went wide, and he stepped in front of his ex-wife.

"No, no, no," he said. "I already know what you're about to suggest."

"What is she gonna suggest?" Logan asked. They ignored him.

"Morgan, we don't have many other options," Meya said to Sydney.

"It'll be dangerous out there," Sydney said. "We still aren't completely sure of what else that thing's capable of."

"Who's the pilot?" Greene cut in. Like Logan's, his question was ignored.

Meya placed her hands on Sydney's shoulders.

"I'm well aware of the risks," she said. "I'm also aware of the dangers of leaving that thing to roam out there." Sydney looked out to the lake, begrudgingly listening to what she was telling him. He didn't want to give in; he had just gotten her back, and though he wouldn't say it, he did not want to suffer losing her again. Worse, he didn't want to mourn her. Meya put a hand on his face and redirected his gaze toward her. They locked eyes. She knew what he thought. "I can do this," she said.

"If this doesn't work, I'm gonna hunt that bastard ex-boyfriend of yours down," Sydney said. Meya smiled.

"It was really just a few dates," she said. "It didn't really go anywhere, so you don't really need to be jealous." Sydney tried not to show it as he felt a swell of relief wash over him. The thought of her with someone else did not sit well. However, his concern for her safety was still present, and would continue to eat away at him until she completed the task unharmed.

"What are we talking about?" Greene called out. Sydney and Meya continue looking at each other. Finally, he turned away.

"Meya can fly a chopper," he said. His answer served both as a direct response to Greene, while simultaneously vindicating Meya's choice to pilot the chopper. Greene clapped his hands and looked to the heavens.

"Oh, thank goodness!" he exclaimed. "Wow, ma'am, you are a lifesaver."

"I'm most familiar with the hospital's helicopter," Meya said. "I'll use that one. Morgan, if you could take me there, we can hook up the lure and then I'll fly it back here."

"Then we'll commence once you arrive," Greene said.

"I would get started soon," Logan said. "We only have a little bit of daylight left." Sydney did not share their enthusiasm for the idea; rather, he almost resented it. Suddenly, the dangers of the chopper pilot's position suddenly felt more real, and a hundred times more dangerous. With the chopper lure being his idea, he now hoped everything would go perfectly well. If not, he would never forgive himself. He snapped back into reality when Meya tapped him on the shoulder.

"Would you drive me to the hospital?" she asked him.

"Alright," he said. He regained his composure and looked at Greene and Logan. "We'll take the truck and attach the lure to a cable. When we get back, we'll begin." He looked at Meya. "Don't fly over here too quickly. I'll need time to get back here."

"Don't worry," she said.

"Alright. Let's get moving," Sydney said. With Wilkow's help, they moved the lure into the bed of the truck.

Both Sydney and Meya partially regretted their idea to attach the lure themselves after getting another whiff of the smell. Wilkow climbed into the bed of the truck to continue applying more of the bait mixture. Normally, Sydney wouldn't allow this, but understood it needed to be done.

He glanced one last time at Meya, who looked back at him. The smell crept in, and spoiled their moment.

"Alright," he said. "Let's get going."

"Please," Meya said, pinching her nose shut. Sydney started the truck and drove them out.

CHAPTER 27

Dave Culverhouse sat in his parked truck, hidden behind a thick wall of trees. Through the brush, he watched the local boat dock, waiting for the two RPD patrol officers to move along. For the past twenty-four hours, the officers kept constant watch over the lake to prevent people from going out on it. The officers moved on foot, and moved dreadfully slow. They stood at the dock, chatting with one another for what seemed like forever. Dave found himself starting to lose patience, until they finally moved out of sight.

He looked around for anyone possibly nearby before slowly moving his truck closer to the lake, with his boat in tow. The area was guarded by woods and created a narrow road to the dock. He maneuvered his truck to back the boat into the water. Before backing it all the way in, he stopped the truck to check his assortment of weapons. He packed his 500 Mossberg Shotgun, AR-15 6.5 Grendel, and his trusty Smith & Wesson 686 revolver. The sound of a vehicle engine caught his attention. He briefly froze in worry that it would be someone who would report him. That concern quickly went away after he recognized the rusty grey Dodge pickup.

"Oh great," Dave said as Luke parked his truck next to his.

"Hell yeah," Luke said.

"What are you doing here?" Dave asked. He already knew the answer.

"Gonna kill me some fish!" Luke proclaimed. He pulled a rifle from the back seat of his truck and lifted it proudly into the air. Dave squinted as he looked at the brown Ruger compact rifle. His jaw lowered with awe.

"What the hell is that?" he questioned, a hint of frustration edging his voice. Luke stared confused for a moment, and held his gun at mid-level, pointed down.

"It's my new gun," he said. "I just bought it." Dave smacked his palm into his own forehead.

"That's a .22!" he said. Luke looked at his rifle, seemingly surprised at the revelation.

"Oh…"

"Oh?" Dave said. "What did you do? Just pick out the first gun you saw?" Luke made a nervous grin. Dave smacked his palm into his own face a second time. "Oh my God, you did." He lowered his hand and started laughing. "What do you plan on shooting with a .22? Bluegills? Squirrels?"

Before Luke could answer, another truck started coming down the pathway. Dave could see the face of the driver, and quickly recognized him as one of the rednecks from the bar. The truck towed a twelve-foot johnboat and pulled alongside Luke's truck. With a cigarette dangling from his mouth, the grey-bearded man stepped out of his truck to load his gear into his boat. He stopped a moment when his eyes caught sight of Luke's rifle. He instantly started cackling when he recognized its capacity.

"Now, that's fucking hilarious!" he said with a snort. He looked at Dave. "What about you, son? Is that what you're going out with?"

"He's not with me!" Dave said.

"Hey, man!" Luke said. "I don't have a boat! Let me come out and we'll split the reward. Fifty-fifty!" Dave glared at him.

"You realize I'm packing the real guns, and the boat?" he said. Luke bit his lip at the realization. Dave exhaled sharply. "Fine! You can steer the boat. And the split is eighty-twenty!"

"I can live with that," Luke said.

"Good," Dave said. "Now let's hurry up. Park your truck behind those trees back there. There's a narrow pathway you can squeeze your truck through. The cops won't think to check it. But we gotta move. There were a couple that were here a bit ago, and they might just come back."

"Oh, we got that covered," the older redneck said.

"Beg your pardon?" Dave said.

"I've got some buddies that are gonna stage a little melee brawl downtown," he said. He coughed and pulled his cigarette from his mouth.

Damn, if the fish doesn't kill him, those things apparently will, Dave thought. The grey-bearded man spit and regained his composure.

"What was I saying…uh…oh yeah, my buddies will be staging a big-scale brawl downtown. That'll attract the attention of the cops, so I don't have to worry about them as I kill the fish."

"Ha!" Dave laughed, raising his Mossberg above his head. "You can try." Luke joined in by raising his rifle proudly in a similar manner. Dave looked back at him. "You just ruined the moment by raising that pop-can shooter."

"I agree with Ginger here," the old man said. Dave gave him a coarse stare, contemplating responding with a derogatory remark about age. He held back, instead going with a question.

"When's that brawl gonna start?"

"Just before dark," the old man said. "Be prepared for some stiff competition. All those guys from the bar are getting out on the lake, all over the place. Most of them are waiting for cover of darkness." Dave looked at his watch. It was late in the evening, with limited sunshine remaining.

"As long as they don't shoot each other over it," he said. He placed his weapons into the boat, except for the revolver, which was strapped to his hip.

"You never know," the old man said as he started preparing his own boat.

CHAPTER 28

Sydney and the others all ducked slightly from the downward gust of wind that came down upon them as the chopper passed overhead. Meya clutched the controls and guided the white helicopter over the lake. Hovering roughly seventy-feet over the water, the large white aircraft looked like a massive dragonfly in search of a place to land. Installed underneath the helicopter was a radar detector, designed for short-range sea-surface detection. Linked to a screen in the cockpit, Meya could look for any blips on the screen, which would indicate a large approaching object. The wind gusts from the helicopter's massive rotating blades turned the formerly smooth water surface into a rippling frenzy. Dangling from the open left door was the metal lure. Smothered in Wilkow's chum-like mixture, it hung from a cable that clipped to the front of the lure.

Meya adjusted her headset after slowing the chopper's advance. Sydney had connected her radio frequency to that of the law enforcement officers'. She manipulated the controls, slowly spinning the chopper around until its nose pointed toward the drop-off.

"Alright, Morgan; where should I start?" she asked.

Sydney stood at the edge of the drop-off, accompanied by Logan and Wilkow, who had changed his shirt. Standing off to the side were a few deputies and RPD officers, standing ready with high-powered rifles. Joel sat in the platform of the crane, poised and ready to operate the controls. Sydney lifted his radio up to his lips.

"Back it out to about a hundred meters, lower the lure, and work your way back," he said. "With any luck, the bass will be close by."

"Roger that," Meya said. Sydney watched as the nose dipped slightly and the chopper moved back. With no additional pilot on board to go back and operate the lever, Meya had to use the control pad to lower the cable. She pressed her thumb to a button to extend the hoist arm. Once the arm extended completely, she pressed another button to lower the cable. She watched down through the mirror as the lure reached further down into the lake, until it finally broke the surface.

"I'll have it to a ten-foot depth," Meya said into the radio. She locked the cable in place, and gently pushed the joystick forward. "I'm moving it in now."

The chopper steadily moved toward shore, dragging the lure down behind it. The large oval-shaped metal sheet flipped and turned in the water. Tiny bits of the meaty covering broke away, creating a trail toward shore. Meya kept the chopper's advance slow, and checked the radar screen for any surface detection. Nothing. Once the chopper drew near shore, she turned it around.

"Go for another try," Sydney said.

"Same spot?" Meya asked.

"Try about three-hundred yards south, and a bit further out," Sydney said. "It'll probably take several tries before our fish detects it."

"Roger that," Meya said. The chopper kicked up wind as it glided further down the lake. Sydney watched it turn, and dip the lure into the water once again. Once it was submerged, she dragged it once more toward the ledge. As before, the lure twisted and turned, swirling the water in its path. It took a little over a minute before Meya closed the distance. Once she was close to the ledge, she turned around to move out.

"You'll just gonna have to keep repeating," Sydney said into the radio. He looked over at Wilkow. "You don't think this guy lost his appetite, do you?"

"Have some patience, Chief," Wilkow said. "You said so yourself; it's a big lake. It's going to take several tries before we figure out where he is." Sydney looked at his watch. It was after *8:00*, an hour later than he wanted to get started. He looked at Logan.

"Do your deputies have spotlights?" Sydney asked him.

"We do," Logan answered.

"Good, because we'll need them. The sun will be going down soon." Sydney saw a forlorn expression crunch Logan's face.

"Is it even a good idea to continue this so late?" he asked.

"Yes, sir," Wilkow said. "Like a lot of fish, this is the prime time for feeding. Lower temperatures; less sunlight. Don't worry, he'll eventually show." Wilkow then casually walked away from the officers and looked at the large hook dangling just over the water, nearly a hundred-fifty-feet from the ledge. Impaled onto it was the large slab of beef, coated with Wilkow's mixture for extra scent. He looked up and saw Joel sitting in the platform. Wilkow knew he was still irritated at him for using his brush.

"Hey Joel," Wilkow called up. Joel glanced down for barely a moment, noticing it was Wilkow calling his name. He looked back to the water, pretending he didn't hear him. Wilkow saw through the act and started climbing up the ladder.

"Oh, jeez," Joel said under his breath. Wilkow quickly reached the top and slid the door open.

"Hey…whoa!" he shrieked as he nearly lost his footing. He leaned forward, grabbing one of the levers by accident. Alarmed, Joel grabbed Wilkow's wrist to keep him from accidentally pressing the lever.

"You trying to get us killed?" he griped. Wilkow fixed his footing and straightened himself out.

"Oops," he said. Joel wasn't sure whether the 'oops' was sarcastic or genuine. "What'd I almost do?"

"That lever swings the crane," Joel said. "With your luck, you would have swung it toward the officers over there."

"I see," Wilkow said. "Technically, we wouldn't be the ones killed, since we're up in here…" he stopped, seeing Joel's irritation in his stare, "but I see your point. Uh…what does this one do?" He pointed to another lever. Rather than answer, Joel felt the urge to tell him off. However, he decided to be polite. Plus, he realized it would be helpful for someone else to have a bit of knowledge of the crane in case he needed help.

"That one lifts the main hoist," he said. "You lock it in place with the foot brake down here." He bumped the foot brake with his boot.

"Good tip," Wilkow said. "You'll definitely want to lock it in place when the Carnobass bites on that hook. Let himself wear himself out before bringing him up."

You think I don't already know that? Joel leaned in his seat, counting down the moments until Wilkow would go away. He hadn't smoked in years, but he suddenly found himself dying for a cigarette.

"Why do you call it a Carnobass?" he asked, immediately feeling foolish for carrying on the conversation.

"I went through several names while writing my thesis for possible lifeforms living in these underground lakes that exist," Wilkow said. "I wanted to go with something like Cretaceous Bass, but I figured that sounded stupid."

"Ah," Joel said. "'Cause Carnobass sounds so intellectual." He watched a grin form on Wilkow's face and felt a sporty tap on the shoulder.

"I thought so too!" he said, and started climbing back down. Joel blew a sigh of relief.

Hopeless, he thought.

Meya steered the chopper further out for another attempt. As before, there was no sign of the fish. She repeated the action, taking the chopper out to the center of the lake and working the lure back toward the ledge. Each time proved futile.

****

Over the next hour, she continuously repeated the cycle with no avail. Daylight gradually faded away into night. Spotlights from the crane and patrol vehicles illuminated Hampton's Ledge. Sydney and

Logan both grew increasingly anxious and tired all at once. Mayor Greene sat inside Joel's jeep, sipping on coffee and waiting for word of the bass. Wilkow leaned back against a patrol car. They watched the helicopter bring the lure toward the ledge, stop, and turn back to repeat. With the lack of sunlight, they mostly relied on the chopper's green blinking operational navigation lights. At least the moon was full, which assisted a bit with visibility.

Sydney lifted his radio once again.

"Let's try something different," he said. "Don't keep working it back toward us. Move continuously southward down the lake, and work your way back slowly. Keep about five hundred feet from shore. Think of it as trolling."

"*Roger that,*" he heard Meya respond. She manipulated the joystick to angle the chopper south. From shore, Sydney watched its green lights gradually become seemingly smaller as they moved away.

The crackling of his radio caught his attention. The voice of the evening dispatcher called through the frequency.

"*Dispatch to Chief.*"

"Go ahead," he responded.

"*We're getting several calls regarding an incident taking place downtown. Park Avenue and Market. Reports indicate a massive brawl involving multiple persons. One caller reported someone wielding a knife at the scene.*" Sydney could hear the phone going off in the background.

"Oh, you've got to be kidding me," he said. He clicked the transmitter. "Shore patrol units, I need you all to respond to Park Avenue."

"*Already on it, Chief,*" Officer Larabee responded.

"As dispatch said, there's a reported weapon on scene. Maintain awareness, and keep me informed."

"*Ten-four.*" For the next minute, the radio blared as officers called in their unit numbers in response to the call. Sheriff Logan clutched the mic on his collar.

"I'll need a few units to head that way as well," he said. He let go and looked at Sydney. "Figures; this would happen tonight."

"Tell me about it," Sydney said. "I can't help but find it a little odd."

Meya put on some classic rock on her iPhone to help drown out the drone of the chopper blades. She had slowly pushed south for several minutes. However, her radar screen showed nothing but a blank blue grid. She could sense herself growing impatient. Her joints were starting to ache from the seated position. Her hips felt like they needed to pop, and her fingers were sore from holding the joystick. Of course, her legs were asleep, and she could use a massage in her neck. Meya suddenly felt grateful she did not choose a career as a chopper pilot.

"*Any luck, Dr. Nasr?*" Sydney's voice came through the radio. She keyed her transmitter.

"You're calling me, *doctor*, now?" she said.

"*Sorry, just trying to keep a bit of formality,*" he said. "*Anything?*"

"Nothing so far," she said. "After I complete this pass, I'll work my way north up the other side of the lake."

"*Worth a try,*" Sydney said. Meya stared ahead while she kept moving. It wasn't easy to move the chopper so gradually. Too much of a push on the controls would have it shooting forward. In addition, that was her natural instinct to apply more pressure. Looking straight ahead, she could see the dock lights outlining the south edge of the lake, less than a half mile down. She considered patrolling all the way down, but impatience got the better of her. Her gut instinct didn't believe the fish was down toward that end of the lake.

Screw it. With a twist of the controls, she turned the chopper left to cut across the lake. This area was about three-fourths of a mile across. Reaching the other side would only take a minute if she increased her speed.

In the corner of her eye, she noticed something on the radar screen. A blinking red dot on the edge of the grid. Interesting, it was to the south. Her mind went on alert. She quickly stopped the helicopter and looked back at the screen. The blip had disappeared. Either she had moved just out of range, or the source had moved away. Meya gently directed the helicopter back in a slow gradual motion, keeping the lure in ten feet of water. She watched the screen intently. Nothing appeared so far.

Meya felt her exhilaration start to slip away. She started questioning herself; *did I actually see a blip? Or is my mind playing tricks on me?* She suspected it was the latter.

Then it appeared again, blinking on the right of the screen. Meya's heart raced from a combination of excitement and tension. She took a deep breath, and continued to move the chopper toward the blip. She watched it on the screen as it slowly neared her position.

Then, all of a sudden, that blip swiftly moved to the center of the screen. Meya's excitement disappeared, leaving only tension. She gritted her teeth and pulled up. The helicopter quickly climbed, yanking the lure from the water just as the blip reached the center.

The water erupted below. The enormous mouth of the fish breached the water, reaching for the lure that dangled just a few feet above it. It fell back down into the water, disappearing behind another huge splash. Meya clicked the transmitter.

"Morgan! It's here!"

Sydney was in the middle of filling his coffee cup when the call came through. With adrenaline coursing through him, he dropped the cup and thermos and rushed to the ledge.

"Where? How far out?"

"*Roughly a click south of you,*" Meya said. "*Found him smack dab in the middle of the lake.*" Logan, Wilkow, and Greene quickly huddled around Sydney to overhear.

"Do you think you can get him to follow you back here?" Sydney asked.

Meya guided the chopper several meters up the lake. The Carnobass slowly trailed behind, studying the strange object hovering above the water. Meya stopped the chopper and turned so she could see the fish from her window. She could see its spines flaring over the surface, attached to its enormous bulk. The chopper gradually descended, dipping the lure into the water.

As soon as the lure touched down, Meya yanked hard on the stick to climb again. The bass had wasted no time. It immediately shot forward, barely missing the lure. Meya steadied the chopper.

"I'd definitely say so!" she said.

"Alright, game time everyone!" Sydney said. Sheriff Logan and Wilkow snatched up binoculars and stood at the ledge. Greene stepped out of the van and eagerly joined them at the ledge. In the platform, Joel put his hands on the crane levers, ready to drop the hook. He glanced down at Sydney, who was looking back to make sure he was prepared.

"Just tell me when," Joel said.

"Sure thing," Sydney said.

Meya steered the chopper north, switching glances between the windshield and the radar screen. The Carnobass followed in pursuit, feeling the water displacement caused by the continuous downward gusts of wind caused by the rotating blades.

Meya looked down out her window for any visual on the bass. Continuing to move the helicopter forward, she started to lower the lure. Before the lure even touched down, the water underneath exploded upward. The bass went airborne, ascending several meters upward. Meya shrieked and steered the aircraft to the right. The chopper tilted viciously and shifted. The lure bounced off the side of the creature's mouth. The Carnobass crashed back down into the lake's foaming surface.

Meya accelerated the chopper's speed, keeping low enough to be seen by the fish, but high enough to avoid the fish's high leaps. She watched the screen to be sure the fish was still near.

The spotlights from Hampton's Ledge came into view. *Finally*. Keeping the chopper at the center point in the lake, she kept pushing the chopper forward. Once directly in front of the ledge, she would lure the fish straight to the crane.

She took another glance at the screen. The blip was still there, but much further off. The fish was giving up its pursuit.

"Oh, no you don't," she said. She lowered the chopper until the lure dipped down. She zigzagged, creating all sorts of motions with the lure. For a moment, the blip remained in place. Finally, it moved toward the center of the screen. Meya clicked the transmitter. "We're almost there!" She accelerated, dragging the lure beneath. She crossed the water, a quarter-mile out from the ledge.

"There!" Sydney pointed at the navigation lights in the distance. They could hear the blades chopping the air as they rotated. Although it was dark, they could barely see the shape of the chopper, hovering over the water like a hummingbird. Sydney lifted his radio. "We see you!"

"*I'm coming in*," Meya said. The chopper turned and gradually moved in. Logan lifted the binoculars to his eyes. He focused just underneath the chopper. He could see the splashes by the lure, but nothing else.

"I don't have a visual on the bass," he spoke into his radio. "Are you sure it's following you?"

Suddenly, the chopper lurched upward. The water underneath it exploded as the fish jumped. Its body twisted in mid-air as it narrowly missed the lure. It arched its body, opening and shutting its mouth repeatedly until it hit the water. Logan felt his body nearly seize with shock and awe.

"Disregard," he said.

Sydney felt his heart thump in his chest as the chopper narrowly dodged the Carnobass's attack. With each rapid beat of his heart, the pain in his leg throbbed, worsened by his concern for Meya. He watched as she gradually lowered the chopper and worked her way closer to the ledge.

"Should I drop the hook?" Joel called out.

"Not yet! We need it to come a little closer," Wilkow shouted. "Chief! She needs to lure him in just a little bit more." Sydney took a nervous breath and then keyed his transmitter.

"Meya, come in a little bit more," he said. "Don't take any unnecessary risks."

"*I got this*," she said. She moved the chopper forward, dangling the lure just above the water. The spotlights grew brighter as she neared them. The fish followed, cutting the surface with its spiny dorsal fin. Finally, she was five-hundred feet from the ledge.

From the ledge, Wilkow watched the fins. He could tell the creature was hesitating after several failures in catching its target. He held a spare radio in hand.

"Steady," he said. Without blinking, he kept his eyes on the fin. Finally, it dipped beneath the water. "NOW!"

Meya pulled up. The chopper climbed just as the bass breached. The lure clipped the top of its head as it was pulled out of range. The fish arched downward into the water, angled toward the ledge. Sydney turned and pointed to Joel.

"Joel, now! Drop the hook!" he called. Joel pressed the lever, and the weighted hook splashed down. With another pull of the lever, he stopped the hook in place, just under the surface.

The creature, frustrated and hungry, felt the displacement. Its nostrils picked up the bloody smell, peaking its interest. It slowly moved in to study the potential meal.

Joel moved another lever, gradually swinging the boom back and forth. The baited hook dragged in the water.

"I can't see it," Joel called out. Logan moved to the patrol vehicle to adjust the spotlight.

"No, no," Wilkow said. "Keep the spotlight on the bait. I can see it." The fish moved closer, continuously to investigate the object. The scent grew stronger as it moved in, and its eyes could see the meat through the illumination. It submerged slightly, and with a flutter of its tail, it shot forward.

"Here it comes!" Wilkow called. The fish closed its jaws around the hook and turned. Joel lifted the hoist. The cable tightened, followed by a large metallic groan from the crane. The platform shook violently, rocking Joel in his seat. He pulled the lever, elevating the boom.

"You got him! You got him!" Greene yelled, excitedly.

The nerves in the creature's mouth lit up as the hook dug into its mouth. The Carnobass opened its mouth and shook its body. It rotated in a corkscrew motion, shaking the hook from its mouth before it sank deep enough to embed the barb. The cable went slack.

"Damn it!" Sydney yelled, throwing his fist across the air in anger. Joel started reeling in the cable. The hook lifted above the water. The beef, while ravaged, still hung from it.

"Relax! We still have the bait!" Wilkow said.

"Is it still here?" Sydney asked. He scanned the water, but saw nothing indicative of the creature's presence. He lifted his radio. "Meya? You see anything?"

"Nothing. Hang on a sec," she said. Sydney watched the helicopter slowly descend. "Sorry, I was a little high for the radar detection. It's still here, but it's starting to move away."

"Hang on!" Wilkow said. He ran around to the other side of the crane. The tub of chum mixture was still there. He grabbed a handle on one side. "Somebody give me a hand." Sydney quickly rushed around the crane and saw Wilkow struggling to move the tub. His first instinct was to ask what the idea was, but he knew time was a critical factor. Sydney grabbed the opposite handle and lifted. Wilkow led the way as they hurried to the ledge. Sydney winced at the pain in his leg, despite his attempts to keep most of his weight on the other. They set the tub down at the edge of the ledge.

"What exactly is the idea?" Sydney asked. Wilkow popped the lid off, and immediately the horrendous smell spread like invisible wildfire.

"Giving him a better whiff," Wilkow said. He tilted the tub. Its contents spilled like a red waterfall into the lake.

The smell immediately filled the creature's nostrils. Its brief memory of its previous encounter faded, and its focus was the intriguing scent. The Carnobass turned around again toward shore. Its fin emerged.

"There he is! He's back!" Wilkow shouted, pointing. Joel lowered the hook into the bloody froth, and slowly moved it back and forth to stir the water. The fish was once again interested. It moved closer, pausing nearly twenty feet from the hook.

"He's gonna go for it," Sydney said. The fish slowly moved its caudal fin, ready to generate a burst of speed.

Suddenly, several lights hit the creature. The whole center of the lake illuminated as bright spotlights beamed from multiple approaching boats. Sydney and the others shielded their eyes as the bright lights scanned over the ledge.

"What the hell?" Sydney said. He could hear several voices calling from out in the lake.

"There it is!" someone yelled with excitement.

"It's mine!" another yelled. Sheriff Logan looked out, squinting through the brightness.

"Who the hell are these guys?" he said.

"I have no idea," Sydney said. He turned and quickly rushed to a patrol vehicle. He opened the trunk and grabbed a bullhorn, then hurried to the ledge.

"*Jesus, Morgan! They have guns!*" Meya shrieked over the radio.

The Carnobass sensed the overabundance of water displacement, and circled around to study the approaching boats. The spotlights focused down on it, illuminating the creature's greenish hide. Sydney lifted the bullhorn.

"This is Police Chief Sydney!" His voice boomed as it echoed across the lake. "I order every one of you to vacate the lake. Those who fail to comply will be arrested!" Some of the boats, all of various sizes, spread out, while others grouped up. Most were typical twelve-foot johnboats, while others were a bit bigger. Sydney could hear the rednecks chattering amongst themselves.

Dave Culverhouse lifted his AR-15. He focused the sights a few feet ahead of the dorsal fin. Luke sat silent, keeping his hand on the motor handle. The other rednecks argued amongst themselves on who got to shoot the fish. The situation was getting hostile, with tempers quickly escalating. People on neighboring boats shoved each other out of the way, resulting in a few physical confrontations. Finally, it got to the point of pointing guns at each other. These people, who hours earlier had been drinking together in friendship, had now become mortal enemies.

Dave took advantage of the disorderly behavior. No matter what, that money was going to be HIS. He could see the fin dipping lower into the water as the creature started submerging.

"Screw it," he said. He squeezed the trigger, firing the first of many rounds. The bullets hit their mark, cutting through the water and striking the bass on top of its head. The deafening gunshots silenced all arguments. All guns pointed toward the water.

The creature fluttered from the pricking sensation caused from the bullets cracking its scales. Its curiosity swiftly turned into aggression. The bass targeted the nearest boat. With a flap of its tail, it accelerated with a burst of speed that left the water fizzing behind it.

The two occupants never knew what hit them as their boat suddenly capsized. Both men were flung from their seats. One landed on the bow of a nearby johnboat, splattering the hull with his brains. The other found himself within the creature's jaws, and subsequently, its stomach.

Shouts of fright, disbelief, and determination filled the air. The crackling of multiple gunshots deafened their shouts. They couldn't see the fish, as it had already disappeared beneath the water, causing the men to aimlessly shoot into the water in hopes of landing a lucky kill shot.

The bass angled itself upward, quickly picking its next target. It locked its sights and waved its tail, generating another burst of speed.

A boat in the center of the group flipped, stern over bow. The single occupant catapulted from his seat on the stern, twisting in disjointed motions until he splashed down. All guns turned to the briefly exposed Carnobass, resulting in crossfire. No shooter took regard of the background of his aim. Bullets and pellets shot in all directions.

Sydney, Logan, Wilkow all dove to the ground as a couple stray rounds zipped overhead. Mayor Greene ran and hid behind one of the vehicles. Joel quickly climbed from the platform and ducked behind the crane.

"Who are these guys?" he shouted.

"I don't know," Sydney said. "But I'm suspecting that brawl downtown was a diversion."

Dave ejected his empty magazine and quickly slapped in a fresh one. As he lifted his firearm, a round struck the upper edge of the bow, creating a deep metallic sound, and a spark. Dave flinched, nearly tripping over his seat. He glanced down at the smoking hole in his boat, then turned his eyes out to the several boats.

"Hey! Watch it!" he yelled. He didn't even know specifically who he was yelling at. Nor did anyone likely hear him over the constant gunfire.

The rednecks focused their blind attack into the water where the fish previously emerged. They reversed their boats away, forming a crooked U-shape formation. Several rednecks cheered like cowboys wrangling cattle. They howled, whooped, and whistled as they shot off their weapons.

Several of those cheers turned into bloodcurdling screams as a swell of water lifted behind the formation. In a single ramming motion, the bass toppled over multiple boats like an armored car crashing through rush hour traffic.

One redneck, with an AR-15 illegally converted to full auto, steadied his shaky hands to reload. He watched two of his drinking buddies swim for dear life, only to be sucked into the beast's massive jaws. After several moments, more swells formed in the water, indicating its presence just below. The swells moved closer to his boat. He jammed the magazine in and aimed. He squeezed the trigger, just as the fish rammed his boat from underneath. With his finger still pressed on the trigger, the redneck fell backward, gun tilting toward the sky. A haze of bullets blasted upward. Some would eventually succumb to gravity and fall back to earth, while others pierced the hull of the hovering helicopter.

Meya tilted to the side after one of those bullets pierced the left window, barely missing her head. A series of emergency lights flashed. An engine compressor failure alert light came on near the controls. She felt the aircraft shift from side to side. She fought with the controls to regain stability.

Sydney looked up, seeing the chopper spinning uncontrollably. Without any regard to his own safety, he sprang to his feet. However, there was nothing he could do but hopelessly watch.

With its blades still spinning, the chopper dropped. Meya felt her harness tighten as the motion lifted her in her seat. Every muscle in her body tensed in the brief moment of the fall. The helicopter smashed down. The windshield shattered, the tail became dislodged, and the hull crumpled inward.

The rotating blades chopped into the water, striking the bass. Pain jolted its body, and it immediately dove away, trailing blood and broken scales. The blades continued spinning in the water, breaking into razor-sharp fragments. Like shrapnel from a grenade, the fragments flew out above the water in all directions. Once again, Sydney hit the ground as bits of sharp metal passed overhead.

The shrapnel bombarded the remaining boats. One redneck watched the crash in awe, up to the point where a large section of blade bounced off the water like a skipping stone, and came up to his neck, decapitating him. Another piece embedded itself into the hull of a speedboat. Water seeped inside, and the two hunters on board panicked as their boat started sinking. Their panic increased when they saw a large swell of water nearby, then the face of the twenty-five-foot largemouth. The fish rammed the boat, cracking it in two.

"Meya!" Sydney shouted. There was no response. He clicked the radio transmitter. "Meya! Are you alright?" There was no response. Logan pushed himself to his feet as well. His eyes went to the nearby patrol boat.

"Chief, come on!" he called. Sydney ran to the boat, despite his old leg injury flaring up again. He detached the line and hopped on board behind the sheriff. Logan started the engine and quickly throttled the boat toward the helicopter.

Joel stepped out from behind the crane and gazed upon the crash. The chopper remained afloat, though it was heavily ravaged. He could see from his point of view that the side door was crumpled in, and likely wouldn't open.

A thought came to his mind; *the jaws of life*. He turned and ran to his van. He started the engine and floored the accelerator, immediately pushing the van faster than it had ever gone. Gravel and dust kicked up as it pulled out of the driveway.

Shockwaves of water rocked Dave's boat. He struggled to remain standing as the floor beneath him shifted. He fired his rifle at the nearby fish. He could see its entire right side as it passed through the broken speedboat. Several scales were missing behind the gill cover, exposing soft flesh. Dave adjusted his aim and fired. Blood sprayed from the flesh, and the creature turned toward him, as if it knew Dave was the one inflicting harm on it. He squeezed the trigger again, but realized the magazine was empty.

He threw it down and snatched up the shotgun. He pressed the butt of the weapon to his shoulder, just as the fish lined up to strike. As it sprang forward, he squeezed the trigger. The fish's right eye exploded into a fountain of red. The Carnobass twisted and turned in the water, flapping its body in a painful hysteria. It submerged.

Luke nearly turned blue from holding his breath. Every muscle in his body tensed from the intense frenzy that had taken place before him. The water stilled, and his body and mind slowly came to ease. He stood up next to Dave.

"Did you kill it?" Luke asked. Dave didn't answer; only chambered the next shell. For several seconds, the water remained calm. Luke felt optimism lift his spirits. If the bass was alive, surely it would attack again. Clearly, it had to be dead. He threw both fists into the air, triumphantly. "Oh yeah! I think you killed it!" He shouted. "Yeah! Woohoo! Thirty grand, here I come!"

While he was in mid-sentence, the water along the starboard side sprayed his face as the Carnobass made a leap. Its mouth angled downward, engulfing Luke's entire body in its descent. Dave felt the boat beneath him plunge into the water, taking him with it. He dropped his weapon and instinctively kicked for the surface.

He drew a breath, only to immediately realize it would be his last. The bass wasted no time to turn toward him. Swimming along the surface, it hyperextended its jaws, and sped at him.

"Well shit," he said to himself, as if accepting defeat. He disappeared into the creature's gullet.

****

An oil pressure light blinked near the speedometer as Joel steered the van into the Birchwood Lodge parking lot. The engine shook as he shifted the gear in park. Before he could remove the keys, the engine died.

"Well, I've been in the market for a new one anyway," Joel said as he stepped out. He ran up to the building, and nearly busted down the door to get inside. He hurried into the cleaning station, where his prized jaws-of-life remained on its special table. As Joel grabbed the heavy tool, his eyes turned to his framed Bandolero sword.

"Ah, what the heck," he said. He busted the frame and grabbed the custom-made sword by the sheath. He rushed out the door and carried the items to the docks. A speedboat remained, owned by lodge vacationers. Joel climbed aboard and checked the console. The keys remained.

They probably were in such a panic after the attack, they didn't think to grab the keys. Whatever the reason, it suited him. He loaded the hydraulic tool, rechargeable battery, and his prized sword into the boat. He started the engine and throttled out.

****

Logan had positioned the patrol boat alongside the downed helicopter. Meya was conscious, thought a bit disoriented. Shattered windshield glass had cut her forehead, and the harness had tightened around her chest and shoulders. Sydney tugged at the door, but it was stuck in place.

To make matters worse, there was the unmistakable odor of gasoline. Fuel leaked from the fuel line, floating all around the chopper.

“Damn it, it’s jammed!” he roared. Logan stepped in his place and tried tugging at the door, making no more progress than Sydney. Meya cupped her hand over a cut on her head. Finally, her senses returned to her. She unclipped her harness and tried opening the door from the inside. She did her best to keep her composure, believing they would free her from the entrapment. She looked up from the handle to see Sydney, but her eyes immediately went to the large bulk in the water behind them.

“Look out!” she screamed. Sydney and Logan turned, just in time to see the Carnobass ram the port quarter. Their shuddering boat was knocked into the floating helicopter, rocking both in the water. Logan fell to his knees, while Sydney barely clung to the edge. He pushed himself off and grabbed the throttle. He accelerated the boat forward, drawing the fish away from Meya. Logan saw the Carnobass emerging behind them. He drew his Glock and fired. The bass rammed the stern, crushing the propellers. The boat stalled.

“Shit!” Sydney exclaimed. He drew his sidearm and joined Logan at the stern. They both fired into the water, but the fish submerged again. “Come out, you damn coward!” he yelled.

As if in response, the bass jumped from the water. Sydney and Logan looked up, and saw its huge mass falling down on top of their boat. It landed on its stomach, directly across the center of the boat. The console was crushed, the deck splintered, and the bow and stern bent upward. Both officers grabbed the stern rail to keep from falling. The creature’s weight pushed the boat down. Water quickly seeped over the sides, coming up to their ankles.

Sydney and Logan emptied their magazines into the beast. A few rounds found their way into exposed flesh, while the rest mushroomed against the solid scales. Red strands of flesh dangled from its ravaged right eye, which still seemed to look right at them.

The water was just below their waists. Out of ammunition, Sydney looked down at the various floating objects around him, desperate for anything he could fight with. His foot bumped something solid. A metal box. He reached down and picked it up. Inside was a flare gun and a single flare, mandatory for maritime first responder vessels to carry.

"Oh, what the hell," he said. He jammed the cartridge in and pointed the orange gun at the creature, aiming for the hole in its eye.

"Howdy!" they heard a voice call from behind. They recognized the sound of a speedboat motor and turned around. Without pulling the trigger, Sydney turned around, as Joel pulled the speedboat alongside their sinking patrol boat. "Hurry up!" he called to them. Sydney and Logan ran in the water, practically swimming at this point, and climbed over the side of the speedboat.

Joel saw the fish wiggling free of the boat, about to submerge again. There was no doubt it would immediately try to sink the speedboat before they could rescue Meya. There was only one thing to do. He unsheathed his sword, and clutched the handle with both hands. The three-foot blade glistened in the moonlight.

With a foot on the edge of the bow, he jumped clear of the speedboat, blade pointed downward. Sydney watched in amazement as Joel landed on the fish, perfectly sinking the blade into the flesh behind its gill cover. He clung to the handle as the fish writhed in the water. Its nerves lit up, and sensed the presence of the attacker clinging to its blindside.

"Joel! What the hell are you doing?" Sydney yelled. Joel took a breath as the creature rolled over like a huge barrel. Still hanging on to the blade handle, he resurfaced.

"Having more fun than I've had in years!" he called out. "Get your lady! I'll keep this guy busy!"

"He's insane!" Logan said.

"Maybe," Sydney said. He grabbed the helm of the boat. "But I'm trusting him." He drove the boat to the chopper.

Joel drew a breath as the creature made a dive. His body hovered freely over its left side as he clung to the sword. He felt like a diver riding alongside a dolphin by clutching its fin. Only, he wasn't riding with a friendly mammal; this was a bloodthirsty fish in the middle of a mad feeding frenzy. The creature bounced off the lake bottom, then arched upward. It fluttered its tail and shot toward the surface. It leapt several feet into the air, flapping its fins and tail. The sword dislodged, and Joel fell off and landed into the water. The creature landed several meters away, generating an enormous splash.

Still holding the sword, Joel surfaced. He saw the distortion in the water nearby. The fish was moving toward him. He saw its head directly in front of him. The jaws opened wide, and the gills flared. Joel felt himself sucked underneath the water, into the creature's mouth. *Oh, hell no!* he thought. This was not how he was going out. Just as he entered the jaws, he shoved the blade directly upward. It pierced the roof of the mouth. Joel could feet his feet touching the back of the creature's throat as he hung on. The jaws slammed shut, leaving him in complete darkness.

The Carnobass turned and rolled, unable to comprehend what was going wrong in its mouth. With its nerves firing, the creature swam aimlessly. Joel felt his whole body quake as the creature blindly crashed into the ledge. It hung in the water, stunned for a moment. Finally, it gave up on trying to swallow its meal. It opened its jaws and swung its head. Joel dislodged the sword just as he was spewed from the jaws.

After he drew a breath, he looked around him while kicking his feet to stay afloat. The crane hook was nearly thirty feet from him, just touching the water. Without hesitating, he swam for it.

The bass continued swimming in mad circles, twisting its body as if it was still trying to get rid of the foreign object in its mouth. Finally, it came to a stop. It flapped its gills to circulate oxygen. Its nostrils picked up numerous smells, including that of its own blood.

Joel grabbed the cable above the hook and rested his foot on the beef. He stood straight up, water up to his thighs. He looked back to the crane.

Wilkow made eye contact with Joel. Without either of them saying a word, he understood the plan. Wilkow climbed into the platform, and placed his hands on the levers. He looked through the windshield and nodded at Joel.

Joel looked for any disruption in the water. The lake had calmed down, but his gut instinct told him it was still nearby. Clinging to the cable with one hand, and holding his sword with the other, he clanged the blade against the metal hook. He smacked it again, and again, sending metallic echoes underneath the water.

The creature's lateral line sensed the vibration. Having recovered some of its energy, it curiously turned toward the source of the noise.

Using the jaws-of-life, Sydney and Logan tore the door off the helicopter cockpit. Sydney reached inside, embracing Meya as he pulled her from the seat. The feeling of solid decking under her feet was a welcome one. Logan stepped to the console and began steering the boat to the ledge. Hugging Sydney, Meya looked up over his shoulder. She saw Joel standing on the hook. Fifty feet ahead of him, the creature broke the surface. It came at him, jaws extended once again.

Meya shrieked and cupped her hands over her mouth. Sydney turned and watched in horror.

Joel didn't blink as the Carnobass closed the distance. He measured the gap in his mind. *Forty feet, thirty, twenty...okay now.* He dove down and paddled as hard as he ever had in his sixty-one years of life. The Carnobass passed overhead, biting down on the hook and instinctively turning to run with its "prey." The hook sank into the side of its mouth. Wilkow applied the footbrake, and the cable went taut. The hook sank deeper, embedding the barb.

Seeing Joel surface, Logan turned the speedboat in his direction. Sydney and Meya both reached down and grabbed him by the wrists. Joel nearly fell onto the deck, all of his energy spent.

"So, did you have your fun?" Sydney said. Joel laughed weakly, which turned into a cough.

"I'm definitely not as young as I once was," he said.

Logan turned the boat toward shore. He didn't bother pulling it up to the dock. Instead, he simply lined it up with the ledge. All four occupants climbed over the starboard side, onto the safety of the ledge.

"HEEELLLL YEEEAAAHHH!" Wilkow shouted as the creature fought against the crane. "Now THIS is fishing!" The crane shook as the Carnobass tugged relentlessly. He manipulated the lever to lift the main hoist. The joints and gears groaned, and smoke started billowing from the friction at the upper sheave. The fish fought against the tension, turning left and right to free itself from the unknown force driving it back.

"Hold on," Joel said to Wilkow. "It's causing too much stress."

"Well, what else can we do?" Wilkow said. Sydney watched the position of the fish, then looked to the downed chopper. An idea came to mind. It would be a bit unorthodox, but it would get the job done.

"Can you give it some slack, and use the boom to direct it to the chopper?"

"Ummm…yes," Wilkow said. It was both an answer and a question.

"Do it," Sydney said. Logan, Joel, and Meya looked at him with questioning eyes. Sydney held up a souvenir from the sunken patrol boat; the orange flare gun. Wilkow eased the tension on the cable, and swung the arm of the crane right. The creature gradually moved outward. It dove deep, but exhaustion was consuming its body. Before long, it surfaced again. A force unknown to it pulled it to the right.

The tension continued easing up. The bass, exhausted and half blind, unknowingly bumped into the chopper. Confused, it started ramming the inanimate object.

"Okay, it's there!" Wilkow said. Sydney stepped to the ledge, and pointed the weapon outward. Before pulling the trigger, he glanced back at his team.

"Don't know about you guys, but I prefer my fish barbequed." He aimed the flare gun, and squeezed the trigger. A ball of orange fire shot from the barrel, and hooked down perfectly into the water beside the chopper. The fuel in the water ignited, searing the fish. The fire followed the trail of fuel, eventually reaching the fuel tank. The several remaining gallons lit at once, resulting in a large explosion. The chopper transformed into a massive ball of fire. Heat scorched the creature, while the shockwave displaced every major organ in its body.

The creature's lifeless body floated briefly beside the burning chopper, until its body weight sank it beneath the flames.

Sydney lowered the flare gun after watching the life fad from the beast. *That's for Tim.*

Everyone stood by him at the ledge, amazed at the sight. Each person was exhausted, even Wilkow. Mayor Greene, shaking from intense fright, finally emerged from his hiding place behind the vehicles, and joined the others.

"Damn," he said. He blew a sigh of relief.

"I think I'm done hunting professionally," Joel said. He arched his back to stretch as every muscle ached.

"Me too," Sydney said. Meya put her arms around him and they held each other close.

"What happens now?" she asked.

"I don't know about you guys," Sydney said, "but I'm going to bed. Let the Sheriff's Department handle this one." Logan grinned and gave a thumbs-up.

"I think that's a good start," Meya said. She pressed her lips to Sydney's, and they slowly walked to his Jeep. With her, the pain in his leg didn't hurt so much.

EPILOGUE

Several days had passed after the chaotic incident at Hampton's Ledge that left many dead. Reports flooded the newspapers with the circumstances of the events. One headline wrote of the arrest of Jimmie Stanton, who orchestrated the event that interrupted a major operation to kill the creature.

Sitting in his home living room, Mike Wilkow glanced at the newspaper headline before tossing it aside. He returned to his laptop, and opened his Microsoft Word document, which contained his detailed analysis on the origins of the Carnobass, and the underground world from where it came.

A knock on his door grabbed his attention. He groaned, believing it to be television reporters wanting to commence another interview. For days, they had been bothering him. He saved the document and closed the laptop. He stood up and opened the door.

"Hey guys, I've already told you…whoa!" He exclaimed as he saw Dr. Nevers standing in front of him. Behind him were several men, all wearing sunglasses and black suits. "Hey there, Doc…Dean!" Wilkow said. "You didn't notify the Secret Service about that credit card thing, did you? I told you I was gonna pay that back." Dr. Nevers smiled.

"Not quite, he said. "These men are actually here to work for you." Wilkow stared at him, confused.

"I beg your pardon?" he questioned, cocking his head to the side. Dr. Nevers stepped inside.

"Dr. Wilkow, your research is surprisingly extraordinary. I've taken it upon myself, with the help of other esteemed scientists, and more importantly, government funders, to start our new special project. N.E.C.T.O.R." Wilkow stared, bewildered. For Dr. Nevers, it was perhaps the first time he saw the eccentric scientist neglect to respond with any witty remark. "That underground lake you discovered…we're gonna see what else is down there."

Dr. Nevers turned around and started walking back to the cars. He looked back over his shoulder at Wilkow.

"You coming?"

THE END

CHECK OUT OTHER GREAT DEEP SEA THRILLERS

PREDATOR X
by C.J Waller

When deep level oil fracking uncovers a vast subterranean sea, a crack team of cavers and scientists are sent down to investigate. Upon their arrival, they disappear without a trace. A second team, including sedimentologist Dr Megan Stoker, are ordered to seek out Alpha Team and report back their findings. But Alpha team are nowhere to be found – instead, they are faced with something unexpected in the depths. Something ancient. Something huge. Something dangerous. Predator X

DEAD BAIT
by Tim Curran

A husband hell-bent on revenge hunts a Wereshark...A Russian mail order bride with a fishy secret...Crabs with a collective consciousness...A vampire who transforms into a Candiru...Zombie piranha...Bait that will have you crawling out of your skin and more. Drawing on horror, humor with a helping of dark fantasy and a touch of deviance, these 19 contemporary stories pay homage to the monsters that lurk in the murky waters of our imaginations. If you thought it was safe to go back in the water...Think Again!

CHECK OUT OTHER GREAT DEEP SEA THRILLERS

LAMPREYS
by Alan Spencer

A secret government tactical team is sent to perform a clean sweep of a private research installation. Horrible atrocities lurk within the abandoned corridors. Mutated sea creatures with insane killing abilities are waiting to suck the blood and meat from their prey.
Unemployed college professor Conrad Garfield is forced to assist and is soon separated from the team. Alone and afraid, Conrad must use his wits to battle mutated lampreys, infected scientists and go head-to-head with the biggest monstrosity of all.
Can Conrad survive, or will the deadly monsters suck the very life from his body?

DEEP DEVOTION
by M.C. Norris

Rising from the depths, a mind-bending monster unleashes a wave of terror across the American heartland. Kate Browning, a Kansas City EMT confronts her paralyzing fear of water when she traces the source of a deadly parasitic affliction to the Gulf of Mexico. Cooperating with a marine biologist, she travels to Florida in an effort to save the life of one very special patient, but the source of the epidemic happens to be the nest of a terrifying monster, one that last rose from the depths to annihilate the lost continent of Atlantis.

Leviathan, destroyer, devoted lifemate and parent, the abomination is not going to take the extermination of its brood well.

CHECK OUT OTHER GREAT DEEP SEA THRILLERS

HELL'S TEETH
by Paul Mannering

In the cold South Pacific waters off the coast of New Zealand, a team of divers and scientists are preparing for three days in a specially designed habitat 1300 feet below the surface.

In this alien and savage world, the mysterious great white sharks gather to hunt and to breed.

When the dive team's only link to the surface is destroyed, they find themselves in a desperate battle for survival. With the air running out, and no hope of rescue, they must use their wits to survive against sharks, each other, and a terrifying nightmare of legend.

MONSTERS IN OUR WAKE
by J.H. Moncrieff

In the idyllic waters of the South Pacific lurks a dangerous and insatiable predator; a monster whose bloodlust and greed threatens the very survival of our planet...the oil industry. Thousands of miles from the nearest human settlement, deep on the ocean floor, ancient creatures have lived peacefully for millennia. But when an oil drill bursts through their lair, Nøkken attacks, damaging the drilling ship's engine and trapping the desperate crew. The longer the humans remain in Nøkken's territory, struggling to repair their ailing ship, the more confrontations occur between the two species. When the death toll rises, the crew turns on each other, and marine geologist Flora Duchovney realizes the scariest monsters aren't below the surface.